# Praise for *Nip 'n' Tuck*

'Exhilaratingly, deliciously rude . . . the jokes ricochet off the page, and you have hardly stopped laughing at one before the next zips along' – **Amanda Craig**, *The Times*

'Forget all pretenders to the chick-fic crown, the tiara belongs to Kathy Lette and she's got the novels to provie it' – *Mirror*

'Classic Lette – comic farce laced with wry observation and enough puns to fill a 36D implant' – *Eve*

'Plastic surgery is no longer an exclusively Hollywood hobby . . . and here in this tragicomedy of aging angst, it's revealed in its full glory . . . Lette is famed for her acerbic, fearless wit and this novel certainly won't disappoint . . . beneath its well-toned plot and light-diffusing puns, there beats an angry indictment of ageism and feminism's many failures' – *Daily Mail*

'Chick Lit gets a welcome facelift. Kathy Lette . . . brings such spiky energy to her treatment of the subject of human decay in *Nip 'n' Tuck* that she actually breaks new ground . . . when she caricatures the charlatans of the beauty profession, she is almost Dickensian' – *Observer*

'You would not want to get on the wrong side of this wordsmith: you could find yourself on the receiving end of a devastating barb . . . Dorothy Parker-esque . . . A wisecracking caper with hidden depths' – *Sunday Telegraph*

'So many verbal felicities . . . inventive, spot-on similes . . . real wisdom . . . Lette has put her finger on one of the great sicknesses of our time. Behind the clowning, there are flashes of real anger at our anorexic, looks-obsessed culture' – *Telegraph*

# Praise for *Foetal Attraction*

'I adored Kathy Lette's novel. It is utterly outrageous, irreverant and screamingly funny. She is such an exciting talent, because she has an incredibly pyrotechnic command of the English language, but also has an acute eye for all our sillinesses. I squirmed and laughed and cried' – *Jilly Cooper*

'It's an answerphone on, feet up, family-size-bar-of-Dairy-Milk sort of a novel . . . hilarious, snappy prose . . . who says you can't be witty to be deep? Huh?' – *Guardian*

'Wildly, painfully funny – the jokes pop up like ping-pong balls in a Bingo hall' – *Sunday Times*

'Non-stop mirth from the uninhibited Kathy Lette . . . Intelligently funny, zesty and exceedingly frank' – *Daily Mail*

# Kathy Lette

Kathy Lette first achieved *succès de scandale* as a teenager with the novel *Puberty Blues*, now a major motion picture. After several years as a newspaper columnist in Sydney and New York (collected in the book *Hit and Ms*) and as a television sitcom writer for Columbia Pictures in Los Angeles, her novels, *Girls' Night Out* (1988), *The Llama Parlour* (1991), *Foetal Attraction* (1993), *Mad Cows* (1996) and *Altar Ego* (1998) became international bestsellers. *Mad Cows* was also recently made into a motion picture starring Joanna Lumley and Anna Friel. Kathy Lette's plays include *Grommits*, *Wet Dreams*, *Perfect Mismatch* and *I'm So Happy For You Really I Am*. She lives in London with her husband and two children.

## Also by Kathy Lette

*Puberty Blues*
(co-author)

*Hit and Ms*

*Girls' Night Out*

*The Llama Parlour*

*Foetal Attraction*

*Mad Cows*

*Altar Ego*

# KATHY LETTE

# *Nip 'n' Tuck*

PICADOR

First published 2001 by Picador

First published in paperback 2002 by Picador
an imprint of Pan Macmillan Ltd
Pan Macmillan, 20 New Wharf Road, London N1 9RR
Basingstoke and Oxford
Associated companies throughout the world
www.panmacmillan.com

This edition published for Index Books Limited 2005

ISBN 0 330 49197 0

Copyright © Kathy Lette 2001

The right of Kathy Lette to be identified as the
author of this work has been asserted by her in accordance
with the Copyright, Designs and Patents Act 1988.

5 7 9 8 6

A CIP catalogue record for this book is available from
the British Library.

Typeset by SetSystems Ltd, Saffron Walden, Essex
Printed and bound in Great Britain by
Mackays of Chatham plc, Chatham, Kent

*This book is dedicated to my children,*

*Georgina and Julius, without whom*

*I would look **years** younger.*

'God has given you one face

and you make yourselves another.'

– *Hamlet*

# Contents

# CONTENTS

# CONTENTS

# 1. Introduction: The Pitter Pitter Pat of Tiny Crows' Feet

Let me introduce myselves.

First there's the me who is often found flirting with lettuce fronds on my front tooth. The me who doesn't use hair conditioner because it takes too long. The me who, only this morning, got my antihistamine and spermicide sprays confused. I now have a vagina that can breathe more freely and nostrils I can safely have sex in for at least six hours.

This is the me whose idea of 'working out' is a good, energetic lie down. (There is growing medical evidence, you know, that jogging can make you hot and sweaty.) The me who understands that if shop mannequins were real women, they'd be too thin to menstruate. (I mean, *hello?* There are three billion women in the world who *don't* look like supermodels. And only six who *do*.) Hey, if you're feeling fat, just make sure you always stand next to a heavily pregnant woman – take one with you everywhere. That's my advice. And wear tights that control your excesses the way the Taliban controls Afghanistan.

It's the me who only shaves my legs to the hemline in summer. In winter I'm too lazy to shave at *all*. I wear thick tights and hope nobody notices the spikes porcupining through my Lycra. As for holes? I simply paint my leg in black felt pen. Even when I *do* shear, I always miss a bit and end up sporting a hirsute median strip down the back of one leg. And you could use a curling wand on those pubes. I like my bikini line, goddamn it. It's like having a little pet in my pants. Which is why I favour, at the beach, the Channel-crossing-neck-to-knee *circa* 1922 look. Nothing better than a sturdy, orthopaedic bathing suit.

My other sartorial preference is trackie daks. My motto is – if it fits, *don't wear it*. I like to wear clothes baggy enough to cover an aircraft carrier; teamed with voluminous knickers – yes, my panty-line is always visible. I have a positive allergy to G-strings. Hey, if I needed a curette, I'd bloody well go to a hospital and get one.

The same me who's always thought of beauty as a case of mind over matter – if you don't mind, it don't matter. The me who allows all that ageing *Angst* to fly right under my anxiety radar. The me who doesn't think age is relevant, unless you're like, you know, a Stilton. You never see Ched-dar cheeses undergoing Dermagen soft-tissue augmentation, now, do you?

This me mouths off tipsily at dinner parties that makeup generates more money than armaments. 'And when you think about it, that's exactly what all those beautification products are, really – ammunition in the sex war.' (My girlfriends are usually making 'Who lit the fuse on *your* tampon?' taunts by now.) 'Most cosmetic manufacturers are *French*. What does that tell you? That they're full of bullshit and LOUD about it. *That*'s what.' (You're starting to be amazed that I *have* any friends, right?)

But honestly. 'The *Science* of Beauty' . . . puh-lease. If

these so-called beauty scientists are so bloody brilliant, why aren't they off fixing the hole in the goddamn ozone layer? Given the choice between an episiotomy and listening to a beauty therapist, I'd say, 'Get the scalpel.' It's nothing but protein-enriched witchcraft. The only reason a moisturizer is called a 'miracle cream' is because it's such a bloody miracle that anyone would fork out fifty frigging quid for it.

That's the me who thinks 'free radical' refers to Nelson Mandela. The me who hears myself described as a 'lady' – and reels around looking for the Duchess of Kent. Despite the fact that I'm a presenter for the BBC's *The World News Today*, I'm obviously just impersonating an Adult. Actually, I'm immaturing with age. At work, after I've boiled down the day's events into digestible yet nourishing news bites, I waste entire afternoons thinking up profoundly puerile nicknames for my superiors. After I've reported on the latest volcanic eruption or political corruption, I am often to be found alone in my office, miming along to Destiny's Child singles using my deodorant as a microphone, or hanging out with the makeup girls, making prank phone calls to the Prime Minister's office and Xeroxing our labial regions.

That's the me I like – the one who's been known to drink huge amounts of vodka and wake up stark naked in an unfamiliar nation with nipple jewellery. The me who only leaves a cocktail party when abducted. Or at knifepoint. The low-maintenance, high-value, worldly me who can say in sixteen languages, 'Hey, buddy, I've got an extremely contagious genital disease I'd be only too happy to give you.'

*

But *then* there's that *Other* Me.

That *Other Me* recently rear-ended a police car because I was scrutinizing my face in the rear-view mirror for signs of photo-ageing. This *Other Me*'s body is coated in creams thick enough to trap small domestic creatures – cats, squirrels, passing pet mice, they're all to be found stranded and struggling on my nether regions. Honestly, of late I've been dousing myself in a potion quotient to rival the petrochemical output of Iraq. My husband, Hugo Frazer MD, could develop Gulf War Syndrome from just one kiss. Actually, I'm terrified I'll start some toxic chain reaction by accidentally using a Revlon *décolletage* softener with a Clarins abdominal cellulite gel and just EXPLODE! There'll be bits of me all over the bloody room. Well, at least *those* beauty products will live up to their claims to 'stop ageing in its tracks'.

This *Other Me* feels trapped in a body that is no longer mine . . . which is why I'm wheezing and panting my way to an early death on the hamster wheel of self-improvement . . . And why I've given up the *New York Review of Books* in favour of magazine articles entitled 'Ten Tips For Toning Thunder Thighs'.

This *Other Me* is backstroking up and down the pool of Narcissus, at torpedo speed . . . This *Other Me* feels so ugly that I worry if people so much as glance at me they'll need a cornea transplant, pronto.

\*

What the hell is wrong with this woman? I hear you ask. If her brain were a toy the box would read 'Batteries Not Included'; produced by a company called Morons R Us. I mean, why the schizophrenia?

4

Why? Because I'm thirty-nine.
*That*'s why.

\*

At thirty-nine, you go to bed one night as usual, your normal, scuzzy old self, in your husband's faded Arsenal shirt, with a smudge of toothpaste on your chin and a bit of dental floss still wedged between your fangs, encased in your favourite pair of moth-eaten cottontails, the ones with the hole, the stain and the erratic elastic (just in case you get your period) – only to wake up a Spandex-wearing gym junkie with pores in need of constant rehydration, a personal trainer, a Jungian analyst, a car shaped like a sex aid, a nail technician, a toy-boy fixation and having whole conversations about seaweed facials and tantric clitoral lavage.

Beautification techniques to which you've never given a moment's thought suddenly take up more of your brain space than third-world debt. If I had to choose between starting a new diet and eradicating world hunger, I'd have to ask, 'Um . . . Slimfast or Jenny Craig?'

El Niño and the ensuing environmental destruction are less worrying than the discovery of a new wrinkle. *Wrinkle?* Who am I kidding? I've got enough crows' feet to start a bird sanctuary. Actually, they're not crows' feet: they're bloody great ostrich prints . . . Who let the pterodactyls loose? Apparently they've been stomping all over my face and I didn't damn well notice.

It's as if UFO rays from some outer galaxy have been beamed into your brain making you agonize over, of all things, inner thigh elasticity. Just as quickly all the money in your purse evaporates, teleporting itself into the bank vaults of cosmetic companies. And for what? Some 'wonder cream' that they can't tell you exactly how they make – but, put it this way, two hundred ferrets went *into* the laboratory, and only two hobbled out, and *those* had grown a couple of extra heads and undergone some mysterious sex change.

But who cares? You bloody well buy it anyway. You seem to have developed a chronic inability to say 'No' to Harrods beauty assistants. Puréed pig erections? Yes, please. Ground sheep embryos in a handy, handbag-size dispenser? Hell, yes. Good God, if beauty experts told me to eat my own sanitary towel for an invigorated complexion, I'd damn well do it.

All of a sudden, sunlight, late nights, alcohol, coffee and everything else that makes life worth living are not DC – Dermatologically Correct. With no prior warning, I find myself unexpectedly wanting to put a cosmetic surgeon's kids through private school. Out of the blue, I'm comparing my butt buoyancy to women on ten-foot billboards and making lists of all the females I know who are younger and more slender of thigh than I.

Me, Lizzie McPhee, a woman who could put a builder in a headlock as soon as his lips so much as pursed towards a wolf whistle. Me, Lizzie McPhee, a mouthy brunette who has been known to kick-start her own vibrator.

At least I'm not the only one making such a moron of herself. It seems to me *all* women over thirty-nine – from the double agent who smashed terrorist cabals to the aviatrix who crash-landed on a Himalayan peak – find themselves, contrary to all expectations, transmogrified into demented Barbie wannabes, desperate for an elixir to combat the terrible, incurable disease afflicting females – age. It's not racial but facial prejudice – a discrimination only suffered by women. (I mean, Woody Allen still gets laid, right?) For females, word-play is foreplay. But for blokes? Well, if manners maketh man, make-up maketh woman. And we don't need a phalanx of behavioural scientists to explain why men judge women by their looks. Because they *see* better than they *think*.

Is it any wonder that once you hit thirty-nine a woman's IQ halves when she's within the vicinity of a new beauty product? Why we huddle around the latest anti-ageing cosmetic like an underground movement in touch with the free world?

For females, turning forty is more dangerous than a beach-thong in a big surf.

I blame Mother Nature (two-faced bitch!) and Father Time (bloody bastard!). Yep, those misogynistic killjoys have cut off my pocket money and left me grounded. With those two authoritarian heavyweights ganging up, what chance does a woman have, I ask you? . . . Which is how I ended up here, halfway through my thirty-ninth year, in a pastel-wallpapered, Muzak-saturated hospital recovery room, pulverized, puking and punch-drunk on painkillers. Mummified in bandages, I'm like a Christmas present waiting to be oohed and aahed over at my own unwrapping.

But will I 'ooh' and will I 'aah?' Or will this be the day I'm going to wake up, look at the algae wrapped around my abdomen and the raspberry enema pipe stuck up my bum and say to myself, 'You fucking idiot'?

Bristling with needles and woozy from the anaesthetic, I try to swim back up into consciousness, but am weighted down

by the enormity of what I've done. So much has happened
over the past year to propel me here – adultery, incest, death,
divorce . . . an accident with a do-it-yourself Brazilian Bikini
Home Waxing Kit . . . The facts keep toppling down on me.
I dimly recall that it all began last June, on my birthday.
That's when I first felt that my age was forcing me to hitch-
hike on the hard shoulder. And Life was the lorry that had just
zoomed by . . .

# 2. Are You Sure You Need Only One Cake For All Those Candles?

..........................................................................................................

The thirty-ninth birthday began much as any other day – a cup of cold coffee and a guinea-pig-poo pellet. As I tell my BBC news producer, the reason I'm often ignorant of the latest political development is that my kids always use the morning paper, before I've read it, to line the hamster cage. I have the best-informed rodents in the western world.

My husband Hugo handed me a hurriedly wrapped weed-whacker, for the newly landscaped garden – which had no weeds. 'And they say romance is dead.' I laughed. He was dashing to the hospital to save some poor bastard who'd blown out his carotid artery by driving into a lamp-post and self-ejecting face first through his sunroof.

But in truth, it was this very quality of altruistic dedication that had first attracted me to him. God, what was it now? Ten – no, eleven years ago. I'd smashed my jaw to smithereens when I'd fallen off the Berlin Wall. The only casualty of the Velvet Revolution. (What can I tell you? It's a *gift*.) My then employers CNN flew me back to the London Hospital where I spent the next two weeks watching Hugo Frazer stride purposefully from ward to ward, as though on invisible skis. You see, my husband is a cranio-maxillo-facial surgeon. He jigsaws together landmine victims, excises cancerous tumours or corrects horrendous Elephant Man birth disfigurements, mostly in gruelling twelve-hour operations. His confidence is as broad as his shoulders, broad enough to advertise on. With his big build, blue eyes and engagingly craggy face (as though in training for the vacancy that will be left when Robert Redford's arteries harden), it took me exactly two examinations to fall in love.

We quickly discarded professional ethics and gave in to a passion so hot, so intense that I worried it would affect the global climate. 'We can only hope that Saddam Hussein is not developing a passion like this,' I panted, post-coitally.

Hugo said that he was so elated, so *high*, that he kept expecting air-traffic controllers to ask him to relay his position – which, at that precise moment was on the middle shelf of the medical supply cupboard.

It was clear why I'd fallen for him (basically, Hugo was just like any other bloke you'd meet in a Greek myth). But what I could never work out was why *he*'d fallen for *me*. I think it had something to do with the serious academic circles he frequented at the time. We're talking bookish females. We're talking piles of dandruff forming around their ankles. Which, he said, was why he loved my low laughter threshold. My breezy ability to cut through bullshit like a scalpel through epidermis – something he put down to my being half American and living in the States until I was ten. I think he was also intrigued by my job: the coups; the collapsed dictatorships: me, flak-jacketed, a slick of lipstick on a sooty, sleep-deprived face, bouncing along in my bulletproof bra. 'This is Lizzie McPhee reporting . . .'

It may also have helped that when we first met, I was

accidentally wearing my paper hospital gown, back to front –
you know, the one with the *big gaping hole*.

Even after all these years, as I watched Hugo cross the
bedroom to pucker up for my birthday kiss, I felt a wave of
love wash over me. If I went to see a doctor myself, that's
what they'd diagnose – unfailing love of MD.

My kids – Julia who's nine and Jamie, seven – were my next
birthday well-wishers. As I slathered Marmite on to their tepid
toast, they tore themselves away from brightly coloured cereals
with cheerily abbreviated names like Fruit O' Yes! to honour
me with a collection of tiaras made out of old loo rolls, which
I praised as though they'd just presented me with the Dead
Sea Scrolls.

'Mummy, did they have television when you were alive?'

Hugo slapped his hand playfully over our daughter's mouth.
'Do you remember how thrilled we were when they learned to
talk?' he asked, shaking his head but smiling indulgently.

Jamie was investigating whether the electric fan would be a
good way to slice up his Weetabix more finely.

Hugo, mopping milk from his brow, bent down to give me
a curdled kiss. 'Don't worry. When they become teenagers,
*we*'ll turn to heroin, okay?'

'Do you think that will be strong enough?' I asked, picking
a soggy Nut O Wow! from his lapel.

But he wasn't angry. Hugo adored his children. When we
went out to the opera, he'd call home on his cellphone before
we'd even made it to the bottom of the street to check they
were okay. He knew without looking which child had stuffed
the Malteser up the other's nose. He *never* lost his temper
with them, not even on the terrifying occasion when they

accidentally pulled the inflate tag on the bouncy castle in the back seat of our moving car on the motorway. Not even when he'd been paged urgently in the middle of surgery because the kids had just washed the cats and wanted to know what setting to use on the tumble-dryer.

As he cupped their tiny chins to kiss them farewell, I watched the love spill and ripple across his face and felt a tingling shiver of happiness.

Hugo hastened off to the hospital and the kids trooped reluctantly upstairs to get changed for school, while I attempted a quick clean-up. My kitchen, like me, was comfortable with its lot in life. Chipped skirting-boards from indoor scooting, coffee rings on every surface, a chaos of kitsch magnets attaching homework schedules to an emphysemic fridge. I was just removing the brown blobs in the sugar bowl made from wet cereal spoons, when my older (although she'd never admit that to the outside world) half-sister Victoria breezed by for a quick hit of caffeine on her way to the beauty parlour.

'Oh, shit,' Victoria over-enunciated so that her red lipstick wouldn't come into contact with her perfect teeth, 'it's your birthday. Darling, I forgot. Thirty-nine! Well, for God's sake,' she lowered her voice conspiratorially, as she shrugged off a light suede coat made from many cute, adorable woodland species – no doubt endangered, 'don't tell anyone. Take it from me, the twenty years between thirty-five and forty are the most fascinating of a woman's life!'

I laughed with a mixture of affection and despair. 'You're really sad, do you know that? Really sad and pathetic. You may not have noticed but "growing older" is a Major Lifestyle Trend.'

Victoria is a model and, believe me, this is the woman who put the 'cat' into 'catwalk'. Her *décolletage* is the deepest thing about her. She was humungously famous in the 1980s, but once she hit thirty, her star-wattage dimmed. It had been a good ten years since her face graced the label of a shampoo bottle. Her modelling assignments have now dwindled to shows scheduled in, say, Helsinki, around, oh, *four-thirty a.m.* And her shoots seem increasingly dangerous – you know, the ones that nobody else would touch, Somalia, Belfast, or into the wildest depths of Birmingham. The cold hard truth? My sis was ageing faster than a pair of Prada platforms.

'Actually,' I prised my arm free of her crimson talons, 'I think I'll like the anonymity of cronedom. At forty you can stop worrying about it all and just quietly go to seed.'

My sister eyed me haughtily. 'Don't be rid*i*culous darling,' she replied, peering into a diamanté compact to retouch makeup manufactured by Trowel and Co. 'Turning forty is the major cause of old age.' She flopped on to a kitchen stool and shuddered. 'Age to women is like Kryptonite to Superman.'

'God, Victoria, you make me feel like I'm about to open as the next Norma Desmond in *Sunset* bloody *Boulevard*!' I said, exasperated, hurling celery and carrot sticks into the kids' lunch-boxes.

'Don't pretend you're not worried, Elisabeth. Turning-forty *Angst* is required by international law. All women go through it. And *you* are no exception.' She ate a crumb off the breadboard – which took care of breakfast – and lit up a fag. 'With every other forty-year-old woman feeling used and abused and on the social scrap heap, why should *you* feel any different?' She launched a halo of passively cancerous smoke. 'You'll only alienate all your other women friends.'

'Look, on the Big Day I expect I'll drink too much.' I slapped the Tupperware lids on to the lunch boxes and burped them shut. 'I'll possibly cry and dance naked on a table or two. But I mean it. I like getting older.'

My sister rolled her heavily mascaraed eyes. With their tonnage of eye-shadow, it was a feat of optical weight-lifting worthy of Olympic status.

'No, I *do*. I don't feel scared of life, the way I used to. I don't care if people like me or not. I like myself. And I know my limitations. I no longer expect to win the Nobel Prize for Astrophysics. I will never be an astronaut either. Or do a nude film scene. I will never have sex with Ben Affleck. I will never be beautiful. But one thing I'm *not* terrified of is wrinkles. Or death, come to think of it . . .'

'Darling, wrinkles *are* death.'

'Hugo loves me just the way I am.'

Victoria arched her topiarized brows. 'Show me a woman who's happy about her age and I'll show you the electro-convulsive therapy scorch marks.'

I shook my head at her. As half-sisters Victoria and I love each other, but we're insufferable friends. The only thing we have in common is our shared contempt for our materfamilias. Our mum, a B minus English actress on Broadway, survived a stormy six-minute marriage to an unpublished New York poet, thereby producing Victoria. The closest I came to finding out the identity of *my* father was during an attempt at a sex-education talk. 'Where do I come from, Mum?'

'Brooklyn,' was all she'd said.

Victoria and I presume she only got pregnant as a useful distraction from daytime television. Whenever she was summoned to our headmistress's office, she chose to go to the Caribbean instead. Finally she left us boarding in some scholastic hellhole in Surrey and took off – for ten years. Her favourite little quip was that she was so desperate not to have more kids that she'd put a *condom* on her *vibrator*. (Despite our mother's endless warnings that 'Men don't make passes at female smartasses', we'd both inherited her unattractive talent for tongue-lashing.) She is now ensconced in a Maximum Security Old Persons' Home and has put out an injunction to stop us visiting her.

But apart from mutual disappointment in our mother, you couldn't get two more opposite siblings. Victoria, with her slanted, luminous grey eyes and six feet of slender, photogenic flesh, doesn't look anything like a sister of mine. While I'm a brunette, Victoria is a blonde – and prepared to go blonder. I'd always wanted to be tall and disdainful like her, but instead ended up just short and eager. And it's not only in looks that we differ. Though *I* baked and broiled my way around the beaches of South East Asia during my gap year, I have never once seen my sister in direct sunlight. I tell people she hangs upside down to go to sleep at night. While I tend to think that my body is just there to carry my head around, my sister thinks that her head is just there to enable her to worry more about her body. After studying Liberal Arts at Brown University, I moved to Europe with the CNN job to discover my superficial sibling adorning the British fashion pages.

I caught sight of our reflection in the conservatory windows. I looked as flushed and dishevelled as my sister was coiffured and calm. In order to be ready to go out at nine a.m., she starts preparing at *four*. She's not happy unless squeezed into a size double zero dress. In her *grave*, Victoria will still be wearing a collagen mask and an overnight rejuvenation cream.

I wrestled my electric mane of hair into a rubber band at the nape of my neck. Why was *I* the sister to fall out of the Plain Jane tree and get hit by every bloody branch on the way down, goddamn it?

'Darling, don't forget tonight.' She flicked a blonde frond over her right eye, Veronica-Lake-like. 'It can be your birthday treat.'

My sister was a member of the Vulva Chorus in a big charity performance of *The Vagina Monologues*. Although embarked on the inexorable slide towards the C list, Victoria was digging her acrylic nails in all the way. And appearing at a media-intensive event raising money for a women's refuge was part of her publicity rehabilitation plan.

Her minuscule pink Nokia began to ring and her face lit up as she mouthed, 'Sven,' to me before purring huskily into the phone, 'Darrrrrling, six weeks' absence was *way* too long. My muff's in a huff. So, did you find me any work in America?'

I winced. While I'd retreated into books, Victoria ran away from our bleak, Nicholas Nickelbyed boarding-school at six-teen. She found work as a topless waitress in a Spanish tapas bar, followed by a stint as a 'dancer' in Sophisticats where she was spotted by a model scout. Sven's first words to her were '*You* are 9.9999. If you were with *me* you'd be a perfect ten.' This was her version of events anyway. Personally I think she could only have met her odious boyfriend in a police line-up. Hell, the man had handcuff tan marks.

Twenty years later, she'd now rekindled contact with this 'love of her life' and although he'd re-signed her to his agency, she was desperately hoping he'd marry her as well – a proposal she was busily promoting with sexual favours.

Sven (as in 'Svengali') had changed his name at twenty-two (from Terry Taylor) and had never looked back at his knick-knacked, pebble-dashed council-house past. He'd successfully transmuted a juvenile zeal for nicking women's knickers from clothes-lines into a career as a model agent where women took them off for him. Proving that you can't keep a bad man down, he became the European head of Divine, one of the world's largest model agencies with (as he endlessly boasts) a 100-million-dollar annual turnover. But his Christian Liaiger décor didn't fool me. This was a flamenco spa five-seater Jacuzzi man if ever I saw one. Despite the copy of the *Financial Times* tucked permanently under one arm, I'm convinced his real reading material is limited to back issues of *Big Butt*, *Hog Tied* and *Latex Maiden*. He may have a voice as mild and cool as a kindergarten teacher, but I suspect that if Sven went swimming in shark-infested waters, the sharks would wear chain-mail suits.

I checked my watch and realised that I had exactly thirty seconds to remove squashed bananas from the bottom of gym bags, snap the velcro fasteners on trainers, comb Julia's hair for nits and leave for work. I could have asked my sister to drop off the kids, but she'd only accidentally leave them behind at the hairdresser's. To Victoria, children are like Ikea appliances – you have no idea how much assembly is required until it's way too late. Despite having the maternal instincts of a guppy fish, my sister is the bewildered mother of the beautiful

Marrakech. For the past fifteen years she'd been looking for a loop-hole in her daughter's birth certificate.

I left my sister practically fellating her lover over the phone, herded the kids out of our Hampstead terrace house and was just about to hook myself up intravenously to a bottle of Valium for the school run, when my neighbour from the ramshackle, rent-controlled garden flat next door trampolined towards me on springy Nikes.

'Happy birthday.' Calim Keane grinned. 'I have no idea how old you are but you certainly don't look it.' He plucked the car keys from my hand and replaced them with a plate of cupcakes bristling with candles. 'How 'bout I do the school run?'

Calim was always coming to my rescue. He looked after my kids even when they were contagious and had earned their undying gratitude for teaching them how to make hilarious intestinal noises with their armpits. He'd assisted in the delivery of our guinea-pig's babies. He even came with me to try on swimming costumes; threatening to kill anyone who attempted to get into the fitting room. I kissed his cheek. 'Oh, Cal, *would* you? I am sooo late for work.'

Although he was a hard, Belfast man of thirty-one, a builder by trade, his pale skin was incongruously satiny – the sort of skin that can bruise from walking in the wind. He was also a poet on 'L' plates having published one very slim (to the point of anorexic) collection of verse. I looked affectionately into his speckled eyes, the eyes of a stray cat. And he *was* a stray, really.

'Me ma drank, me da drank, Jaysus, me *dog* drank,' he'd told me the day we'd met over the garden hedge, eight years previously. Abandoned by his father, he had been put into care at the age of four with his brothers after his mum died. When I'd asked him why he'd become a writer he'd replied nonchalantly, 'Oh, huge psychological dysfunction.' Not that he'd had much success. His only book had been published by Remainder and Co. I'm afraid Calim Keane is to literature what the Apollo 13 was to space travel. He was studying English Lit now, as a mature student at Birkbeck College, living on a student loan and working on a novel.

'How's the masterpiece?'

'Me poetic licence has expired. Me muse is unamused. Yep,' he said self-deprecatingly, 'I started out with nothin' and I still have most of it left. How're you doin'?' the lanky, languid, lunatic Celt asked me now, ruffling my hair.

'My sister reckons that thirty-nine is such a nice-sounding age I should decide to hold on to it for at least another decade.'

He snorted. 'Liz, you can't be poised on the cusp of forty for ever. You'll be in a zimmer frame. You know, people will notice.' He tossed the car keys high and snatched them out of the air.

'And *you* can't stay cooped up inside scribbling all the time. You need to be more outgoing. I mean, the home shopping channel operator is starting to recognize your voice.'

'I am outgoing . . . only inwardly. Which is why I was kinda hopin' you'd come to the university ball with me. It's too humiliatin' to go alone.'

'You have *got* to get a girlfriend, Cal. Otherwise the Pope is going to start asking you for tips on celibacy.'

'What woman is goin' to be interested in me? A man who's listed in *Who's* Not *Who*?'

I shook my head wearily and tucked a ginger-coloured curl

behind his ear. Cal's motto in life is 'If at first you don't succeed, give up.' 'Of course I'll go with you, you big Irish bastard.'

'Thanks, shug.' He always called me that. It was a Belfast-ism, short for sugar.

The kids tumbled into Cal's battered Volkswagen. I nosed my orthopaedic people-mover past the snaggle-toothed Dickensian buildings that make up our cobbled cul-de-sac and headed towards the BBC. I'd won my journalistic spurs during the fall of the Communist regimes in Poland, East Germany, Czechoslovakia and Romania. First for CNN. Then for the BBC. At twenty-nine I might have been jumping out of helicopters, but at thirty I was jumping into maternity clothes. Once pregnant, the Beeb had shunted me sideways into *The World News Today*, desk-jockeying behind an autocue. Resigned to Mother Mode, I'd opted for the lunchtime shift so that I could be home in time for the kids.

When I got to the office my girlfriends gave me a card that read 'What can you give the woman who has everything? *Shelves*.' My work was no longer filed on the floor but stacked neatly on a new bookcase.

And I laughed because I *did* have everything, damn it. I was the luckiest goddamn woman in the world.

I'd just come off air when Hugo rang to say he'd be delayed for my birthday celebration. And what life-threatening compli-cation would be keeping him from me *today*? I bantered, affectionately. A tracheotomy and an air rifle bullet lodged behind a child's eye. He promised to meet me at the theatre later.

If I'd known then what I know now, I would have

screamed, 'Don't come! Let's cancel. Better still, let's leave the city and go open a cute little craft shop in the Cotswolds.' But, oblivious to Fate's landmines, I just smiled. 'Sure, catch me up when you can, darling. I'll be holding Vicky's hand backstage.' It was my birthday and I felt blessed with a family life the Waltons would have killed for. I felt suffused with contentment; cocooned by love. 'It's the Old Vic, don't forget. I'll take my car, okay? There's plenty of parking.'

I blew a kiss down the phone, totally unaware that once I drove over Waterloo Bridge, I would find myself double-parked in a parallel universe . . .

21

# 3. Medics! We Have Incoming!

Other than when having sex or giving birth, most women pretend not to have a vagina. *The Vagina Monologues* (no, not a very unusual ventriloquist act) was a theatrical event designed to raise female consciousness as well as loads of cash for battered women.

At London's Old Vic theatre, an assortment of famous actresses, models and writers were performing pieces based on different aspects of the vagina: 'If Your Vagina Could Speak, What Would It Say?'; 'My Angry Vagina'; 'Reclaiming Cunt'; 'Because He Loved To Look At It'.

My sister doesn't have a political bone in her undernourished body. She thinks 'arms control' is some kind of biceps-toning exercise. But this was a chic media event, osmotically providing intellectual kudos plus loads of influential men to lust after her. (The sudden conversion of chauvinistic blokes to feminism had nothing to do with the opportunity to hear Winona Ryder, Calista Flockhart, Brooke Shields and the Kates, both Blanchett and Winslet, talking dirty, of course!) Victoria, a B list celeb, was not pleased therefore to find herself sharing a dressing room with A list Hollywood soap star Britney Amore, totteringly perched atop two needle heels, whimpering and simpering in a little-girl-lost voice about her gorrrrrgeous new boyfriend. While the men backstage marvelled at Britney's butterscotch body and emerald green eyes, her female co-stars were more ruthlessly objective. 'Her thighs are so liposuctioned, it looks as though she had one leg amputated and just split the other in half,' hissed my sister.

But nothing aroused more speculation than the Case of the Disappeared Bottom. *There was no bottom.* Ms Amore was hindquarterly challenged. It's a mystery as to how the woman sat down. Since the buttocks had been sliced off and the brain was missing as well, my sister and I gigglingly deduced that we had a new definition for 'lobotomy'. Nor was the irony of her appearance at the fundraiser lost on us. With all of Britney Amore's rhinoplasty, liposuction and silicone mutilation, well, if *that*'s not a Battered Woman, hell, *what is*?

Although it was a feminist event, nothing makes women bond faster than having another woman to bitch about. As Britney took her cue to go on stage, the other female performers in the wings were cackling and chortling. The only thing missing was a cauldron.

'You know how you get a huge mouth like that?' my sister sniped. 'You have fat from your bum injected into your lips.'

'Then the woman is literally talking out of her arse,' I volunteered. Cue more cackling. Tittering, we peered through the gloom, shielding our eyes against the theatre spotlights, to see the daytime drama diva, famous for her stethoscope-fondling as head nurse in the soap opera *Tell Me Where It Hurts*, cooing to the audience about what her vagina would wear if it could. But I was more intrigued by what *she* was wearing. Britney was the reverse of an iceberg: ninety per cent of her was visible, most of it between her clit and her clavicle.

'That's not a dress,' I murmured to Victoria. 'That's a cocktail napkin.'

My sister, who favoured the husky-voiced Lauren-Bacall-tightly-belted-mackintosh-narrow-waisted-pencil-thin-skirt-defined-shoulder-pour-me-a-martini-rhinestone-studded-cigarette-lighter look, ran her critical eyes the length of my body before quirking a tweezed brow. '*You* can talk. So, what is it? Hideously Awful Polyester Pants Day?'

What *I* saw as a well-tailored pants suit, Victoria saw as appropriate for a Stalinist machine-gun parade. I watched her slide one long leg through the slit in her starkly tailored dress. 'Who designed your outfit exactly, Elisabeth? *Blind people in a dark room?*'

I bridled. 'I'm a news journalist. I don't think it would be appropriate to start purchasing my clothing from the – ' I prodded a finger in Britney's direction, ' – Aspiring-Actress-Unbelievably-Revealing-Figure-Hugging-Clothing Shop.'

Britney sashayed towards us in the wings to the sound of lusty applause. Her metallic blue mini skirt was so tight you could see the three-course raisin she'd had for lunch.

'It's not a female,' I murmured. 'It's a pool cue.' I smiled politely at her as she passed. But Britney was not a woman's woman. With Herculean effort, her mouth moved into some kind of lipsticky grimace. It was a smile that could have irradiated soft fruit.

There were so many celebrities in the cast that most of the friends and family of the performers had elected to schmooze backstage rather than actually to see the show, resulting in an impromptu party. The pool cue made her way towards the hospitality table in the wings, walking at a deliberate tilt, hips thrust forward to accentuate her slim thighs, leaving behind a trail of gawking males. I saw Hugo arrive, dump his briefcase then beat the other men to hand the actress a glass of the warm Spanish wine (otherwise known as Grout Remover) obligatory at charity events.

'So,' goaded my sister, 'does Hugo *play* pool?'

'Don't be ridiculous, Victoria,' I scoffed. 'The woman's blouse is as sheer as her brain ... I mean, *look* at her.' I gestured towards Britney Amore, who was pouting her collagened lips in my husband's direction. 'She's just a charisma wrapping a vacuum. Hugo says that the brain is the greatest erogenous zone. Well, a woman like *that* has got the IQ of a lower primate. Hugo loves me for my mind,' I asserted smugly, 'not because of my butt buoyancy.'

My big sister gave me that irritated stare siblings reserve for each other. Victoria could never find the time to nag her only family member as often and as effectively as she would have liked, especially about Letting Myself Go.

'You're letting yourself go, Elisabeth.'

'You're the one who's let herself go – mentally,' I called out as she donned a red feather boa and glided majestically towards the stage to take her place in the Vulva Chorus. 'At least I'm well-read.'

'Yes,' she said, over her shoulder, 'but your ass is as broad as your mind.'

'Well . . .' I groped for a comeback '. . . your mind is as narrow as your waist.'

But my barb did not have the desired effect. 'It *is* narrow, isn't it?' she gloated, before sailing into the limelight.

Hugo seemed to be the only man in the wings who was not

drowning in the pool of drool surrounding Britney Amore. The TV soap star had declined Hugo's Chateau Grout Remover with a lecture on deadly pesticides. She then tried to prevent him sampling the hospitality meatballs.

'Stop!' she exclaimed. 'Yer stomach may be sayin' yes! But yer colon's sayin', "*Are you insane?*"'

Looking her directly in the eye, my husband devoured three koftas in one bite. 'Hitler was vegetarian. Enough said?'

Turning her back on him in apparent disgust, Britney proceeded to hold forth to the rest of us about her upcoming stage appearance at the National Theatre. 'Actin',' her Texan accent had a velvety rasp, like the tongue of a big cat, 'is ninety per cent talent and forty per cent brains.'

My husband snorted derisively. 'Is that what you think? If you'll pardon the exaggeration, ' he added, with disdainful suavity, handing me the beaker of tepid *vino* the actress had rejected.

Britney Amore shot him a wary look from beneath heavily beaded lashes – so thick it looked as though the tarantulas that were obviously nesting in her eyebrows were doing stretch aerobics with their many mohair legs.

'Am I missin' somethin', hon?' She turned to me, placing her manicured hands on her sticky-out hips and cocking one little foot up on to its towering heel.

'I'm terrible at maths too,' I explained, kindly. 'But, um, I think you'll find that ninety and forty is a hundred and thirty per cent.'

'Ah-*huh*.' She widened her eyes at me as though I were retarded. There was an alluring contemptuousness about her which took my breath away. 'And that's exactly what I give, honey-pie.'

Yeah, along with chlamydia, *honey-pie*, I thought, my good-will evaporating.

'Acting these days,' said Hugo a bit pompously, 'is a hundred per cent about looks. Now that the National Theatre is in a state of collapse, the only way they can get bums on seats is by casting actrines from TV soap operas – preferably with a scene where they take off their clothes. I guess it was hard to find a Shakespearean role that required full-frontal nudity. Ophelia's last swim, perhaps . . . ?'

I giggled. 'Can I Ophelia up?'

Britney met Hugo's gaze with defiance. 'I ain't never had a red-blooded man complain about *my* bodkins forsooth.'

Her scrum of male admirers, having ignored my bad pun, laughed over-heartily at her worse one. Except Hugo.

'Achievement doesn't depend on physical perfection,' he elaborated. 'Beethoven was deaf. Milton was blind. Stephen Hawking is in a wheelchair. Physical perfection means, well, nothing much, actually.'

I gave him an imploring glance – one of those oh-there's-nothing-wrong-with-my-partner-that-a-good-funeral-wouldn't-cure looks, an expression perfected by wives over the centuries . . . He completely ignored it – a response perfected by *husbands* over the centuries.

'We're totally aware of racism and sexism these days. But 'lookism' is one of the most pervasive, albeit most denied, prejudices.' Hugo ran his hands through his tawny mane of hair, which reared back off his broad forehead. 'Society confuses beauty with goodness. Police, judges, juries – they're all more lenient towards pretty women.'

Britney snapped her gum belligerently. 'Yeah, well, *sex* discriminates against the un-att-rac-tive.' The elasticated twang to her Texan vowels jarred discordantly with Hugo's rounded, ringing tones. 'I reckon a lady's gotta make the most of what she's got, ya know?'

'Well, here in *Europe*,' he responded, pointedly, 'we have a much more sophisticated approach to life. A woman who ages well is a thing of beauty.' I can't say I appreciated the way he draped his arm limply across the back of my shoulders, with all the passion of a beach towel. 'And those who fight it, ugly.'

There was a baited quality to the air. The actress bristled. But before she could run him through with her stiletto, the last chorus of *The Vagina Monologues* faded. After the curtain calls, everyone was ushered upstairs for the post-show party.

A slightly shell-shocked minister from the Department of Culture and Sport and the usual collection of Labour-supporting and toupée-sporting beer barons and tax exiles were approaching the benefit gala like draftees crossing a minefield. Feigning feminist sympathies, yet terrified that they were about to be savaged by a feral Fallopian tube, their smiles were snap-frozen on to bewildered faces. To unnerve them further, on the table in the centre of the room rose a six-foot cake in the shape of a pudenda. Between the two pink marzipan labia majoras pouted the particularly moreish, sugar-coated labia minora. The whole ambrosial, raspberry red cunt-fection was crowned by a delicate candied clitoris, which nestled temptingly beneath the piped icing pubes.

Guests hovered hungrily, in lip-licking salivation . . . until they realized that they'd just been subjected to an account of infibulation from a Somali victim. It had been a harrowing monologue from her heart and what was left of her vagina, which had made complaints about western sexism seem trivial. Shuddering at the memory, nobody dared wield the knife to cut the cake. Eventually, ravenous guests unhygienically took to gouging out chunks with surreptitious fingertips.

'I know he's here *some*where.' My sister anxiously scanned the throng, looking for Sven. 'I couldn't believe it when he said he was coming tonight. I mean, this is *not* his scene at all. I think he's finally on the brink of proposing! The night before he left for the States he said we'd look cute on a wedding cake together! I so want to be happily married like you, Lizzie.'

I was about to point out that Sven was really not my cup of slime when a whiff of aftershave strong enough to dissolve igneous rock forewarned me that the patron saint of Fake Tan Man was in the near vicinity. I swivelled and, sure enough, Sven appeared, a gold chain glinting amongst the hairs of his toasted torso. Though thinning on top, he wore the pre-requisite ponytail, which straggled down the back of a shirt darker than his tie. Inhabitants of the lower slopes of showbiz genuflected before him.

'Well, here I am! What were your *other* two wishes?' he oozed, in a silken voice.

'Sven, darrrrrling.' My sister kissed him proprietorially.

'Vicky,' he daubed his mouth with a satin handkerchief, 'let me wipe off a place for you to sit.' Sven's easy charm was negated by his cold, slow, unblinking eyes – which he rested, in turn, on each woman in the room. The scrutiny was so intense, so calculated, it made me feel as if he was assessing which of us to eat first, were we ever adrift in a lifeboat.

'What the hell are *you* doing here?' I asked him icily. 'Your views on women date back to the Jurassic period.'

'I couldn't miss out on seeing my fiancée in action.'

Victoria beamed at me. But when we turned back towards Sven it was to see him tentacling an arm around the minuscule waist of Britney Amore.

The atomic bomb on Hiroshima had less impact than this conversational detonation. My sister made a third-stage-of-labour face.

'Your – your fiancée?' she stammered, trying hard to digest the unsavoury information. (Probably all she'd eaten that day.) She was as crushed as the marzipan clitoris Sven had just circumcised from the cake with his penknife and was now devouring whole.

'Christ, you've only been in the States for six weeks!' I said, amazed. 'I mean, where did you get her? *A fiancée-vending machine?*'

Victoria's daughter, Marrakech, chose that moment to bound up to us. 'Mum! You were amazing.' She hugged Victoria with an enthusiasm usually reserved for foliage in the path of a bulldozer. 'I'm so proud of you. You're, like, finally using your fame to help the less fortunate . . .' She kissed me too. It was like being greeted by a Labrador pup – all limbs, wet mouth and yelps of joy.

My niece, devoid of her Doc Marten boots, combat trousers and beanie, had at last allowed her thick golden hair to fall free. Marrakech, who is desperate to be Taken Seriously, is a bottle brunette. Much to her mother's horror, she regularly dyes her blonde locks a mucky dull brown.

'This is *your* daughter?' Sven asked, amazed.

'So they tell me,' Victoria said, almost inaudibly. To preserve her unlined visage, my sister kept her emotional thermostat at a constant sixty-two degrees. And yet from the play of muscles beneath the surface of her face, I could see just how much Sven's marital announcement had mortified her.

'But she's grown so much!' Sven let his eyes slide down to focus on the teenager's stupendous bosom. And it was more than a professional appraisal.

'Yes. Who would have thought that beneath the chick-pea halitosis and hand-knitted bulky jumpers lurked a beautiful fifteen-year-old,' Hugo teased.

'*Thirteen*,' my niece amended strictly, nodding towards her mum.

My sister's anti-gravity precautions include not only bribing the Passport Office to allow her an airbrushed photo but also making her daughter pretend to be thirteen for the last two years.

'Anyway, beauty is superficial crap, it just makes you into a decorative object. A vase with tits.'

'Your breasts remind me of Mount Rushmore . . . My face should be among them. I'm a president too, you see. Of your mother's modelling agency.' Sven winked at her. 'You don't mind a bit of tasteless humour, do you? I do so love to whip these liberals into a froth of indignation.'

'I hate my boobs. They only attract one-track-minded creeps. Phallocrats. And penetration is oppressive.'

'Marrakech,' chided her mother. Victoria was holding

herself very still, as if she were an overfull glass of wine that might spill at any moment. I winced for her. Despite our differences, there's a fine silver umbilical wire uniting us. Something to do with all those childhood years of crawling to the bottom of the bed, shrieking with laughter about something ridiculous our mother had said, snorting, howling, muffling our hilarity with our nighties. Something to do with all those years whispering sad secrets beneath those covers, holding each other because nobody else would.

But Sven looked far from displeased at Marrakech's feisty outburst. He'd made a career out of bedding women – two thousand at the last count (his). Running the European division of Divine put him in prime position to play the Cuntmeister. And working with teenagers allowed him never to grow up. At fifty-six, the man was a senile delinquent. Peter Pan with the Lost Girls.

'Phallocrats, eh?' Sven repeated, lasciviously. He eyed my niece hungrily. Think fluffy pink bunny, I thought, think python.

'I agree wholeheartedly,' said Hugo. 'I'm so glad I married you, Lizzie. Men who marry beautiful women are heading for an early grave. Men married to plain women live an average of twelve years longer. Looks *can* kill!'

Victoria clucked her tongue in utter horror on my behalf. But I merely laughed.

I punched my husband's bicep good-naturedly. 'Thanks very much, you sweet-talking bastard. And on my birthday, too.'

'So it's ya birthday? How old are ya, hon?' Britney came out of her sulk to miaow at me.

32

Victoria spluttered, unable to believe one female had asked another female that question in public. My sister maintained that the best way to tell a woman's age, was *not* to.

'Thirty-nine,' I stated, with matter-of-fact pride.

Britney who was approaching thirty, but I'm not sure from which direction, recoiled. 'Hon, your cake must be *collapsing* from the weight of candles. Hell, you'll need *two* cakes!'

Briney Amore obviously had some good points – if you like rottweilers. But before I could share this insight with her, the guest speaker from the women's refuge, who were benefiting from the show, took to the podium. Terrified that any talk about women might make mention of cramps or secretions, the various well-fed corporate cowboys, so desperate to appear PC, could not disguise their drinking-straight-whisky expressions.

Next to me, Sven absentmindedly rearranged his testicles in their too-tight pants and murmured to Marrakech. It might have looked to others as though he was scratching his dick but, considering where he kept his brains, it was clear to me that the man was just thinking. Edging closer, I overheard him offer her a modelling contract. 'Modelling agencies are ruthless and cut-throat . . . especially the good ones,' he bragged, marinating in his own testosterone. 'You are a 9.9999. If you were with *me* you'd be a perfect ten.'

Where had I heard *that* before? As he was a friend of her mother's, Marrakech's crescents of black lashes blinked back at him trustingly.

The heavy summer air seemed suddenly freighted with unbearable tension. As the speeches monotoned on (it was the turn of the Big Businessmen now: a particularly pinstriped one took the microphone to feign feminist sympathies in the talk version of karaoke – talkaoke) I grew a surface of awareness that made my skin crawl. Half an hour later I could feel the beginnings of a headache gnawing at my temple. Was there a doctor in the house? I looked around for my husband. When I couldn't see him, I decided to brave the backstage labyrinth of corridors, locate Victoria's dressing room, fetch my bag and flee. I planned to call Hugo's mobile once I was in the car. He had probably zipped off to an emergency op. As I pushed past the throng, the party seemed like a movie set. My mind was zooming in and out, the shutter of my eye's lens clicking and whirring.

If I really *had* been in a movie, though, water would have started shaking in a glass to warn me that something Very Big and Scary was about to happen. Completely oblivious to the fact that my life was about to change for ever I pushed open Victoria's dressing-room door. When the door swung wide to reveal a naked Britney tongue-kissing my husband I saw stars. And I don't mean the Melanie Griffith, Glenn Close, Gillian Anderson performers either. Oh, no. In that split second I discovered more celestial firmaments than an astronomer with a Hubble telescope.

'Lizzie! Oh, Christ. It's not what you think . . .'

I tried to retreat from the room, but it was as if my entire central nervous system was being remote-controlled by a puppeteer. My hands, legs, arms, mouth all jerked awkwardly trying to ape real human movements. My heart was beating so loudly and quickly, I felt sure they could see it pulsating in and out of my chest cavity like a character in a Merrie Melodies cartoon. The very air seemed to shiver, as though in recoil from the scene.

'Remember me?' I finally squawked. 'I'm whatshername –
*the mother of your two children.*'

Hugo had leapt back as though electrocuted. His fly! Oh,
God, was his fly open? 'Have you just had sex with That
Woman?'

'It was only a kiss.'

He was beside me in a trice, tossing a lick of hair from his
handsome face with a flick of his head and whispering, 'Look,
if George Clooney suddenly asked you for a kiss, you couldn't
turn it down, could you? I mean, look at her.'

I followed my husband's gaze towards the chaise, where
Britney lay, supine, laughing insouciantly at my suspicion. Her
legs were as long as the limousines she used in lieu of them
for transportation. Her tangerine-coloured tresses set off her
lightly sautéd tan. The icing on her cupcake of loveliness
were her breasts: 32D, I reckoned, at an envious glance, and
as buoyant as the bubbles in the champagne flute from
which she nonchalantly sipped. The woman was so perfect
that she kept fit, no doubt, by doing step aerobics off her own
ego.

That was when I caught sight of my own reflection in one
of those dressing-room mirrors studded with merciless bulbs.
My uncollagened mouth was as open as my unrehydrated
pores. Britney draped a silken arm across her ample chest.
Even her elbows were moisturized, for God's sake. *My* skin
was like stucco. You could make a bloody patio out of me.

'Yer see, hon,' she gloated, in a belated but cruel response
to my earlier Ophelia crack, 'beauty may only be skin deep –
but ugly goes right down to the bone.'

It was then that the wave of ageing *Angst* engulfed me in

one gigantic roar. Why was I born so plain? Why was I born at all? Happy bloody thirty-ninth birthday to me.

'I came looking for you . . . She was changing. And . . .' Hugo panted '. . . we just naturally seemed to have a make-it-all-up kiss. I mean, she is a star,' he shrugged, 'and I'm a man—'

'Don't kid yourself.'

'A normal red-blooded man who—'

'Well, your DNA suggests you're a male,' I shrilled, 'but your behaviour is more that of a rutting elk.'

'Really. I don't know what came over me—'

'Britney Amore, apparently.'

Embarrassed to be having a marital meltdown in front of *Her*, I backed into the hall. Hugo followed, making defensive noises about it being just a brief exchange of saliva. ('I'm innocent, officer. I just tripped and fell and my tongue ended up embedded down this woman's throat.') On the drive back to north London he delicately turned the knife of accusation I had held against him. Hadn't I noticed that we'd fallen below the national average sex wise? My diaphragm must be home to at least three strains of mould spore from under-use. But once home he promised fulsomely never ever to go near her again, and I good-naturedly promised not to tell anyone about his misdemeanour – especially Sven. It was just a kiss. It meant nothing, I did understand that, didn't I?

My brain understood, but if my vagina could monologue it would have only one thing to say: you lying, cheating, hypocritical bastard.

# 4. Too Old to Lambada, Too Young to Die

A woman of thirty-nine prides herself on her worldly smarts. We know never to order anything on the menu described as a 'medley of'. We know that any product's packaging which reads 'easy to assemble' will contain more components, screws, wires and thingamajigs than a NASA space shuttle . . . And that husbands are prone to pork younger women. Okay, I know what you're thinking – not *all* men fancy eighteen-year-olds . . . You're right. Some fancy *sixteen*-year-olds. It's a given. Still, every time I thought of my husband's betrayal it felt as though a slavering wolverine was trying to claw its way out of my abdomen via my oesophagus.

Hugo? Between the legs of a woman he'd met for only ten minutes? Hugo Frazer MD, the man who's so terrified of diseases that he wears a condom while masturbating? Hugo Frazer MD, who showers before taking a bath in which he uses separate washcloths on different parts of his body so as not to cross-contaminate from one orifice to the other? Who gargles after oral sex? Hugo Frazer MD, whose body is so sterile, a bacterium would die of loneliness there? But there he was. The Howard Hughes of Husbands, discovered with an unprotected part of his anatomy inserted into a vagina monologuist. But *was* it just his tongue in her mouth? Or had he also explored a more unmentionable aperture of this strange woman's body? Was this the same man who, when making love to me, stopped at timed intervals to check his own pulse and respiration rate? Post-coitus I've often felt that, like a kindly children's GP, he was going to give me a jellybean for saying, 'Aaargh.'

The next morning, as I jockeyed for position among the designer jeep gridlock of horn-happy mothers late for Hampstead school runs, steering with one hand because I was leafing through an architecture book to find inspiration for the Greek temple I was planning to construct from ice-lolly sticks at subsequent traffic lights (why is it that kids never tell you about their homework until they're half-way out the door?), I paused to change gear with my teeth, while simultaneously fielding light, frivolous topics like 'If God made us, then who made God?', and balancing a Corinthian column between my legs with an ice lolly under each armpit, I found myself pondering a profound question: why the hell did I ever get married?

Adultery only happened to other couples. I'd read that it was on the increase, but I'd never dreamt my Hugo would cheat. We were completely entwined – emotionally, economically, socially, physically; spun together like silkworms. I just couldn't believe he could do this to me.

Two traffic fines and a dented bumper later, I delivered the kids to school. Just as I contemplated returning my family to their manufacturer to request a new model (because this one was obviously faulty) Julia and Jamie drowned me in kisses so wet the assistance of surf lifesavers was required. And a great poignancy squeezed into my bones as I felt full of freshly minted mother love. Kids have that way of just slipping in between your heartbeats. And Hugo, the man I'd loved most of my adult life, was their father. I had loved him so hard and for so long, it would take a restraining order to keep these feelings out of my heart. I loved the competent way he steered me through crowds, a sturdy, protective hand in the small of my back. I loved the fact that he always knew just how much to tip. I loved the inky arabesques of his handwriting on those indecipherable prescriptions. I even loved his singing voice, which sounded as though he was chewing off his own foot. I loved him because he was worthy and good. My man had made his name in a charitable cause, helping children injured by land mines, for heaven's sake. And, by God, I was going to keep him. I would start by abiding by his wishes and being absolutely one hundred per cent lip-zipped discreet.

'Hugo played doctors-and-nurses with that soap actress from *Tell Me Where It Hurts*.' I sobbed into my mobile five minutes later.

There was a beat of silence on the other end of the phone. 'Elisabeth, you've been sniffing your kids' homework glue again, haven't you?' diagnosed my half-sister.

'Or maybe it was just a vigorous exchange of saliva . . . I'm not sure. You must promise not to tell anyone, Vick . . .' I swabbed my leaking eyes with a sleeve.

'Darling, I hate gossip – but don't tell anyone I said so! Your secret is safe with me.'

'Yeah, you and Matt Drudge.'

'I won't tell anyone, darling . . . Well, only about twenty or thirty thousand of my closest friends. Where are you?' she barked.

I glanced out of the window at the sooty Victorian buildings, recognizing, between hot tears, the Planetarium. 'Marylebone Road. Why? What are you up to?'

As if I needed to ask. My sister is a petted frequenter of many salons – nail, face, body, groin – but she is most renowned for her long blonde tresses. And, believe me, it costs over two hundred pounds a month to get hair that natural.

Her crimping salon was literally one street away. 'But I'm . . .' I glanced at my Swatch. 'Jesus! *Very* late for work.'

'That Uberslut! What are you going to do to her?' Her husky voice went metallic and staccato as it broke up on my mobile.

'I'm pondering the Uzi machine-gun, hostage-taking and gradual-posting-of-bits-of-her-body-for-ransom option.' I lurched my large family car into an illegal double-yellow park outside the exclusive salon. 'That option looks quite attractive at this point.'

'You can't hate Britney Amore as much as *I* do. Have you any bloody idea how long I've been grooming Sven for marriage?'

'Vick, come on, you didn't have a real "relationship" with Sven. You just had three hundred and sixty-five one-night stands with the same person.' I cut the ignition.

'But I need a man. A *rich* man. I have designer footwear needs! Then there's the clothes – Moschino, Versace, Valentino. That John Galliano dress alone was three and a half thousand. All put together by my very expensive stylist, of course. Underwear – La Perla – we're talking a hundred and fifty for matching bra and pants. Then there's two thousand a year gym membership so that the body looks good *in* the La

Perla. Prada shoes – plus yoga, acupuncture and osteopathy to recover from *wearing* Prada shoes. A weekly personal masseur – fifty pounds. Facials once a month, seventy-five. Weekly nail technician specializing in transfers, piercings and varnish airbrushing, fifty-five. Pedicure, forty-eight. Hair-cuts, eighty pounds a trim, not including highlights every fortnight with seventy-pound white-truffle moisturizing shampoo . . . *Darling, people who say that money can't buy happiness just don't know where to shop.*'

I was walking through the crimpers now; phone cupped to my ear. It was a posh inner-city salon where they dyed your hair in the same sort of organic stuff they seemed to serve for lunch. It was what Cal called bullshit millennium food – balsamic this, sourdough that, wood-fired everything else.

'I am going to win Sven back, Lizzie. At all costs . . . Which is why I'm forking out for a few little procedures . . .'

Her lips came into view first. They were twice as big as they had been last night. These were childbearing lips. Swollen and bruised purple, it looked as if two velvet beanbags had been velcroed to my sister's lower face. I skidded to a halt. 'What the hell . . .' I dropped my mobile phone on to the mock marble floor where it skittered beneath the kneeling Filipino pedicurist, who was busily separating my sister's toes with wads of tissue. A manicurist, also of third-world extraction, was kneading Victoria's left hand as her right propped open a glamour mag at a page entitled 'Hasta La Vista Body Hair'. Victoria's entire cranium was wrapped in tin-foil plumes, which a colourist was lacquering in foul-smelling bleach. But it was the lips that demanded total optical astonishment.

'Beauty,' Victoria's velcro beanbags proclaimed, 'is one of

the most lovely and natural things money can buy . . . For God's sake! Don't kiss me!' she shrieked, shrinking. 'Can't kiss anyone until my own tissue grows around and locks the scaffolding into shape.'

'Yeuch!' I backed off. 'Way too much information.'

'In a couple of months, apparently, it will feel normal to both eat and talk again.'

'Oh, well, *that*'s comforting.'

'The doctor used alloderm. It's a sheet of human collagen taken from dead people. They feed the sheet through a small incision and—'

'Lips to die for.' I shuddered. 'Literally.'

'It's the Julia Roberts look.' Actually it was the I've-got-a-vagina-sutured to my face look. 'Sven will love it.'

For a moment, I pondered Sven's fifty-six-year-old gargoyle excrescences. 'Victoria, have you actually *looked* at the man lately? He's so hirsute he needs *nostril* mousse. What's fore-play for you two? Combing nits out of his back hair?'

'Any man on the *Sunday Times* Rich List looks exactly like Brad Pitt to me.' Her face flickered and tensed. 'I'm tired, Lizzie.' The normal swagger in her voice was extinguished. 'And I'm lonely. I'm so lonely I've started to talk to my daughter! Speaking of which, Sven offered to sign Marrakech and that bloody little egg-head turned him down. Can you believe that? And he's not happy with Britney Amore. He really opened up to me last night.'

'And let me guess, confessed to a few major felonies?'

'You've got Sven wrong. He's charming, he's polite—'

'What? He says "please" before he rapes you?'

'He's realized that he's always loved me. He told me, right after we . . .' Her voice trailed off.

'Right after what?' I asked, flopping exhausted into the leather swivel chair beside her.

My sister took a deep breath. 'Right after we made love last night.'

I gazed at her, stupefied. 'Am I the *only* one not having sex around here?' I finally managed to blurt, modulating the outburst when I realized that every neck in the salon was craning in my direction.

'It's all right, darlings,' Victoria announced to the gawping patrons. 'She's just having an out-of-marriage experience . . . Look on the bright side,' she lowered her voice, 'you'll lose *so* much weight now!'

I shook my head in disbelief. 'You have *way* too much time on your hands, Victoria, do you know that?'

She then leant into my ear. 'Sven's going to dump the Fellatrix *pour moi*.'

I felt a sickening sensation in the pit of my stomach. 'Oh, God. If Sven leaves Britney Amore for *you*, that will leave *her* free to steal Hugo!' It would be the mating version of Musical Chairs.

'You're just going to have to make more effort, Elisabeth. You *are* at that age when husbands start to go off you.' She swivelled me towards the bank of mirrors. 'When are you going to Do Something about yourself?'

'Um . . . how 'bout never?' Still, I was startled by the haggard, sleep-deprived, tangle-haired visage peering back at me. Could an adulterous husband do that to you? 'You *know*

I don't like looking at my reflection.' I slapped her hand off my arm and turned my back to the glass.

'Yes. You and Dracula. It's not normal, darling.' She leant into my face and scrutinized it ferociously. 'Look how leathery your skin is. You should have a handle on your arse!'

'Have you got any idea how annoying you are?' I growled at her. 'Skin has only one function. It's to stop your insides from slopping out everywhere. Why can't you just let nature take its course?'

'What?' she shuddered. 'Downwards and outwards? Nooooo, thank you.'

'Look, it's true. As a teenager I desperately wanted to be super-glamorous, like you,' I said, glimpsing the clock – I couldn't believe I'd missed the morning news conference just to enjoy the sharp end of my sister's tongue, 'but I had problems with still wanting to eat at least once a day. Now if you'll excuse me I—'

'Which is why you've ended up old and dull with nothing to regret.'

This was an old refrain I'd put up with since my book-wormed boarding-school days. I felt my blood boil. 'Oh, yes, all those venereal diseases I missed out on as a teenager, the hangovers and heroin addictions I never experienced. I look on them as the "wasted years",' I retaliated flippantly.

The colourist encased Vicky's tinsel turban between radiator bars. 'I warned you,' my sister tut-tutted, pursing her lilo lips. 'It's not Life that begins at forty, it's Death.'

'Oh, shut up, Victoria. You're making me feel like the female version of Keith Richards. Now, I really must get back to the Real World. And listen, sis, by the way – the lips? I'm all for collagen injections.'

Her two inflated, fleshy Dunlop tyres mouthed, 'Really?'

'Yeah. They provide so many hours of harmless entertainment for the rest of us.' And with that, I took my cellulite and my crinkles and stomped the hell out of there.

'Let's see if you feel that way once you turn forty,' she called out after me.

'Once and for all, forty is not old,' I tossed over my shoulder.

'Only women who are about to turn forty say that. It's a terrible age. TOO OLD TO LAMBADA, TOO YOUNG TO DIE.'

*

All the way to BBC Television Centre, I massaged my poor, battered ego. I had lived. I had learned. I'd had experiences. I had earned these crows' feet, goddamn it! Isn't experience as valuable, in professional terms, as having young skin?

Yeah, *right*. And Cher is ageing *naturally*.

The first blow to my fragile confidence came when I dashed into the doughnut-shaped building known as the Beeb to find myself being taken aside by the production team – Raphael, Crusoe and Dweezil. (It was like working for the Ninja Turtles.) They were PR-ed, upstart, X-generationers (as in X-tremely arrogant), who could pat you on your back to your face while kicking you in your face to your back. Raphael was sorry, he palavered, that I'd missed that morning's meeting because there had been a long discussion about 'image' during which it was decided that I should be shifted from the prime-time slot and replaced by a blow-waved anchorman recently poached from Channel 5.

At first I presumed it was just another instance of There But For the Genitalia Go I.

But no. His appeal, Raphael insisted, was not that he had balls, but that he had what the producer called 'TVQ' – Televisual Quotient. In other words, he was young.

I felt a brittle, crumbling sensation inside. 'Why? Does it make the news any better?' The office was open plan and all my colleagues were periscoping over their flimsy, carpeted partitions, straining to overhear the conversation.

'I'm being demoted for someone prettier!' I announced to them all, as I tried in vain to lasso my extravagant tendrils of hair back into a ponytail.

'Demoted is such a negative little word, yeah?' the acned Raphael condescended, sucking on a pen that was probably twice as big as his dick. 'Think of it more as a staff *feng shui*. We could offer you *Playschool*? That whole mum thing. You can relate to that, yeah?'

Despite the profound sense of loss engulfing me, I squared my shoulders. 'Screw you and the ageist policy change you rode in on. Now, if you'll excuse me I'd like to go and spend some more quality time with my wrinkles.'

Which is why I left pretty much as I'd arrived – fired with enthusiasm.

\*

I know you'd have to be a Trappist vegan celibate not to get hurt in Life, but losing my hubby and my job in twenty-four hours did seem one visit too many from the Fuck-up Fairy.

Bumper-to-bumpering back along Euston Road, arms clenched around the steering-wheel, I tried to contain the anguish I felt inside. I rang my sister and ascertained her location – a shabby photographic studio in Camden. I drove straight there to find her erotically draped over a couple of seventy-year-old men wearing cardigans.

'What the hell are you advertising?'

'Viagra. It was all the agency could get me. *Now* do you understand why I need to be rescued by something tall, dark and Sven-like?'

'Well, don't give any Viagra to Sven. He'll only get taller,' I said caustically.

'Ha bloody ha. So what's up?'

When I'd numbly reported the change in my employment status, her voice shivered. 'Christ, Elisabeth. Well, you really can't afford to lose your husband now. If you're not going to improve your looks, then you'd better get bloody good in bed.'

A hollow laugh escaped my lips. 'Hugo and I've been together for eleven years. To us, "good in bed" means not snoring, farting or taking all the covers.'

'Really? I always thought Hugo might be quite imaginative in the sack.' She paused to pout for the camera, looking exactly like one of those tribal women on the Discovery Channel with plates in their bottom lip. She really should have been advertising tableware. 'Has the passion really gone?'

'Put it this way, my birthday present was a weed-whacker.'

'A weed-whacker? Bloody hell. Then you have *got* to get more creative in bed.'

'What are you suggesting? *Origami*?'

'No! Toys, games, fantasies, French ticklers, benwah balls, banana-flavoured erecto-gel . . . Become alluring and sensual. Sex keeps you young. And it's terribly good for your complexion.'

All the way home up Haverstock Hill (and much to the amusement of other motorists), I practised alluring and sensual facial expressions in the rear-view mirror. After a particularly jubilant response from a group of schoolboys at the traffic lights I rang Vicky back. 'Posing provocatively in latex lederhosen is *not* the way to intrigue a husband like mine. Think about it. What first captivated him? My composure while under fire. I was too shell-shocked to fight with him last night. If I can just keep my dignity and not get all desperate . . .' the car moaned around the corner of my cobbled street '. . . Hugo will have enough space to take a fresh look at me, to remember what he loved about me in the first bloody place. I mean, what could be more attractive to an errant husband, I ask you, than a cool, in-control wife?'

It was then that I crashed into the red pillar-box. I wasn't hurt, but the sheer shock of it made me slump over the wheel and sob uncontrollably. A blur of raggedness tumbling through the passenger side door slowly resolved into the shambolic shape of Calim.

'Jaysus. Are you okay?'

'I'm having a pulmonary embolism, but apart from that . . .'

'What's goin' on?'

'Oh, nothing much. I've lost my job and . . . and my sister just told me that I have the erotic appeal of a dental-floss dispenser.'

He grinned coyly, rummaging through his pockets for a

crumpled tissue. 'J'know what men really find excitin' in bed? A woman who's confident enough to enjoy sex . . . and you're a confident woman, Lizzie.'

I blew my nose. 'You've been to say-the-right-thing school, haven't you, Cal?'

'But it is true, Lizzie. Bein' sexy is more to do with bein' at ease with your body than anythin' else. I don't know any woman with a perfect body . . . but I know loads of sexy ones. A woman who's really juiced up, whatever her shape, is more erotic than a woman who walks backwards out of bedrooms.'

Like airbags in a car, sensitivity in a man is an optional extra. And Cal was clearly top of the range. I squeezed his arm. 'Are you sure you're not gay?'

'Hey, I'm so in touch with my feminine side I'm startin' to complain about me wobbly thighs. Lemme help you out of there.'

Since the driver's door was wedged up against the post-box, I had to slide across the console. It was then, to add insult to injury, that I got impaled on the gear lever. The symbolism proved too much for me. 'Hugo . . . was . . . unfaithful.' I started sobbing again.

Cal reeled. 'No! Who with?'

'Britney . . . I can't even put her name in my mouth, I mean you never know where it's *been*. The Artist Formerly Known as Slut.'

'Amore? Britney Amore? Christ almighty.'

'Yes. The actress from *Genital Hospital*. I walked in on them. He said it was just a kiss, but his hand was between her legs. She was naked. And I'm pretty sure his fly was at half-mast. I couldn't tell if he was zipping it down, or – or zipping it up.'

My mobile phone shrieked. It was Jamie's teacher, Ms Savage, reminding me that I'd promised to go on the afternoon excursion to the British Museum. 'You signed the return slip and tore along the dotted line at the bottom,' she reminded me sternly.

'School,' I said, staggering out of the car. 'Excursion. I forgot.'

'Tell her you can't go. Tell her you're a meningitis carrier.'

'Only a certificate of death – a recent one – would be an acceptable excuse for Ms Savage. Could you drive me?'

Hampstead is built on one of the few high hills in London. The sunshine had vapourized and the city below us had become so grey it looked veiled in gauze – a perfect meteorological match for my mood. In minutes the sky darkened and a passing storm shattered on to the streets. Puddles hissed beneath car tyres. Cal pulled me into his battered Volkswagen with the bumper bar sticker 'Who cares who's on board?' On the dashboard was a hand-scribbled note declaring, 'No radio. Already stolen.'

'I'm going to stick a sign on *Hugo*,' I said, 'reading, "This is *not* an abandoned husband".'

'Obviously,' Cal said, trying to concertina his six-foot frame behind the wheel, 'I'm only drivin' this wee car to prove that I have an enormous cock. You do understand that, right?'

As he contorted into the driver's seat, I lectured myself quite sternly. It was no good looking for my self-esteem in Lost Property. I could compete with that Slutcicle. I had a vivid, quirky imagination. Whereas Britney was a No-brow. She was ninety-eight per cent personality free. She was Bimbo-

50

lite. One week and he'd be sick of the bland taste of her. Whereas *I* was a complex carbo of a woman. A nourishing, filling, well-balanced meal. I could make Wildean epigrams. Do cryptic crosswords. I knew the square root of the hypotenuse. *She*, on the other hand, was nothing more than a mattress with breasts – something to lie down on while having a shag – president of the Vaginal Discharge Self-Help Group. Our relationship was based on more than just tawdry sex. We had a deep commitment. Goddamn it. *I* was a return-slip-tear-along-the-dotted-line-at-the-bottom signer! I was not going to degrade myself by trying to compete with the likes of *her*. It was good in a marriage to create a little intrigue, but that didn't mean greeting my husband at the door in edible undies.

Cal finally squeezed into take-off position and shook his mad hair. Water drops flew off his curls like spangled jewels. As he careered down the street, contenting himself by making helpful corrective gestures at other drivers, I felt a rekindled faith in my husband. I'd overreacted. Birthday blues had made me feel vulnerable, that was all. Maybe it really *was* just a kiss. And what was that, after all? Just the anatomical juxtaposition of two orbicularis oris muscles in a state of contraction. It was clear that Britney Amore was nothing more than a fly on the windscreen of my life.

Awash with relief I rang Hugo to tell him how much I loved him. The hospital said he'd gone home for lunch. I rang the cleaner. She said Hugo had called to say he'd be staying late at the hospital.

We were outside Jamie's school gates. 'Where to now, ma'am?' Cal asked, doffing an imaginary hat.

'A whip emporium. Pronto. I need to buy benwah balls, banana-flavoured erecto gel, French ticklers and a vibrator with forward and reverse gears.'

Another thing a worldly, smart thirty-nine-year-old woman needs to know: up against a Sex Goddess, principles and profundity are about as useful as a eunuch at a whipped-cream orgy.

# 5. If I Can't Have It All, Can I At Least Have Some of Hers?

.................................................................................................................

The female orgasm is more of a mystery than the continued career success of George W. Bush. But, by God, I was determined to have one with my husband. An Academy award-winning one – better than any two-bit telly actress could pull off.

After a quick detour to a sex shop called Sssssh, Cal had dropped me, late, at the British Museum so I could go into Mother Mode. We got home from collecting Julia to find a message on the answering-machine from Hugo, saying he'd be back at seven. I consulted my watch. That gave me one and a half hours. In between burning chicken nuggets and checking math homework, I ran to the bathroom, showered and shampooed. I pffted with that spray and pffted with another, powdered armpits and nose, painted fingers and toes, trowelled on moustache bleach and spatulaed off depilatory creams. Then, finally, I shook out the lingerie I'd bought (with Cal fiercely guarding the changing room), threaded myself into the tight lace teddy, took a deep breath and dared to glance into the mirror.

Due to the pleasure of breast-feeding two children (thank *you* Penelope Leach), my boobs were like day-old party balloons with all the air leaked out. The most popular technique for flat-chested women to make themselves look ridiculous is the 'Wonder-bra' – so-called because as soon as you take it off, you wonder where the hell your tits went. My boobs were now strapped up on my neck someplace, like a couple of spare double chins.

Steeling myself, I let my eyes creep cringingly downwards. Well, it looked like that weed-whacker Hugo gave me was finally going to come in handy. A pelt of pubic growth sprouted from each leg hole. It was amazing my pudenda hadn't been awarded National Park status. Snapping open the crotch press-studs, I immediately took to my pubes with a pair of the kids' project scissors shouting 'Timber!' Ten minutes later I sneaked another look. Now my entire vulva just looked ragged. Oh, my God! And one of the pubes was grey! I cropped closer still. Soon the general effect was of a moulting shag rug. Frantic, I kept on trimming and shaping. Now my spiky fanny resembled a sea creature disturbed in a rock pool and preparing to attack. It gave 'bad hair day' a whole new meaning.

My eyes slid lower. Oh, God! My thighs were spilling over two black stocking tops like lava from a flesh volcano. Flinging the teddy floorwards, I tore off the nylons. Unfortunately, what lay beneath was acres of white flesh. Luckily, by rummaging in the bathroom cabinet, I found an old bottle of fast tan. While the kids yapped around me, demanding to know why their fingers and nostrils had to be kept apart when they so obviously *fitted* and whether sneezes were really 'your soul trying to escape', I slapped and slurped the tan on to my anaemic skin. There, that would do the trick.

But forty minutes or so later (after I'd explained to Jamie

that only his Aunt Vicky was allowed to pick her nose – and then only from a catalogue and postulated with Julia on the theological concept of after-life) what had seemed richly Mediterranean in the privacy of my own bathroom had begun to look Rajhneeshi under the bright rays of late-afternoon sun. In fact, my 'tan' pulsated. It radiated – but more tandoori than tanning salon. I looked as if I was wearing a tangerine wet-suit, with darker elbow patches, knee-pads and ankle straps.

Heart palpitating, I checked the time. Six forty-five. Hugo would be home in fifteen minutes. After I had packed the children off to Cal's next door garden to shoot some hoops and horse around, I frantically pumiced myself with a nailbrush while panic gnawed at my insides. No luck. I took to my poor body with a pot-scourer, exfoliating myself down to a pretzel. Still no improvement. Followed by a sand blaster. But still nothing. Just orange. I looked like a distress flare. People could employ me at the scene of a boating accident.

Oh, boy, did I feel sexy now. It was clear that I was soon going to be mastering *The Kama Sutra For One*. In desper-ation I reached for the sex aids. The benwah-balls brochure promised orgasmic bliss. But what it didn't say was that inserting these chrome bowling balls would be like childbirth, only backwards. And with no epidural. And once I'd put them in, would I ever get them out again? If not, I was in for the most embarrassing airport security metal detector search ever. By the time I gave up, panting and exasperated, I was so depleted with exhaustion that I had to eat the banana-flavoured erecto-gel.

With the sound of my husband's key grating in the lock, I leapt on to the bed to lie sensuously among pillows that I now noticed were splattered with squashed chicken nuggets. Eyes darting urgently downwards for a final check, I saw that my bright orange body was decorated in tiny handprints from where the kids had been clambering up me earlier. A trail of little paw marks had developed with Polaroid speed up both legs. Even stranger, I seemed to have hirsute toenails. Oh, God! My pube trimmings had fallen into the wet nail polish and dried there. As much as I yanked and pulled, they remained cement-rendered. So much for being 'alluring' and 'sensual'! Distressed, I shoved my mohair feet under the sheet, which I tugged up over my puckered, baby-marked belly. I could hear Hugo's step on the stair; he always came straight up to change out of his suit. Perspiration was beading my top lip. Dry of mouth, I licked my lips – only to discover I was still wearing moustache bleach. Dry-retching from the poisonous taste, I wiped it with the nearest thing to hand – which I identified too late as my expensive new lingerie. But then I gawked into the bedside mirror to see that the bleach had been on so long it had turned my top lip albino. It neoned out at me from my reflection – an iridescent white. Bloody hell! I also had a stress pimple erupting on my nose. Now *there*'s a good look – wrinkles and pimples. *Thank* you, God. To complete the seductive image, I then noticed a nasty underarm shaving rash. Worse, although I'd hidden my aggressive sea creature in a pair of delicate silk scanties, the spikes were poking through. Jesus! My pubic hairs could now shred a man, like Parmesan on a cheese grater.

I ripped off the scanties and balled them up behind the bed. By the time Hugo's hand was on the doorknob, I was in such a panic I was tempted to drink the nail-polish remover with which I was desperately attempting to scrub off the pubed toe-varnish.

Get a grip, girl. My husband loved me because I was the loyal and devoted mother of his children, goddamn it. I suspected that the Texan Pant-snake Charmer had probably asked him to *Tell Me Where It Hurts*, so I needed to be fierce in pointing out that my adoration was not based on infatuation but on feelings that had grown during a real, in-sickness-and-in-oh-God-not-the-flu-again? relationship. I had to let him feel that, yes, I could live without him – because hey, I was a vibrant, independent career woman (despite the temporary set-back of being unemployed). But also that I'd definitely rather not. Needing him was not the same as being 'needy'.

I clutched the erecto gel, which promised to 'animate the phallus'. In just moments my Hugo's penis would be so damn animated it would be signed up by a cartoon network.

I parted my lips into a warm and welcoming smile, lit up my eyes with love, vibrantly arranged my facial muscles into an independent-yet-needy look and turned to face my darling, dearest husband . . .

# 6. You Turn Me On Like a Cuisinart, Baby

························································································

'Oh, fancy a quickie, do we?' my husband said, in a voice meant to discourage.

'As opposed to *what*?' I retaliated, hurt. (This was *not* going to plan. I was *supposed* to be demure and desirable.)

'I knew you'd get all vindictive about last night. It wasn't my fault.' He flumped on to the edge of the bed to shuck off his shoes. 'The woman threw herself at me.'

I groaned. 'Men always think women are hot for them. You could be stabbing a man repeatedly with a carving knife in the cardio-artery-vascular thingo and he'd still be thinking, Oh, wow, she really fancies me!'

He tugged impatiently at his tie, wrenching it from around his neck. 'I fell prey to her transient glitter and I'm sorry,' he said wearily. 'But that kiss meant nothing to me. I love *you*, Lizzie.' But his voice seemed thin and diffident.

'Huh! You only love yourself, Hugo Frazer. When you come, you call out your *own* name!' (*Oh, good one, Lizzie. I was obviously a graduate of the Andrea Dworkin School of Desirability.*)

It was his turn to bristle. 'So, what are you saying exactly? That I have a big ego?'

'Oh, is *that* what's blocking out the sun?' I shielded my eyes and squinted melodramatically.

'I'm trying to be emotionally honest. I thought you women liked men who're in touch with their feminine sides?'

'Yeah, as long as it's not on another female.' I couldn't help the bitterness in my voice. I'd wanted to be digni-bloody-fied, but anger was bubbling up and beginning to haemorrhage all over our oak-panelled sleigh bed. We were obviously having the fight I'd been too stunned to have the previous night. 'By the way, it would be nice if you used some imagination in bed now and then.'

'Oh, you mean I should imagine its good?' He turned his back on me to peel off his pinstriped trousers.

I was crushed. 'Are you insinuating that I'm not good in bed? Maybe I should go and get a *second opinion*.' I squirmed in embarrassment as Hugo tossed back the sheet. My whole pudenda looked like Astroturf. You could play mini-golf down there.

But worse than him noticing was that he didn't. He hadn't even clocked that his wife was orange.

'No.' He sighed, yawning elaborately. 'You're a very proficient lover.' Lying down, he gave my thigh the kind of perfunctory pat you'd give an old family pet.

'Proficient!' I reeled back as though he'd poured acid all over my body. '*Proficient?* The Nazi invasion of Belgium was *proficient*.'

'Well . . .' he groped verbally '. . . reliable then.'

'Reliable? That's *worse*. Mussolini's *trains* were reliable.'

'Well, reliable as in every Friday.'

'I'm too tired the rest of the week!' I counter-attacked, turning my back on him and curling up into the foetal position. 'Looking after *your* children. *I'm* the one who attends the school assemblies to hear the reports on 'energetic events and their ergs'. *I*'m the one constantly reeking of Plasticine.'

'That's just an excuse and you know it. The big secret is just how much married women hate sex. That's the great thing about having a baby, you don't have to make love for months afterwards. To most wives "sexual freedom" means the freedom not to have sex. "Not tonight darling, I'm Having It All in the morning."'

'I don't know why I bother to take precautions.' I extracted my diaphragm in one dextrous move and slapped it on to the side table. 'I mean, an oral contraceptive is a conversation with you, Hugo.' I threw myself out of bed and into my old silk dressing-gown, recalling, with a pang, the lace panties I'd bought for what I'd intended to be an erotic encounter.

Hugo hauled his bulk to a sitting position on the side of the bed. I noticed, dismayed, that he hadn't bothered to take off his socks and vest. A gloomy silence descended on the bedroom. A dismal picture of the Slough of Married Despond mocked us from the mirror above the mantelpiece. 'If our marriage was a restaurant, we'd be in the non-smoking, vegan-only section . . .' I sighed . . . 'unlike the All-You-Can-Eat-For-Free-Finger Buffet you devoured at the party last night.'

'Let's not fight, darling.' He moved towards me. 'It was nothing more than a pheromonal incident . . . Are the kids at Cal's?'

'Yes . . . A what?'

'Pheromones. A hormonal smell that stampedes your glands and demands that you kiss that woman immediately.'

I eyed him glacially. 'Couldn't you just breathe through your mouth?'

Hugo spread his hands in a conciliatory gesture. 'Men are trapped, Lizzie. Deep within the cortex of a man's brain . . .' now his warm, capable hands were kneading my knotted shoulders '. . . instantaneous judgements are made to ensure that we respond to beauty.' He undid my old dressing-gown then placed his penis in my palm as methodically as he'd hand a scalpel to a surgical nurse. 'And, yes, such behaviour is cruel and shallow, but it's momentary, instantly regretted and, most importantly, *not our fault*.' He moaned in expectation as I knelt down.

I cupped my husband's splendid penis in two hands and addressed it wistfully. 'What was a nice thing like you doing in a slut like that?'

'I wasn't *in* anybody. She was having trouble with her zip. That skirt was so tight it could only be removed by a surgical procedure'.

'Oh! How convenient! And there you were with your bedside manner. How *could* you, Hugo?' I stood up, letting go of my old friend. 'That woman's so manhandled, so fingered, so *pawed*, she could be exhibit A in the forensics department of Scotland Yard!'

'Kissing's not that big a deal, is it? I mean, for Christ's sake, these things happen every day.'

'Yes . . . in *Las Vegas*!' I harrumphed to the bed and flopped back down on it. 'A kiss, Dr Frazer, is a contraction of the mouth due to an engorgement of the dick.'

'Oh, listen!' Hugo cupped a hand to his ear. 'Do you hear

that yelping noise? Oh, wait. It's just *you*, barking up the wrong tree.'

'Yelping?' I withered. 'Hey, if you want to get rid of me, throw a stick. Obviously I'll run after it. Let's see if I can catch a frisbee with my *teeth*.'

Hugo rubbed his furrowed brow as he followed me back to bed. 'Why does a woman always misconstrue innocuous statements to mean her husband wants to be rid of her?'

'Oh, so *that*'s what Britney is – an innocuous statement?'

'God, I don't know.' His hand was on my nipple rolling it half-heartedly between forefinger and thumb. 'I don't know why I did it, Liz. Maybe I'm having a midlife crisis.'

'Well, you're definitely giving *me* one.'

'It is well documented, dearest – the medical phenomenon of the male menopause.' He ran his hands soothingly down my body and between my legs, spreading my lips with the deft precision of a gynaecologist undertaking a routine cervical smear. 'The craving for emotional intensity, the desire for heart-fluttering human drama . . .'

'Couldn't you just have gone whitewater rafting? Male midlife crisis! What a load of crap. It's nothing more than ovulation envy.'

'Please forgive me,' he begged penitentially. If his voice had had legs it would have been on its knees. 'I'm really, really sorry. You're the only woman in the world for me.' He picked up my diaphragm, folded it in half like a letter and posted it between my parted thighs.

But jealousy had sidled in and taken up residency. 'What really upsets me is how you could fancy *her*. I mean, the woman has the cognitive ability of – of limp lettuce.'

'Generous mammaries don't necessarily mean she's a bimbo,' he said defensively, stroking my thighs.

'And just to establish that she's not a bimbo, she's chosen to appear nude in various men's magazines.'

'Only *Playboy*, darling,' he teased my clitoris with his fingers, 'and they interviewed her because she is actually disarmingly intelligent.'

'Meaning she faked rapt attention while you bullshitted on,' I decoded, fuming as I rolled away from him.

'She seemed very interested in my work . . . and, she's written a book.'

'What kind of book?' I looked at him amazed.

'A cookbook.'

I laughed violently, convulsively. 'An *actress* who's written a *cookbook*? What does it say: "Take fingers, put down throat, regurgitate"? "Take one line of cocaine, place on paper, snort"?'

'She's going to give you a copy – '

'I bet it lists the calorific value of sperm from various movie moguls. The Casting-couch Special,' I hooted.

' – when she comes for dinner,' he interjected, tentatively, propping his head on his folded arms. 'The week after next.'

I leant up on one elbow and gawped at him, uncomprehending. 'Dial-A-Mattress is coming to dinner? And when exactly did you issue this invitation?'

'When I rang Sven today – to discuss a project – *she* answered.'

'Listen,' I said stonily, 'just because I've lost my job doesn't mean I'm going to become a professional wife.'

'You lost your job? Why?'

I hadn't meant to blurt it out like that. 'I'm too old,' I grieved, my bravado evaporating. 'Apparently they're tearing down buildings that are younger than me.' I clutched a pillow to my abdomen. 'Next time I get on a bus, the *driver* will offer me his seat.'

'Darling, that's preposterous. I'm appalled. Tell me what happened.'

'Anyway, why on earth would you be interested in any of Sven's projects?' I probed suspiciously, but the fight had gone out of me. The crushing humiliation of losing my job had left me as limp as an eighties perm in a sauna.

'It's a business proposition he put to me at the party last night.'

'What business?'

'Sven's agency is going to donate some money to my charity for landmine victims . . .' His eyes shifted, evasively. 'And anyway, we need a little "lifestyle surgery", you and I, starting with some entertaining. It may have slipped your attention, darling, but I am a highly respected surgeon. I need to be part of a "power couple". Plugged into the social socket. When we first met you were so dynamic! Maybe losing your job is a blessing in disguise. You could devote your energies to becoming one of London's leading hostesses. A Domestic Goddess. A Trophy Wife!'

I looked at him aghast. Oh, where was my husband? My lovely, gentle man? My steady, wise and witty Hugo? The holder of the World Indoor Record for Lovely Husbandliness?

'As a couple we could give credibility to an idea Sven has had for a . . . health clinic.'

'A *what*?'

The phone rang then – something to do with an airlift of Chechnyan children who needed immediate surgery – and, moments later, Hugo was reinstated in his suit and headed back to the hospital. 'Have a think about the cuisine,' he called, from half-way down the stairs.

I tugged the blankets over my head. Anxieties clung to me like a wet shower curtain. He wanted me to be a suave and dynamic dinner-party hostess? Just on the very day I'd become a newly signed-up member of Losers Anonymous? Why didn't I become a sophisticated 'Trophy Wife'? A 'Domestic Goddess'? Why didn't *he* just plop on to some shore and evolve?

Bugger it, there was no way I would play little wifey at a dinner party for *her*. Apart from the fact that Britney had recently devoured my husband, it should be illegal to have to cook for someone who's written a cookbook. Anorexic women like her should be skewered on a toothpick and eaten as an hors d'oeuvre. That's what I would tell Hugo when he got home. End world hunger – eat an actress.

Besides which, catering wasn't my forte. (Even though I could now grate Parmesan on my pubic area.) I'd only ever once attempted anything beyond cold cuts and then I'd nearly fallen into the blender and made a crudité of myself. No bloody way would I do it. Domestic Goddesses who say they get high on housework have obviously been inhaling too much cleaning fluid. Definition of a 'hostage'? A woman who has to cook for damn visitors.

# 7. When You Wish Upon A Michelin Star

The notion of wives doing all the cooking and housework is no longer publicly fashionable. But I know for a fact that it goes on behind closed doors.

Two weeks later, on a hot Sunday night in July, with the kids still not bathed and in bed, I endured the usual hostess panic that since nobody was going to turn up there'd be too *much* food; or if they did show they'd have new lovers or lawyers in tow so there'd be too *little*; or everyone would have food allergies, which would mean either insulting me by *not* eating my dinner or eating the meal and throwing up over each other. I called for Cal to help me with the children and catapulted back into the kitchen just in time to catch the cats stripping the last of the sesame-seeded seared tuna out of the salad. All that remained was a little sad spag and a frond or two of wilted seaweed. Any hope of a cordon-bleu sensation bit the gastronomic dust.

'Listen, Cal,' I said, when he bounced in five minutes later to find me desperately rummaging through the freezer, 'I'm just not up to going to your uni ball any more. Why don't you ask Victoria?'

'*Victoria*? She'd never go out with the likes of me. This modelling business your sister's in, well, it's all about contacts.

Right? Entrée into places. Stuff like that? Well, the only entrées I've got access to are on a menu. Oh, sure, I can get entrée . . . as in prawn cocktails and canned soup. I can get the power table at McDonald's with a minute's notice.'

'That's all right. Victoria doesn't eat in public anyway. Models live in a state of permanent terror that they might actually develop some muscle tissue.'

When Hugo arrived to find his wife armed with a hair-dryer trying to defrost eight chicken breasts, he gave me a homicidal look. I'm not exaggerating. If looks could kill, I would have been donating my organs to medical science right there and then. Actually I wasn't sure if he was angry about the chaos, or that I'd invited Victoria without consulting him. (Victoria would never forgive me for denying her a Close Encounter of the Sven Kind.) Hugo says my sister doesn't visit, she *invades*, which she was doing right now, cascading into the kitchen in a swirl of silk scarves and duty-free bags.

'Alcohol! Quickly!' She seized my glass of Pinot Grigio.

'What's the matter?'

'I have just spent the last week modelling muu-muus for drunken electrical engineers in Dubai. If Sven doesn't marry me soon, my next gig is glamour-posing for amateur photographers in Milton Keynes.'

'Is that so bad?'

She slumped despondently over her wineglass. 'Darling, it's Kosovo without the perks.'

'I know something that will cheer you up. Cal's planning to ask you out.'

Now it was Cal's turn to shoot me a homicidal look.

67

'Ah . . . yeah.' He nervously readjusted the worn leather belt on his Levi's 501s.

Victoria placed her manicured hands on the hips of her spray-on snakeskin trousers. 'Put it this way, Calim,' my sister replied, 'if I were naked, you'd bore the pants *on to* me.'

'Victoria!' I snapped. She might have severe PMT (Post Modelling Tension), but there was no need to take it out on my best buddy.

'Okay, so it's no to sex,' Cal replied gamely. 'How 'bout some indiscriminate heavy pettin', then?'

'I'm not being rude.' Victoria sighed. 'It's just that you're so insignificant.'

Beet-faced, my loyal friend took a small bow. 'Ladies and gentlemen, that last act of abject humiliation was brought to you by Calim Keane. Excuse me, but I have a date to read bedtime stories.' He left abruptly, bounding up the stairs two at a time.

Before I could shove my half-sister down the waste-disposal unit, Victoria exclaimed, 'I suppose the fact that Britney has rather en*or*mous tits is a rather ex*a*sperating detail.'

'God.' My stomach churned. 'Is she really so brazen that she's actually turned up?'

'I just passed Jabba the Slut parking her Porsche. Forget the *chicken* breasts, Elisabeth, and just concentrate on your own.' She thrust her hand down my bra and hoicked my tiny tits to the top of their lace cups. 'Leave It To Cleavage. That's the only show men are really interested in.'

I glanced in Hugo's direction over by the wine rack, where he was scrutinizing vintages – my husband could put the bore into Bordeaux. 'Victoria, Hugo is *not* a breast man!'

On cue, the largest pair of mammaries in the northern hemisphere glided into view. It was like a photo-finish in a blancmange bake-off. The female to whom the Siamese soufflés were attached followed some five minutes later. My husband's eyeballs pogoed out of their sockets and boinged! into her bra cups, where they gambolled around in the throes of ecstasy before boomeranging back socketwards.

'You were saying?' crowed my sister.

When Sven waylaid Britney with kisses on the kitchen threshold, I thought it was an opportune moment to retreat with Victoria for some tandem toilet time.

'For God's sake, don't let on that you know about Britney and Hugo. He told me not to tell you. He wants me to be suave,' I bleated, plonking my posterior on the lavatory seat. 'I can't be suave.'

'Of course you can, sweetie. All you have to do is stand still and look brain-dead . . . Hurry up, I'm *bursting.*'

'I have a degree. I can't look brain-dead.' I washed my hands while Victoria took her turn to pee.

'Try winsome, then. Britney does a terrific winsome.'

'How?' I handed her a toilet roll.

'You just look like a neutered dog. You keep looking at him till he pats you – and then you take his leg off. That's my number one Useful Girlish Tip,' she philosophized, pulling the chain. 'The only other way to keep a man happy are a few Martha Stewart Moments in the kitchen. Oh, and some feminine mystique.' She paused to fart before sashaying out of the bathroom. 'Men love that.'

WANTED – Suave, sophisticated, winsome, discreet, dynamic 'Trophy Wife' with enormous cleavage. Must be an experienced Michelin Star cook and general Domestic Goddess, appropriate for Power Coupling. Applicants without feminine fucking mystique will not be considered.

I fastened my face. It was going to be a bumpy night.

# 8. Many a True Word Is Spoken Ingest

There is only one certainty in life: things always get worse before they get worse.

And so it was that the woman who made Jessica Rabbit look two-dimensional was now wriggling into the kitchen in a pair of leopardskin pants – Britney Amore wore so much jungle print clothing you really couldn't date her without taking malaria tablets. 'Hi, y'all!' she said, with such euphoric bubbliness that it was impossible that class A narcotics weren't causally related.

'You remember my *husband*,' I said coldly (postscripting a mental mutter, 'last seen sprinting up Mount Lust').

'Hel-*lo*,' enthused Hugo, almost concussing himself on the elevated pan rack in his hurry to stand up.

'So, where are the kiddos, hon? I was simply *dyin'* to play with them.'

God! Not content with stealing my husband, she now wanted to win over my children! My throat was on fire with misery. And what, I wondered bitterly, would a dumb-ass broad like her play? Remedial Scrabble? Join the *Dot*? 'They're in bed,' I said, primly.

As Hugo congratulated Britney on the critical reception accorded her extended nude scene in the National Theatre's production of *Hamlet*, I tried not to look at her bra-less chest. They weren't breasts. They were speed bumps. And they had all the men at the party – Hugo, Sven and some low-life Italian friend of his whose handshake left me begging for Dettol – crawling over to the social kerb.

'Do you think she's had a boob job?' I whispered to my sister.

'Noooo.' Victoria rolled her eyes sarcastically. 'Under her clothes she's obviously wearing some kind of anti-gravity device.'

'I mean, what's holding her up?' I marvelled. 'Wire? Glue? A team of specially trained fleas?'

'Now, boys, don't let me monopolize y'all. Its embarrassin', isn't it?' Britney confided to Victoria and me, in mock cama-raderie. 'If only I could make myself less desirable.' She looked me up and down, enquiring solicitously,'How do *you* do it darr-lin'?'

I was only half recovered from my coughing fit when Marrakech breezed into the kitchen. Britney immediately fell upon the teenager, kissing her ardently on both cheeks. 'Well, I am now officially a lesbian because *you* are so *gorg*eous! No wonder Sven's offered you a modellin' contract. I can see why!' She stepped back to appraise her young rival. 'How old are ya, Princess?'

Marrakech shrugged. 'I'm not sure. I'll check. How old are you *today*, Mum?'

I held my breath.

A curtain of blonde hair fell languidly over my sister's smoky left eye. 'Thirty-one,' she announced confidently.

There was a collective throat-clearing at this revelation.

'You don't believe me, do you? . . . You just can't believe I'm that old.'

Sven grabbed my sister's photogenic butt. 'Tell me,' he chuckled smuttily, 'is this seat taken?'

I would have liked to grip him warmly too – *by the throat*. Hugo, nervous about Sven's presence, laughed with exaggerated heartiness. It wasn't like Hugo to be so sycophantic. Would he really feel so guilty over just a *kiss*? With my chest tightening, I whacked the half-thawed chicken into the wok and stir-fried the shit out of it – not exactly what you'd call a Martha Stewart Moment – and downed my glass of wine in one long gulp.

'My offer still stands, Marrakech,' Sven said, trailing after her. Honestly, the man was more adherent than a stay-fresh mini pad. 'I'd be happy to give you the lay of the land.'

'Let's just hope that's a figure of speech and not a sales pitch,' I confided, *sotto voce*, to the chicken breasts. I gave one a tentative prod. It had the consistency of a Pamela Anderson implant but it was warming up vaguely, thank God.

'You simply cannot let this opportunity pass you by, Marrakech,' Victoria insisted. 'Your beauty is a gift.'

'Yeah? Well, I want a refund. I wish I were really plain so that people would treat me, you know, *normally*.'

Even though she'd had her hair snipped to a monkish Still-Born-Again-Christian crop, Marrakech was as stunning as ever.

'Besides, after I leave St Paul's I'm thinking about going to Oxford to do a Ph.D. on human-rights abuses in the American Correctional Services – it really sucks over there. What do you reckon, Aunty Liz? Should I model instead?'

Hugo glanced at me sharply. I dodged the oil spitting up

from the pan. 'Well, sure . . .' I said, chug-a-lugging his vintage *vino*.

My husband breathed a sign of relief.

'. . . if you want a career where you starve yourself to death, wear stupid shoes and get bossed around by men with huge beer bellies and minuscule brains,' I concluded.

My husband's tufty eyebrows beetled in annoyance.

'I agree with Aunt Lizzie. Modelling's bollocks. It's, like, the worst job in the world.'

'Not the worst,' I put in. The guests all looked at me expectantly, hoping I might now redeem myself. 'Manually masturbating caged animals for artificial insemination would, technically, be a tad more repugnant.'

My niece chortled – a reaction not remotely shared by the others, especially my husband, who was mouthing, '*Power Couple*,' and '*Domestic Goddess*,' at me, with narrow-eyed annoyance.

'Beauty is a curse,' Marrakech said emphatically.

Britney gasped. 'But, hon, a woman without beauty is like . . .' she groped for an analogy '. . . is like . . . well, it's like *Macbeth* without the balcony scene!'

The other guests assumed tactful expressionless faces but Marrakech actually laughed out loud.

A suffocating silence filled the room. To break the tension, Hugo began shepherding guests into the dining room. I was so rattled I'd already downed a bottle of wine on my own, which meant that I was feeling too happy to remember to put the rice on. Oh, well, I groggily rationalized, nobody really likes rice anyway.

As I circumnavigated the round table at a trot, depositing

glasses, placemats and butter dishes, Sven tried to introduce the aftershaved offering he'd brought in lieu of the customary bottle of wine. The solarium tan, the bottle-tinted hundred-pound hair-cut, the Versace suit and diamond ear stud, the flawless dentition bar one glistening gold tooth – the man had international money launderer written all over him. 'This is Tony "Knuckles" Milano – a *potential investor*,' he stressed. Investor in what? Landmine victims? I was distracted by Hugo's desperate demand for the placement. Shit! The placement! I improvised, ensuring a mad Musical Chairs scramble for seats, which allowed Britney to insinuate herself into the seat between Sven and Hugo, and Victoria to slide in next to Sven. Before I could hyperventilate over these two particular disasters, I realized I'd forgotten to put the dishwasher on earlier, meaning we'd have to resort to the second-best porcelain – a motley crockery collection comprising little chipped plates with bunnies running around the edge, complemented by a canteen of blunt butter-knives.

Back to the kitchen I trudged. Panicking, I heaped half-cooked food on to everyone's plates, except Victoria's of course: she declined to eat. ('Go on,' I urged her, placing spaghetti strands vertically on her plate, for a more slimming effect, 'you can always regurgitate it later.') I finally collapsed into my chair to hear Sven holding forth.

'Yep, the fad for plastic surgery is sweeping through post-forty-year-olds the way a fart sweeps through a jam-packed elevator. All the experts now agree that beautiful people actually do have a better life than the "fuglies".' For Signor Milano's amusement he translated. 'Fuckin' uglies.'

'Ap*par*ently we beautiful people are more loved,' Britney

batted her long lashes in a perfect neutered puppy-dog impression. 'We even earn more. Up to twelve purr cent. That's what Hugo told me,' she added serenely.

Victoria raised a told-you-so eyebrow at her daughter, who was shredding her paper napkin into confetti in her lap.

'What do *you* earn, hon?' Britney asked me sweetly. 'Oh, shoot! That's right! I heard you lost your job. Silly ol' me. I forgot. Too old weren't you? . . . An' now you're tryin' to stop Marrakech from havin' a job too.' Everybody looked at me. I felt like a parachutist in a skirt who'd forgotten to wear knickers.

'At least we know how she gets herself to vomit up her food,' Victoria whispered to me, while I tried to retrieve my jaw off the parquet floor. 'She just listens to herself *talk*.'

But then it was my sister's turn to flinch as Sven rewarded his girlfriend with a peck on her luscious lips and Britney adhered to his mouth with a smack of sticky fuchsia lipstick. Victoria speared a bit of chicken from my plate and shoved it unceremoniously down her throat. My sister, eating solids? I gave her look of astonishment. 'I'm eating to compensate,' she mumbled between chews.

'What for? *Hunger?*' What others saw as a cryptic superiority in my sister, I knew to be nothing more than a sad and desperate irresolution – coupled with starvation.

Hugo, smiling, bent towards my ear. I thought he was going to thank me for going to so much trouble. Instead he hissed, 'Elisabeth, this chicken is still frozen in the middle! Go back into the kitchen and *do* something!'

A drunken lurch to the kitchen and a rummage through the

freezer produced nothing but a packet of themed fish fingers in the shape of Disney characters. 'What the hell?' I muttered vengefully and, while waiting for the chicken oil to reheat in the frying pan, dumped the fish fingers into a Pyrex dish and nuked them to death in the microwave. *Chef will be serving the fish tonight in a lovely sauce we call haemorrhage of ketchup.*

'What *is* it?' Britney, the cookbook writer, asked moments later, peering dubiously into the bowl I placed before her.

Sven prodded one with a jewelled forefinger. 'Braised bag-lady's tampons?' he hazarded.

'The dietician said I should put some weight on,' Britney smugged. 'I try, I *really* do but . . .' She shrugged in defeat, before presenting me, rather pityingly, with a copy of her damn cookbook.

My husband gave a bewildered shake of his noble head.

I met the collective critical gaze of my guests defiantly. 'It's a . . . Seafood Medley. A concoction of batter cunningly fused with marginally aquatic foodstuffs and configured into comic characters. Post-gourmet,' I ad-libbed, '*Cuisine ironique.*'

'Eatin' to excess takes ten years off your life anyway,' Britney pronounced superciliously, pushing away her plate.

'Aye, but it's the worst ten years, isn't it?' said Cal, tumbling through the dining room to fetch glasses of water for the kids. I pulled him into the chair next to me. He rocked back and pivoted on two chair legs, one cowboy-booted foot cocked across a denimed knee. 'It's the incontinent, droolin', depressed years. I mean – who needs 'em?' Cal gave a crooked smile, his fluorescent-toothpaste-coloured eyes crinkling with kindness.

I laughed. The candlelight gave an underlay of gold to his mussy red hair, which surely even Victoria must notice. 'You are allowed to smile, Vick, you know. Go on. He's funny.'

'No,' she said firmly. 'It will only lead to lines.'

The potential Italian investor glanced at his Rolex.

'Which brings me neatly to the point of tonight's little soirée,' Sven spieled urgently, desperate to get the conversation back on track. 'All women want to live to a hundred, but not past the age of thirty-five. Baby-boomers are being nipped and tucked and sucked and lifted—'

'And chopped off?' Marrakech sliced her knife savagely through a lemon. 'If I didn't have these humungous tits, people would take me seriously.'

Sven was openly salivating . . . and it couldn't have been over the themed fish fingers. 'You see?' he gloated. 'Every woman wants to be different from how she is. Younger or prettier or smaller titted or *bigger*.' He looked at me pointedly.

My eyes slitted venomously. Is there anything quite so annoying as having your physical shortcomings criticized by a man who should be imprisoned for persistent chest hair exposure? Hugo shot me a wary look. Yeah, yeah, *Trophy Wife*, I reminded myself, biting my tongue.

'Do you know what the cosmetic-surgery industry raked in last year? In the States alone? Three hundred and fifty billion,' Sven trumpeted. Tony 'Knuckles' Milano stopped looking at his Rolex, which cheered Sven up enormously. 'They reckon money makes you miserable – but I reckon I could be miserable quite happily. What do you think, Hugo? Wouldn't you like the *chance* to see whether money could make you happy or not?'

My husband, oblivious to Sven at that moment, seemed to be pretty damn happy already. His head was bent towards Britney in a pianissimo aside. Britney was stifling hysterical laughter. You would have thought it was Billy Connolly whispering in her ear-hole. She pulled Hugo's hand towards hers as she rocked back with mirth, ensuring that my husband was buried up to his eyeballs in cleavage. I felt the heat of anguish burn into my face. As he hauled himself out of there, wearing a grateful smile, I was Joan-of-Arced in jealousy. If that actress didn't get her hand off my husband's thigh the only 'cast' she'd be in would be made from plaster after I pulverized her.

'Jaysus. Is that *her*?' Cal tossed his head in Britney's direction. 'How the hell could anyone get into such a tight pair of pants?' he whispered to me.

'A glass of champagne usually does the trick,' I grumbled back.

'But cosmetic surgery joints, we have them all over Italy,' said 'Knuckles' Milano. 'Once Interpol gets your mugshot, a new face is quickly advisable. So why fly to Harley Street?'

'Because we're a Longevity Clinic. With a whole anti-ageing ethos. Including cryogenics. Quite handy for gunshot victims,' Sven jawed on.

'Ugh. Isn't that where they freeze your noggin?' cringed Marrakech.

'Oh, yes. I give very good head.' He winked at my niece. 'Neuro-suspension for fifty thousand bucks. A hundred and twenty thou for the whole bod. Plus, for the living, the ultimate in professional plastic surgery, with the services of renowned, world-famous cranio maxillo facial surgeon,' Sven verbally drumrolled, 'Dr Hugo Frazer!' He spoke my husband's name in the sort of reverential tones usually reserved for the miracle of birth or the Second Coming.

The pinch of salt I'd discreetly been adding to Cal's meal became an albino mountain. 'Hugo, don't tell me you've been taking those mindaltering drugs again?' I joshed.

My husband pushed away his untouched plate and busied himself in opening more bottles. This dinner was starting to resemble a Kennedy family reunion. Being on call, though, he was the only one not drinking.

'You are joking, right? Hugo? You used to say that on the integrity scale cosmetic surgeons are ranked right down there with syphilitic ulcers and politicians.'

Britney uncapped a red lipstick shaped like a bullet and took aim at her Cupid's bow. 'Beautification of the body is among the oldest established practices of mankind,' she parroted, pausing to run Jungle Red over her lips. She was rewarded with another kiss from her fiancé, prompting my sister into an even more frantic food-spearing frenzy.

'Hugo, why don't you just fall into an open sewer and drown slowly?' I was beginning to understand that 'drunk' is the future of 'drink', but pushed on regardless. 'It would be a more dignified end to your career than working with *Sven*.'

Sven canted a brow. 'Yes, I am an agent of Satan, but my duties are largely ceremonial,' he quipped, smiling wickedly at Marrakech.

On Sven's far side, Britney was convulsing with laughter at Hugo's latest whispered witticism. Suddenly my Serious Spouse had turned into Billy Connolly, Robin Williams and Steve Martin all rolled into one hilarious bundle.

'So, how much investment would you need from offshore?' persisted Mafia Man, swigging back another full glass of Montrachet. Under the table, Sven gave Hugo a stealthy but self-satisfied thumbs-up signal.

My husband – going into business with Sven? As a supportive, loving, caring wife I just had to say something – something like YOU'RE FUCKING INSANE. But determined to be a Leading London Hostess with the Mostest, I dipped my remark in disinfectant and said, instead, 'But don't you think all this worry about wrinkles is slightly ridiculous?' A sea of blank faces turned towards me. Except Hugo, who was strafing me one of those I-Married-a-Moron expressions. 'I mean, wrinkles are a result of laughter . . .'

Sven scrutinized my face before concluding. 'My dear, nothing's *that* funny.'

As the rest of the guests chortled, Car leant into me and asked in a steely voice, 'Do you want me to punch his lights out?'

'Ya know, hon,' Britney simpered, 'a face-lift would simply transform you!'

'Yeah. From a woman in her late thirties to an extra in *Planet of the Apes*. How could you let Sven talk you into something like this without first talking it over with me?' I beseeched my spouse.

'Actually, it was Britney's brainwave that we go into business with your hubby,' Sven clarified.

Britney? Wasn't Sven pulling her strings? I'd presumed that the actress was so ventriloquial, her fiancé might just as well have put his hand up her ass and started working her mouth. 'It was Britney's idea?' I gasped, reappraising her.

'Of course, she gets all her most brilliant ideas during sex,' Sven preened, 'because she's plugged into a genius!' Sven laughed uproariously at his own joke, then looked lasciviously at Marrakech, obviously hoping she'd also like a stroke of genius.

'Oh, well, I'll always be a dumb brunette, then, 'cause I'm celibate,' Marrakech announced. 'I mean, what's the point in having a relationship, yeah, when statistically, in one out of every *three* couples, one partner is cheating?'

The air was suddenly polluted with guilt. An uneasy smog of silence settled on the table.

Feeling me tense up beside him, Cal gallantly attempted to rescue my party from the social minefield into which it had strayed. 'Ninety-nine per cent of statistics are made up, you know . . . just like that one,' he drawled.

Hugo gave a fake laugh. 'I don't know what all the fuss is about with affairs. I'm sure I'd be very understanding.' He fired off a meaningful look in my direction. 'If it ever happened to *me*, that is . . .'

'Really?' Victoria retorted loyally on my behalf. 'I'd shoot my spouse in the head with a small handgun. Or maybe just the woman he was cheating on me *with*.' She glowered at Britney.

Britney's gaze remained impassive, her smile serene.

Sven's yellow wolfish eyes glinted at me. 'What would you do, Lizzie, if Hugo was unfaithful?' He fired up a cigar.

'I . . . I . . .' I wanted to respond, but Hugo was pulling that passing-a-kidney-stone expression.

'She'd divorce him,' Victoria answered, looking daggers at her brother-in-law. 'No. She'd kill him and *then* divorce him.'

'Really, hon?' Britney asked, amused, ostentatiously waving away Victoria's cigarette smoke. 'You'd divorce him?'

'And why are *you* so concerned, Princess?' Sven probed suspiciously.

Hugo and Britney were overtaken by a sudden simultaneous desire to count the pinenuts in their salads.

'It's all hypothetical anyway because Lizzie and I are faithful,' Hugo assured the guests. Now it was my turn to be riveted by pinenuts. 'Because I know the secret of how to keep a woman happy.'

'And, by God, does he know how to keep a secret!' Victoria let loose a husky guffaw.

By now I'd chewed my lip into pâté. Oh, well, at least I finally had something interesting to serve up to the guests.

Cal's breath was hot in my ear. 'How can you just sit there and listen to this crap?'

'I'm under sedation,' I told him, braving a smile.

'I am blessed with a very happy marriage,' elaborated Hugo, arms spread expansively along the backs of the chairs on either side of him.

'We'll have a real happy marriage too,' cooed the actress, seductively snuggling up to Sven. Victoria started bayoneting more food off my plate. Her fork prongs were literally flying back and forth in front my face. 'I'll like nothin' more than havin' sex with the Hubby.' Britney playfully pinched Sven's cheek.

Victoria's fork froze in mid-air. 'The fact that its not, strictly speaking, *your* hubby is by the by, I suppose,' she said, with all the subtlety of a Scud missile.

My husband looked at me with such intensity that I felt like a new strain of bacteria beneath a microscope. Now he knew that I'd told Victoria about the illicit nude kiss.

'Meaning?' demanded Sven, extinguishing his cigar in his wineglass with a hiss.

Hugo was so rigid he might have been mistaken for a waxwork at Madame Tussaud's. 'That's Victoria's idea of a little joke.' The waxwork spoke, nerves and anger jockeying for dominance in his voice. 'But women can never remember the punchline of jokes.'

'No,' spat my sister, 'because we marry them.'

Hugo was up on his feet in one swift movement and looming down upon her. My sister was up too, the wine in her glass already arcing towards Hugo, who dodged sideways, ensuring that most of the Chianti *classico* splattered down Milano's designer suit. Sven manacled Britney's upper arm, demanding to know what all this fuss was *really* about. Hugo was shaking Victoria vigorously by the shoulders.

While male disdain is the traditional response to sisters-in-law, throttling them is a whole other matter. 'Hugo, stop it! Cal, stop him!' Cal sprang at my husband. The piratical way he was dressed – torn T-shirt, threadbare denims and down-at-heel leather boots, made him look quite threatening – prompting 'Knuckles' and Sven to roll up their sleeves and lurch to standing positions, fists flying. It'd be so much easier if men just had antlers, really.

With so much smoke coming out of people's ears it took me a while to notice that it was also coming out of the kitchen. Shit! The oil! For the chicken! I'd left it on the stove. Somehow I doubt that Martha Stewart uses her smoke alarm as a *timer*. *Today's recipe – take one Domestic Goddess then skewer on sacrificial altar*. Where was some cleaning fluid to inhale, when I needed it?

As the smoke alarm wailed and Hugo accidently ejaculated the fire-extinguisher foam over the guests, there was an abrupt scooting back of chairs and a mass exodus for the door. Our visitors were as flustered in their departure as they'd been calm and collected in their arrival. Bags, coats, car keys, mobile phones – there was a mad scramble for paraphernalia, then a dash for the door, led by the Rolexed Knuckles. I got the vague impression that London's latest 'Power Couple' had just blown a fuse, big time.

First my husband's infidelity, then getting the flick at work and now burning down my own kitchen to publicly launch a new taste sensation – Cordon Noir . . . I think it is fair to say that I had turned into one of the unluckiest girls in the world. Hell, if I fell into a bag of dicks, *I*'d come out sucking my *thumb*.

# 9. It Is as Bad as It Gets and They Are Out to Get You

.......................................................................................................................

'When exactly were you planning on letting me know that you'd chosen to redirect your precious medical expertise into stuffing plastic whoopee cushions into women's chests?' I asked Hugo, as soon as he got back from driving Victoria home. (She was only being loyal: I'd *insisted* they make it up. After all, blood is thicker than Beaujolais.)

'I wanted to meet the people involved first,' he said, throwing off his jacket. 'I was going to talk to you about it after that. How thoughtful of you to set aside this specific time to humiliate me in public, Elisabeth, before our sole investor.'

'His nickname is Knuckles. What does that tell you? That he's wearing a monitoring device around his ankle – *that*'s what. Hugo, cosmetic surgery is the most wasteful use of human potential outside of, well, outside of *modelling*.'

'For God's sake, Lizzie, I'm going to be a cosmetic surgeon, not a Nazi medical researcher! It's an exciting field. Great strides are being made as the medical community becomes increasingly aware of the benefits of—'

'Getting rich? Come off it, Hugo. You're a brilliant doctor.' I took his hand in mine. 'You should be saving the lives of some indigent people somewhere remote and tsetse-flied. When we met you were principled. You were . . .' My husband

wavered in the heat of my scrutiny. For a moment I flashed
back to how he was then, striding those hospital corridors like
a conquistador, his mission to liberate people from their pain.
I felt a pang of nostalgia for those pre-Montrachet days when
we spent the rare nights he wasn't on call with unpublished
poets who leant towards philosophers of triple nomenclature
and struggling musicians who just leant. *Now* I had to put up
with his gynaecologist golfing buddies who boasted so wittily
about 'doing eighteen holes' before lunch.

'We don't need more money. We've paid off the house.
I mean. What's the difference between a million pounds and
twenty million pounds?'

'Um . . . a Lear jet, an island, a couple of helipads. Look,
I'm sick of the ugliness and poverty of the NHS. I've spent
half my life working with patients who are suffering from some
disease I can't quite put my finger on – and would much
rather not, come to think of it.' He winced.

'No. You'd rather go into business with a man who watches
videos entitled *Shaved Frankenhookers*. God, he's even engaged
to one.'

'This is all to do with Britney, isn't it? Because it was
her idea. I keep telling you, I am not remotely interested
in her.'

'Oh, that was an escaped python writhing in your trousers
all night, then, was it?'

'Lizzie, Sven's offering me a chance to grow, professionally,
intellectually . . .'

'Hugo, this is *me*. Your wife. The only interest *you* have in
"personal growth" is your morning erection.'

The door squeaked. Jamie, all bleary-eyed, stumbled in

wearing his luminous Bart Simpson pyjamas. 'Why are you and Daddy fighting?'

'We're not fighting, love,' I comforted, scooping him up in my arms. 'We're just having a slightly raucous conflict resolution, that's all,' I said, for Hugo's benefit.

A few seconds later, there was a muted thump of bare feet padding down the stairs. Julia appeared, her eyes wide with dismay. 'You're not going to divorce, are you? I'm the only kid in my class whose parents are still married.'

Hugo snatched up his BMW keys from the bowl on the hall table. 'It's up to your mother. If you don't trust me, Lizzie, what's the point?'

'Where are you going?' I felt panic gripping my throat.

'Out.'

'At one a.m.? Going out to Her,' I said, impulsively.

'With your usual impeccable judgement, you seem to think this is an appropriate conversation to be having in front of the children.'

Hugo strode down the hall. With the kids clinging to my knees as though they were drowning, I trailed after him. Why are men so like mascara – running at the first sign of tears? When I spoke, I felt as if I was dubbing a film. 'Don't go.'

But his high horse had galloped in, and he simply swung up into the saddle and rode off on it.

I sat there, amid the dinner party detritus, cradling my seven-year-old son and nine-year-old daughter. Despair flooded into me like the sea into a scuttled vessel.

After a while, I settled the kids back into their beds. I sloshed the alcoholic leftovers into a glass and slugged it down in one gulp. With rain pecking at the windows, I sat weeping

88

in the gloom. At two a.m., with still no sign of Hugo, I resorted to dunking the kids' teddy-bear biscuits into a glass of whisky and chewing off their soggy ears. He couldn't leave me. I'd go mad with grief, like Ophelia . . . God, I'd been one of the castaways from the wreckage of my own mother's life, and now I was about to make emotional driftwood of my own dear babies. By three a.m. it was a case of 'Can I Trade My Life For What's Behind Door Two'? How I longed to cuddle up inside my *old* life, and go to sleep. At four o'clock I dragged myself fully clothed into bed. I rolled over and over for the next two hours, until the sheets were twisted tighter than a French plait. How had this happened to me? When? Where? What had I done wrong? Obviously, there *is* a God and he'd just found out that *I* was an atheist. My husband, who spent his life patching up bodies blasted by anti-personnel munitions, had placed a sexual incendiary device right in my path. Britney Amore had blown up my known world. I was maimed. And things would never be the same again.

When he still wasn't back by dawn, I knew that Victoria was right. The reason men have that tiny hole in the end of their cocks is so they can think with an open mind.

# 10. Husband Uncertainty
# Syndrome

..........................................................................................................

$A$nd so it was that I found myself being tutored by Dr Love – *but on a Doctor Crippen fellowship*.

Hugo returned the next day without a word of explanation. For the rest of July and way into August it was a case of take heart, put in trash compactor, turn on. Was he seeing her? Or wasn't he seeing her? I became obsessed. Life lost its humour. The six o'clock news was getting more laughs than I was. I was so absent-minded I drove to a job interview with my briefcase on the roof of my smashed-in people-mover; I'd search for an hour for my sunglasses before finding them perched on the top of my befuddled head. I took to wearing those sunglasses even after dusk, to hide eyes that were as pink-rimmed and watery as a lab rabbit's. I forgot my children's names and then, when I remembered their names, I couldn't remember why I'd summoned them.

I took to calling myself 'the Patient'. *The Patient has a philandering doctor-husband, but no other abnormalities.*

I tried to keep myself busy. I catalogued my shoes in alphabetical order. I checked the crisper and threw away anything that moved without being touched. I picked my *Desert Island Discs* list. I looked up synonyms for 'depression'. But despite not wanting to turn into a walking, talking wronged-wife cliché, I finally succumbed to the urge to nitpick Hugo's bank statements and wore off a valuable fingerprint pressing redial. I told myself I was only interested in Hugo's happiness – so interested that I went through his diary to see who was the reason for it. Soon I was spending all my waking hours wallet-snooping and underpant-sniffing. Not to mention the constant nagging – 'You're still seeing her, aren't you? Well, go on, then! Contract the antibiotic-resistant bacterial strain of your choice and pass it on to your wife. Why not?'

He would return a few barbed comments about paranoia and pathetic behaviour. In the space of a few weeks, we'd turned into the sort of couple who indicate the happiness of their marital union by giving each other head injuries with the nearest household implement. I secretly envied the patients he touched so tenderly. I began to wish I could tread on a bloody landmine. But in effect I had: my mind was flying apart in all directions.

By September our marriage took on the weighty, soft-boned weariness of anaesthetic. My husband's feelings for me seemed to fade in and out like a wartime broadcast. And I sat huddled, twiddling dials, desperately trying to pick up a signal: 'Receiving, over and out.'

I tried talking to him.

Me: 'We never talk any more.'

Him: 'What do you want to talk about?'

Me: 'The fact that you never want to talk to me any more. See? Even now, you're not listening.'

Him: 'I hate it when you say I'm not listening. I was listening enough to hear you say that I'm not listening, wasn't I?'

I tried *not* talking to him – turning my back on him in bed, serving meals in silence. But after a week I couldn't bear it any longer and begged him to make it up with me.

He just looked at me blankly. 'What?' he asked, perplexed.

*He hadn't noticed.*

In that marital desert I became an emotional camel, able to survive on one kind word for days. One night, as we carried the kids up to bed from the TV room, dreams flitting across their faces like shafts of sunlight, I reached for my husband's hand and he squeezed mine in return. His face relaxed into a smile and hope pole-vaulted into my heart – until he yawned elaborately. What I'd taken for fondness was merely fatigue.

I tried not to get too emotionally het-up. I avoided all Nora Ephron films on the grounds of emotional stability as well as taste. I tried to stop Angsting over breast size – but found myself ordering a D cup of coffee at the café. When I wasn't sleuthing through Hugo's private life (and, believe me, I did everything but dust him for fingerprints) I just sat around reading one of the many self-help books entitled *Why Husbands Hate Their Wives and Leave Them And Why It's All Your Fault, You Fat, Middle-Aged Frump*, volume 26.

When Victoria rang one morning to ask what I felt like doing, I said I wanted to crawl into a cupboard with a martini shaker. I was drinking so much alcohol that if I'd given a urine sample it would have had a swizzle stick in it. Really, under the circumstances, I was coping rather well – apart from the stomach acid condition, fine. But I was obsessed with suspicions of Hugo's infidelity. I could talk of nothing else, even when Cal confessed that there actually was a woman he felt passionately about. 'While we're on the subject of you meeting the love of your life . . . do you think it's possible Britney's better in bed than me?'

'Would you stop obsessing?' Cal demanded. 'I really think I'm in love with her, Lizzie . . . Hell, I'm so in love I'd eat her pedicure shavings.'

'Okay, okay . . . but while we're on the subject of pedicures, perhaps it's the elasticity of her pelvic floor? I bet he trampolines off it. After all, Britney hasn't ruined *her* body having *his* children.'

Though Hugo maintained he wasn't seeing Britney and I tried to believe him, doubts were constantly slipping into frame, like the tedious relative who sneaks into the background of every family photograph.

During the night when I'd stir to pat his side of the bed – expecting the warm hollow of his broad back – my hand would settle on an Arctic expanse of sheet. It's common, I know, for insomniacal partners to move to another room, but usually not in another *house*. (Hugo would explain, in a long-suffering voice, that he had been working late setting up the Longevity Clinic.) I tossed so much in bed I could have made myself into a salad. One night when restlessness catapulted me into complete consciousness I rang Victoria – she always stayed up three hours later than everyone else because 'calories consumed just before bedtime are double calories and have to be burned'. She responded that if I wanted to keep Hugo interested I would have to put in the 'grooming hours'. She promised to be over first thing in the morning to begin my instruction.

*

Cal insisted that if anyone needed grooming it was Hugo, as *he* was the one who'd behaved like an animal. 'The man couldn't travel to the States without going through quarantine . . . How *is* he, by the way?' They'd avoided each other since Cal had thrown a punch at him at the dinner party from hell. 'I suppose the life-threatening humour of the situation passed him by did it?' he asked, grinning sheepishly.

Cal was at my place fixing Jamie's Nintendo. 'Those instruction manuals are the Japs' revenge for losing the Second World War,' he gasped. 'But what about you, Lizzie? Can I put *you* back together at least? How are you doin', shug?'

'I'm fine,' I replied, 'apart from chronic Husband Uncertainty Syndrome.'

'Why don't you leave him?'

'*Where?*' I said, sarcastically. The tone of my voice was mimicked by the whiny snarl of the coffee-grinder. 'Why on earth would I leave him? I gave up my career as a foreign correspondent for him. Hugo is everything to me.'

Cal, embarrassed, shuffled his frayed trainers along the tiles of my newly refurbished kitchen – the rubber of his soles was Kleenex-thin from scuffing. 'Hey, it's perspicacity like that which separates the hack from the Pulitzer Prize-winner,' he added self-deprecatingly, raking his hands through wiry curls, which erupted chaotically from his cranium.

The ground coffee beans hissed as I scalded them with water. I thrust the cafetière at him in annoyance. The kids whooshed through the kitchen on their Microlite scooters. Cal went cross-eyed and pretended to garrotte himself, making them shriek with laughter. 'I keep telling you to ignore everythin' I say. I'm an uneducated yob, yer know

that. Although I think there was an F in metallurgy somewhere along the line.' He hooked his thumbs in the loops of
his blue jeans and tilted his head until it rested on the back
of his chair. 'The only thing I know for sure is that if this girl
I'm mad about—'

'Tell me who she is, Cal. Don't be so cagey.'

'There's nothing to tell yet – except,' he garrotted himself
again, 'if she doesn't sleep with me soon, I'm gonna contract
carpal-tunnel masturbation syndrome.'

*

'You're just going to have to make more effort,' Victoria said,
flicking at my sombre trouser suit. 'Look on it as a fashion
opportunity. A marital crisis gives you *carte blanche* for the
kohl-rimmed eyes and austere but sexy short-skirted look. And
sunglasses to give the maybe-I've-been-crying-maybe-I-haven't
image.' She'd finally made it over by mid-afternoon (men had
been known to get their master's degrees in engineering while
waiting for Vick to get ready to go out). 'Darling, *must* you
slavishly adhere to fashion favoured by Gestapo wardresses?'

Self-consciously I did up the buttons on my crisp white
shirt. While my sister was more your feather boa and Manolo
Blahnik kind of a gal, I sported the minimalist and monochro-
matic. 'I am not fashion-deficient, thank you very much.'

'Elisabeth, look at yourself. You're wearing a suit the colour
of leaf mould. If you fell over in the park, people would think
you were compost. Your clothes are a desperate cry for help,
darling.'

'Think so? See, I feel *you*'re always overdressed – being so
*wrapped up in yourself*.'

But that night when the kids and I decided to surprise Hugo by collecting him to go ice-skating, the surprise was on us. Britney Amore was in his hospital office. 'Just for a check-up, darlin'.' She pouted, looking sultry in a wisp of thigh-high black silk and red satin sling-backs.

'Really? After hours?' My heart thudded anxiously against my ribcage. Had she been examined, X-rated, then sent home?

She eyeballed my denim overalls, torn T-shirt and hiking boots. 'Oh, look, it's Frontier Woman. Hon, whatever "look" were you going for? Well, hon, *you missed*.'

And so began my medley of self-improvement.

Despite my protestations to Victoria that I would never allow myself to become more than healthily obsessed with triple hydroxy fruit peels, despite my endless lectures to her that here we were, ninety-three million miles from the sun on a podgy little rock, with a population of six billion people, spinning at the rate of one thousand miles an hour, busily stockpiling enough plutonium to blast us into another galaxy completely and all *she* could worry about was pore-clogging – despite all this – the presence of Britney Amore on the heterosexual horizon had jolted me into a bitter realization.

I was running seriously late for my Pathetic Female Under-achieving Conference.

# 11. *Never Darken My Dior Again*

The humiliations began sartorially.

'Do you have anything in my size?' I timidly asked the louche young woman in the Harvey Nichols tog emporium.

She looked me up and down and emitted a disdainful sigh bordering on disgust, never having seen anything quite so revolting in her department – certainly nothing alive. I was tempted to bow down before her immaculate presence and plead to be deemed fashionable enough to dare to drape some of her precious, horrendously overpriced garments over my unworthy hide. But before she could call the fumigators, my sister floated into view. The shop assistant immediately lit up, piling sequined handkerchiefs (oh, my mistake, they were *dresses*) emblazoned with the designer's name into my sagging arms.

'Who do these designers think they are, putting *their* names on *our* clothes?' I whinged. 'Why can't we put *our* names on *their* clothes?'

Victoria dragged me into a cubicle and stripped off my jeans. The shop assistant's guarded amusement soon turned into astonishment and finally full-scale pity as she tried, with gritty determination, to ruche my size twelve body into a size eight outfit. I squeezed my eyes closed. When I dared to peep open a decade or so later, it was to find myself shoved into the plaid - mini - skirt - long - socks - and - satchel - thirteen - year - old - nymphomaniacal look: a curious choice for a *thirty-nine-year-old*.

The shop assistant's eyes widened in horror. For *her*, someone like *me* dressing in Christian Lacroix was obviously the equivalent of putting caviar on a Colonel Sanders.

Next came a diamanté cocktail frock, with a split from ankle to ass and a low dip in the back more commonly associated with 'builder's bum.'

I shivered. 'It's October. How will I keep warm? A flannel tampon?'

The assistant now turned her pitying gaze upon my sister.

'You're right,' Victoria adjudicated. 'It's definitely not you.'

But a fringed leather bikini ensemble apparently *was*. The pale, pudgy woman in the mirror looked a lot like me, only sadder. The sadistic fluorescence highlighted every blemish. The sensible panties I'd been ordered to leave on poked above the bikini bottoms – not exactly adding to my seductiveness. Nor did the fact that when I re-dressed and stormed out of the cubicle, the plastic crotch hygiene strip had adhered to the seat of my trousers (a fact I didn't discover until I was half-way through a job interview with *Sky News* some hours later.)

I fossicked in my bag for a Bounty bar and devoured it whole.

'Wouldn't it be great,' my sister caught up with me on the down escalator, 'if height was like weight and you just stopped. And stayed there. For ever. But it's not. You're just going to have to diet, darling. So, what shall it be? The Grapefruit? The Israeli? The Protein Only?'

'Find a diet that doesn't actually involve eating less and we'll talk, okay?'

I had always refused to become like my sister, constantly on the bathroom scales, her day ruined if the wrong numbers came up. But that night, when we got home from the school play and were undressing for bed, I noticed a bruise on Hugo's inner thigh that couldn't be explained away as a golf-related accident. And when we made love later, he insisted upon turning out the light. I knew then, as we went through the motions in the dark, that in Hugo's mind it was Britney Amore with whom he was having sex . . . And she was getting many more orgasms than *I* was! The next day it was straight on to starvation rations.

# 12. Having Your Cake and Not Eating It Too

The restaurant to which Victoria took me for lunch was Ethiopian. 'I'm too guilty to eat here! I'll just have a grain of United Nations-supplied rice, please, and a fried fruit-fly.'

'That's the whole *point*, darling. When it comes to guilt trips, I'm your travel agent. The lentil salad is excellent.'

I glared at the menu, my stomach growling with irritation. 'Victoria, only yogis who've been fasting for five years are ever hungry at the sight of a lentil.'

'What about a soya bean and tofu roll?'

'Um . . . no, thanks. And not because it looks like a long-dead dog turd either.'

Victoria ordered for us. In due course, the plate of fat-free tofu burgers arrived. They had the appearance and texture of melted bowling balls. The dish was accompanied by an organic salad. After two bites I realized that 'organic' is a scientific term for 'ferociously chewed by things with many legs', some of which – judging by the crunch against my teeth – had actually made their home in what I was attempting to digest.

'A slim, attractive wife means a happy husband . . .'

'The trouble is,' I snapped back, 'like most women I know, I'm a meaty size twelve, and there's nothing worth wearing in more than a two.'

'Well, the good news is that if you throw up four times a day for a week, you could easily fit into a size six. If you only throw up twice a day, it's going to be a ten,' my sister elaborated, straight-faced. 'It's vital that you lose weight, Lizzie . . . I could go on about it . . .'

'You *do*, actually,' I said, extracting a Mars bar from my bag and inhaling it.

'If you won't start eating sensibly, then it's time for the gym. If you don't want to lose him, you've got to get down to your fighting weight.'

'Exercise!' I scoffed. 'The only exercise *you* ever do is skipping – skipping breakfast, skipping lunch, skipping dinner.'

'You must get in touch with your body.'

'Mine's not all that communicative. If I *do* hear from it, I'll let you know, OK?'

'All it takes is a little cycling on the stationary bike.'

'Stationary bike? What am I? A giant gerbil?'

'Don't knock it, Lizzie,' my sister said airily. 'The Thigh-master is one of the best dates I ever had!'

'Men never even knew about cellulite until we started whining on about it. I hate exercise. My tights may run, but not me.'

But that night Hugo was four hours late coming home. And worse: he came home cleaner than he'd gone out. I had to ask myself some hard questions. Like, why shower at a conference on Ludwig's angina? Even more unsettling, wasn't that new blemish on his buttocks caused by sheet burn? The kind of sheet burn that only comes from making love on inferior linen? Let's just come out and say it: *cheap motel linen.*

And it was time to don the Lycra leotard.

# 13. What Am I? A Hamster?

.....................................................................................................

Victoria immediately put me on an exercise regime so stringent it made a cross-country Iron Man triathlon look like a walk in the park.

'All right! So, how far did you run, sweetie?' My sister clicked off the stopwatch as I hurtled, asthmatically, to the ground at her feet on Hampstead Heath.

'I – believe – at – one – point – I – passed Greenland.'

By the end of October, the slick of wet autumnal leaves made it too dangerous to run on the Heath. I was forced instead to pound up and down the nearby streets. But a few days of that were quite enough. 'If God had meant us to run on roads, he'd had given us four-wheeled toes,' I reprimanded my sister.

When winter descended we retreated indoors. All the women at the gym on Finchley Road seemed to be in some secret, snazzy-leotard competition, the straining thongs lifted and separated their butt cheeks into startlingly strange new formations. I watched my sister leg-scissoring and arm aerobicking on the cross-country ski machine, her pale ponytail jauntily boing-boinging behind her with each happy step. She seemed oblivious to the terrifying warnings plastered across the machine. 'IMPORTANT – See Your Doctor Before

Attempting To Mount This Machine'; 'Use at Own Risk'; 'Stop Immediately Whenever You Feel Faint!!!'

'If you become a quadriplegic, I am *not* going to spoon-feed you for the rest of your life. Is that clear, Victoria?'

I preferred the ButtMaster session. The trick was to find the most crowded class and wedge yourself between two female athletes, allowing them to do all the bouncing and jumping and simply carry you along.

Yoga also appealed – mostly because I tend to like any exercise that allows you to lie on the floor and go to sleep.

By the end of that first week, I was lacerated by Lycra rash on bits of my body primarily reserved for giving birth. I was aching with tit-chafe from all that jiggling. I had cycled, run and rowed to nowhere hour after exhausting hour, enough to make Sisyphus's ground-hog day of boulder-pushing-up-that-bloody-hill seem relaxing. It was then, after all this, that I stepped on to the scales, with Victoria craning expectantly over my shoulder. We both stared, excitedly, then dumbstruck, at the luminous green numbers.

'You're the only person I know in the world who puts *on* weight while exercising,' she said finally. 'Come on, sweetie. You mustn't give up!' she encouraged, following me as I stormed out of the gym.

I was so busy yelling at my persecutor to stop pursuing me, that I didn't see Cal until I bumped smack bang into him coming out of Books Etc. He steadied me, gripping my forearms. 'Hey,' he joshed my sister, 'haven't I grovelled pathetically at your feet somewhere before?'

But my sister looked at Cal with no sign of cognition. 'Be a slob and lose your husband, Lizzie. See if I care.' Now it was her turn to stomp off.

'Vicky!' Cal teased. 'I've slipped myself some of that date-rape drug, Rohypnol, so you can have your way with me, okay?' He flung back his arms dramatically, closed his eyes and puckered his lips.

But my sister didn't look back. Even I was too demoralized to laugh. Enticing aromas were wafting over from the bookshop café. The thing about exercising to lose weight is that it makes you so damn hungry. I dragged Cal into a chair. 'I want to talk to you about Hugo.' Calim suddenly looked as wilted as a roadside salad. 'But first I want a fat-laden, I - don't - give - a - stuff - what - I - eat - because - I'm - a - liberated - woman, mono - sodium - saturated - fat-fat-fat - gooey gorgeousness with some pesticide - coated grains harvested by oppressed migrant labourers on the side,' I told the waitress. 'Same for you, Calim?'

The wilted roadside salad shrugged.

'As certified by the Albanian Food and Drug Administration,' I added, in an effort to cheer him up. 'What? No quip? No rejoinder? No pun?'

'It's crap about humour bein' a woman's favourite element in a man,' Cal said with melancholic acerbity. 'I've quipped. I've *bon*-ed. I've *mot*-ed. And nothin'. Not a thing! Not even a peck on the cheek. I mean, my lips are gettin' grovel-chafed.'

I didn't like the fact that it seemed to be Victoria who'd brought on this precipitous mood plunge. My leg jerked as though hit by a neurologists hammer. 'Your Mystery Woman,'

I probed, trying to neutralize my horrified inflection. 'She won't go out with you?'

'For her I don't exist. I'm too dull, aren't I? Maybe I need to adopt an inner child – as long as it has references. I must know whether or not it's gonna clean up its room.'

*My* inner child was about to throw up. I'd encouraged Cal to ask my sister out but hadn't thought he'd get serious about her. 'You know, the hardest part of addiction is admitting that you have a problem.'

'I am addicted to this certain girl, it's true. She's fantastic. I want us to use really insipid pet names in public. I want us to talk to each other in totally irritatin' baby voices. I want people to roll their eyes whenever we're around.'

'Um, can I get you something. A beer? A glass of wine? A *psychiatrist*?'

'But what woman would want me? I'm skint. The only lucrative form of writing is ransom notes. Maybe it's time I stopped wankin' and went back on the building sites.'

'But isn't that why you became a writer? Chiefly on the grounds that it didn't involve any heavy lifting?'

'Yeah, but, you know, money talks and what I want it to say is "Hi, I'm from Planet Shag."'

'Excuse me.' I snagged the sleeve of a passing bookshop assistant and drew her attention to the adjoining stationery section. 'This man has just been diagnosed as a clinically depressed masochist, the same day his best friend has decided to kill him for giving up on himself – have you got a Hallmark card to cover all of that?'

'Stayin' with a husband who sleeps around on you – actually

I think *that* way clinical depression lies,' Cal said, stuffing his hands into his pockets and loping out of the bookshop.

\*

'Do you think staying with a husband who sleeps around on you – well, do you think that's the way clinical depression lies? I do *not* want to be like Mum,' I confided to my sister later that day, in her minimalist Conran kitchen, a completely superfluous room in her Regent's Park apartment. My sister looked at me blankly. 'Oh, I know our childhood wasn't tough. Not in that walk-barefoot-twelve-miles-to-school-while-foraging-for-roots-and-churning-your-own-butter way.' I made another verbal stab at it. 'But it was, in a bitter and miserable and rather pissed-off way. Don't you think?' I was pacing now. 'Because we were a couple of fathers short. I don't want that for Jamie and Julia.' Victoria gave an almost imperceptible nod. 'Hellooo?' My sister seemed to have taken a Stepford Wife pill. 'What is *wrong* with you today?'

'Botulism,' she said mechanically, her lips barely moving. 'Inject . . . into facial . . . muscles. Stop . . . wrinkles.'

I rifled through my brain. 'Isn't that the bacteria the Home Ec teacher told us to avoid in canned goods? Quick!' I dragged her towards the stove. 'The only cure is to boil you for fifteen minutes.'

'Paralysis short term,' she monotoned. 'Book for treatment. My spa,' ventriloquized the Android. 'Procedure only . . . good till Department of . . . Health gets . . . wind and closes it . . . down.'

'You'd make an Easter Island statue look animated, do you know that?'

Her stilted voice squeezed through lips set in invisible cement. 'Sweetie, I only wish it had been available the *first* time I turned forty.'

I looked at her, stupefied. 'Botox is a poison! In the Gulf War Saddam Hussein squirted it on the Iranian troops! He used it to kill Kurds.'

'. . . At least they would have looked lovely.'

'Victoria!' I slapped her. 'Call me old-fashioned, but I have never really thought there's much point in being beautiful if you're like, *dead*.'

'Want . . . to . . . keep . . . man . . . interested . . . sexually . . . got . . . to . . . do . . . body . . . maintenance.'

'Really?' I replied jadedly. 'I've never noticed that it was very difficult to get men to have sex. With anything.'

'Good . . . 'cause I've seen your armpits . . . You're not woman . . . You're yeti.'

'Victoria, there was a period in my life when I had no cellulite, varicose veins or unsightly body hair. Of course, I was *eight* at the time. *This*,' I gestured at my body with its curves, creases and baby marks, 'is what women look like . . . Real Women. I mean, fifteen and a half million size twelve British women can't be wrong. I will wax by tomorrow,' I assured her. 'Or *maybe next summer*.'

If my sister could have arched an eyebrow, she would have. Instead, she thrust a thick piece of cardboard under my nose. It was an invitation to Sven's Young Model of the Year party. 'Hugo going – to impress investors,' she said, with great effort. 'Britney too . . . So should you . . . Looking sensational.' Seeing me waver, she picked up the phone. 'Book now . . . 'fore lose nerve.'

'You already have. In your stupid face.' I snatched up my bag. 'I am never ever going to a spa with you. Is that clear?' I declared, with invincible repugnance.

Of course Hugo wasn't seeing Britney Amore. Their encounter was a meaningless aberration, I decided, as my car crawled uphill with the Hampstead traffic. Whereas *we* were devoted, long term. Didn't we have joint pension schemes? Hadn't we planted gingko bilobas? Weren't we planning to spend our final years chasing the winter sun on a Caribbean cruise ship with a questionable cabaret?

But that evening, Hugo insisted on introducing new sexual positions into our R-rated repertoire. When my inner thighs had recovered from something I am positive he called the 'Rotating Helicopter', he then suggested the 'Full Cream'. It was when I found myself flipped on top, my legs closed, facing the ceiling, with Hugo's hips undulating against my butt, his hands nipple-twirling and clit-tweaking, that I started getting that who's-been-sitting-in-*my*-chair-sleeping-in-*my*-bed-fucking-*my*-husband feeling.

And the next day, when I was queuing at McDonald's for the kids' Happy Meals, I looked at the security camera TV screen to check my posture for permanent chiropractic damage. And I was shocked by what I saw. Losing your husband to another woman can lead to bad hair, bad temper and mutton-dressed-as-lamb looks, including too-tight jeans and too much eyeliner. I decided right then to follow Victoria to the Maharishi Tranquility Spa for 'harmonizing beautification'. At best I'd get rid of my blackheads. At worst, I'd be inducted into a weird cult and offered up as a human sacrifice to some unforgiving God or other. Hey, what did I have to lose?

My capitulation might also have had something to do with the fact that later that afternoon I'd attempted a home leg and armpit wax because it was cheaper than going to a beauty salon.

Or so I'd thought.

*Cost of salon waxing*: £25.

*Cost of home wax*: £865. Itemized as follows –

(1) Burnt crockpot: £45

(2) Hydraulic hose for removal of wax from kitchen crevices after crockpot exploded: 75 quid. (Note to amateurs. Don't leave wax on stove to simmer with lid on.)

(3) Mini-cab fare to Accident and Emergency: £25

(4) Psychiatric trauma counselling: £720

It was time to get in touch with my Inner Wallet.

# 14. Is That a Wallet in Your Pocket or Are You Just Pleased to See Me?

There is a very fine line between 'beauty regimes' and mental illness. Unlike a snake, I don't enjoy the sensation of my skin crawling. But by the end of two days at Victoria's beauty spa, witnessing acid peels, fat grafts and liposuction, I was positively reptilian.

The Tranquility Spa was a minimum-security prison, with palms. The manor's crumbling façade cruelly mimicked the epidermal exteriors of the females filing through its portentous portals. It was situated in the manicured environs of the Chilterns. Inside, synthetic tinkle-tinkle harp music seeped serenely from the velvet-upholstered walls. Bovine, pampered Kuwaiti princesses bobbed comically in the heated pool, the fleshy bubble-wrap of their bloated thighs afforded round-the-clock protection by whippet-thin security guards.

The walls of its antiseptic treatment rooms were lined with posters featuring women just like us – except that they had *ENORMOUS* boobs with no hips, cellulite or body hair. Believe me, only chemo patients have less body hair than models. It was in these torture chambers that I spent my first day. I had my buttocks pummelled by a Swede called Igor and my lymphatics drained by what – judging by her white garb, austere smile and remote eyes – could only have been a high priestess, who asked me, as she snapped on rubber gloves, if I'd ever really been able to relate to my lip-liner?

On day two, when I was sure I didn't have one remaining pore it would be possible to put your hands in and rummage around, Victoria bustled me off to a 'Tranquility Suite' where I marvelled at row upon row of embalming fluids glistening in glass sarcophagi. Surely there couldn't be enough skin in the world to absorb all these moisturized globules? This place had everything to reverse time, bar a Tardis.

Another high priestess diligently began her application of a phantasmagoria of facial potions that were going to cost more than my wedding reception. They also hurt like hell.

'Jesus Christ!' I gasped, slapping her hand away. 'Is that a moisturizer or a flame-retardant furniture treatment?'

She responded with a mechanical spiel bloated with quasi-scientific guff I didn't know – 'peptides' and 'peroxidation,' 'excisor enzymes' and 'benign solar keratones' – before concluding haughtily that it was also a barrier 'to keep out irritants'.

'What? Like bullshitting beauty clinicians?' I muttered.

Victoria, who had just breezed into my suite, sent me a slit-eyed look. The pharmaceutically sombre clinician who followed her whipped off my sheet. As I lay there exposed to the room in nothing but a pair of paper panties, she made a perfunctory prod of my pale flesh. She then ran long white ghostly nails over the shelves of coloured vials as though consulting a ouija board. Finally she decreed that what was necessary in my rather tragic case was an Intensive Thigh Unit with skin caviar (real beluga). The price? Two hundred and fifty quid.

Victoria confirmed the sagacity of this advice with an earnest nod.

My mouth dropped open. Obviously the Tranquility Spa was not so much about getting in touch with your Inner You as getting in touch with your Outer Bank Manager.

'Why bother buying the products and having the treatments?' I groaned to my disapproving sister. 'I mean, we might as well just record the sound of a cash register opening and closing.'

'It's not so expensive,' Victoria reprimanded crisply, smiling apologetically at the priestesses. With both hands she shoved me back on to the treatment table in to the giving-birth position.

'Yeah, you're right. No more expensive than, say, *maintaining a space programme.*'

'And could you please Do Something about her bikini line.' She pointed at my bristly toothbrush pubes. The haphazard regrowth resembled the pelt of a balding bandicoot. 'I'm amazed Hugo doesn't get rug burn.'

'Not wax!' I squeaked, recoiling. I still had third-degree burns from that nasty home treatment incident. 'Hot wax is only meant for cars.'

'Wax? How very "last century", *madam*,' patronized the beautician, busily strapping her head into yellow welder's goggles. Before I had time to protest, I was attacked by some kind of Tactical Pube Napalmer. I discovered, in that agonizing moment, that laser hair removal is nature's way of promoting the Natural Look.

Trouble is, it's so hard to make a run for it with only a flimsy pair of paper panties between you and police arrest for indecent exposure.

'Victoria! Victoria! Help!' I tried unsuccessfully to swivel from my supine position. 'Where is my sister?'

The beautician waved her harpoon in the general direction of an adjoining cubicle. 'She's having dermabrasion – a very simple and effective beautification procedure. Now, stop behaving like a baby. It's only a laser.'

'Tell *that* to Luke Skywalker.' My protests were drowned out by the buzz of her machine as she resumed her excruciating incineration of the hairs around my groin, with a light beam powerful enough to vaporize a bulldozer.

When she finally lifted the welder's goggles above her forehead (having doubtlessly introduced a vast array of long-term inoperable cancers into my system) and my squeals had stopped reverberating unharmoniously through the entire Tranquility Spa, I unplaited my toes to hear my sister making a high-pitched, squawky whine akin to a walrus giving birth.

'What the *hell* are you doing to her in there?' I gasped, ready to spring to the rescue.

'Skin resurfacing.'

'What is she? A *road*?' It transpired that my sister was involved in a facial resurfacing project more extensive than the Birmingham bypass.

'You're next,' said the over-rouged beautician in her bogus lab coat. 'Now, would you prefer a chemical peel to get rid of your horrid T-zone? Or are we looking at a laser vaporization of the outer layers of that exhausted complexion?'

Horrid? Exhausted? A beauty consultation performs instant dermabrasion upon your self-esteem. Suddenly the door that separated our suites yielded and my sister staggered in. I gagged. The 'simple beautification procedure' had obviously involved being scoured by steel wool soaked in acid. Her face was red, swollen and lumpen with gunk, which I cringingly deduced was singed flesh. What beauticians call 'dermabrasion' most of us know by its original term: medieval torture.

'Oh, Victoria, what have they done to you?' I cried out, mortified.

'Face facts.' My sister's voice was brutally shrill. 'We live in sick, airbrushed times. No woman can afford to be left on the shelf looking exactly how God made her!'

'But why destroy the years of good-lookingness we have left by worrying about staying good-looking?' I glanced from my sister, whose face resembled a burnt pizza, to my own sorry pudenda – which could have been likened to a hairless lab rat. 'Have you ever considered what you could do with the hours you waste exterminating body hairs?' I grabbed my jumper, jeans and shoes. 'Female defoliation is a futile struggle against the forces of nature.'

The beautician cringed. 'Body hair is bestial.'

'Well, then, please excuse me everyone while I skulk back to my lair.'

*

God! How had I allowed Victoria to talk me into trying to preserve myself in amber? What *was* I? An *insect*? I was just throwing myself into my car when she burst out of the manor behind me. At least, I think it was Victoria. Eyes hidden behind sunglasses despite the icy drizzle, face eclipsed by a sombrero-style hat and surgical facemask, it might have been Michael Jackson.

I fired the ignition. The Whacko-Jacko lookalike wrenched at the car door so violently I thought it would snap off.

'You can't go to the Model of the Year party looking like that. Do you want to lose your husband?' I glimpsed the thick oozing skeins of blistered flesh beneath my sister's mask. 'Do you want to feed him on a plate to the Texan Trouser Hound?'

'Hugo said he's not seeing Britney Amore. I don't need to spy on him.' I wrestled the door closed and put the car into gear.

'Is that right?' Victoria screeched, pressing what was left of her face up against the glass. 'Well, just make sure you check for MSB tonight.'

I looked at her blankly, crunching to a halt on the gravel driveway.

'Maximum Sperm Build-up,' she decoded, flinging open the car door once more. 'You've been away for three days. If he's been faithful, well, there should be gallons of sperm, darling. Geysers of the bloody stuff . . .'

Her voice trailed after me as I skittered down the wet drive, door flapping. I'd had enough of paranoia. It was time to get a grip. Wasn't Hugo a good husband and father? Hadn't he volunteered to take Julia and Jamie to Thorpe Park for a few rides on 'Twirl Through The Air Then Projectile Vomit' so I could have some quality time with my big sis at the spa?

As the scribble of roadside trees gave way to the derelict factories of outer London, I abandoned my plan to attend, all eagle-eyed, Sven's party, in order to check my affair radar for beeps. In fact, as soon as I got home, I insouciantly insisted on performing oral sex.

115

'That was sensational.' My husband sighed, falling back on to the pillow after a final convulsion.

I nodded, mutely, confidently trying to gauge the quantity of sperm in my mouth. I wasn't remotely worried. Hell, no. I was cocksure. Literally.

'Really passionate and romantic,' he added, stroking my hair.

'Ah-huh,' I muttered, as I ever so romantically tried to fathom how I could subtly manoeuvre myself bathroom-ward to spit his ejaculate into the sink to more accurately calculate his spermatozoa output. 'Eally oantic. I eed oo ee.' I dashed to the bathroom.

'You what?' he called out after me as I spat into the sink. 'I need to pee,' I repeated, staring gob-smacked at the white porcelain. Because it wasn't the geyser I'd expected. But a tiny, teeny trickle.

And it was *déjà vu, all over again.*

'You know, Hugo, I think I will come to Sven's party tomorrow after all.'

'My love, do you really think that's wise?'

A vision of my husband between the legs of Britney Amore hit me square in the chest. 'Oh, yes.'

'But there'll be a lot of celebs there. Madonna, Jeffrey Archer, Al Pacino . . . He has a hair-loss condition you know. Alopecia.' He leant against the bathroom door as I tore my toothbrush bristles to and fro across my gnashed teeth. 'We're trying to raise money for the clinic so I really need to impress these people and well, you're bound to say something irreverent and raise a few eyebrows.'

'Right. And now you're a Cosmetic Surgeon, that's *your* job.'

'Come on, Liz. You were born with a silver foot in your mouth, admit it.'

Talking of things in mouths: 'Listen, Hugo, I need to know something . . .' I insisted, seriously. It was time to confess that he was married to a spermicidal maniac.

'Yes, Lizzie?' He turned to me, smiling contentedly – and then, as usual, right on cue, his pager went off. It was call-us interruptus, an emergency summons from the hospital.

But was it the hospital? Or was it Her? Hugo's job gave him such a perfect excuse to slip away. As I listened to his car engine sparking in the dark, the pendulum of doubt swung back and forth. I burned with jealousy. What fresh hell was this? What *stale* hell? Because this was the same old hell over and over again. That's what made it hellish. Oh, how I suddenly craved that £250 pot of La Prairie Skin Caviar . . .

**Medical update – the Patient has been depressed ever since the doctor she loves started bloody well sleeping around in the first bloody place**. The Surgeon General, I decided at dawn after yet another sleepless night, should issue a warning that marrying doctors can be seriously hazardous to your health.

# 15. Long Day's Journey Into Shite

What has one hundred and eighty breasts, wants to be appreciated for its brains, hopes one day to start that degree in Sanskrit, looks unspeakably beautiful in a bikini and is desperate to meet rock stars and save the world?

A modelling agency.

What kind of dress code could I expect for a party to celebrate the winner of the Young Model of the Year? Latex? Leather? Nipple rings? . . . Or something more casual? Since Hugo's insinuation that I would never 'blend in', I was determined to prove him wrong. Discarding outfit upon outfit on the bed I reminded myself not to mention alopecia to Al Pacino. Hugo was right. If I had a shoe for all the times I'd put my foot in my mouth, I'd be the Imelda Marcos of NW3. But not tonight. Tonight I was forewarned.

Because my darling husband had gone without me, I had to talk my way into Sven's Mayfair town-house. There seemed to be a strict door policy, enforced by muscle-bound minders with roid-rage, of not admitting any woman who was wearing more than lip gloss and a staple. The fringed leather bikini dress that Victoria had made me buy just passed sartorial muster. Skulking inside, I followed a woven mass of voices up the marble staircase to the Romanesque indoor pool.

Sven's lavish mansion was a jungle-themed eyesore of animal-skin rugs and erotic figurines. The trophy heads of elk, stag, deer and black rhino should really have been replaced with those of the top models he'd shot to fame. Clad in torso-and-tush-hugging ensembles, they wafted perilously by, hipbones first, their skyscraper heels giving them a dizzying tilt. You really had to be HIV positive or have an eating disorder to fit into dresses like that, I realized, as I watched model after model wave away food with elaborate indifference.

Models make even normal women feel like Sumo wrestlers. Pausing beneath a mock proscenium arch, I sucked in my stomach so hard it was bulging out the back of my ribcage. I jutted my pelvis out as though about to enter the World Olympic Limbo Event. I pouted, scowled, put one foot gingerly in front of the other – and slipped a disc in less than two seconds. While the models moved with a floating, graceful gait, my limbs were so heavy I felt as if I was wading against a tide. I clickety-clacked loudly across the marble floor on spike heels sharp enough to disembowel a ferret, only half drowning out the Corrs' song 'We're So Young', which pulsated, mockingly, from inbuilt speakers. So much for 'blending in'. I felt as unobtrusive as a G-strung lap dancer at Buckingham Palace.

Sven was using this awards presentation to pimp for investors so the guest list included corporate lawyers, rich accountants and self-made advertising men trying to look like someone out of their own TV commercials; men like 'Knuckles' Milano, for whom furry dice dangling from their rear-view mirrors would not be a mortifying embarrassment. The party was padded with such people – air-kissing acquaintances who, even if they weren't celebrities, looked as though they should be.

Sven's snorty horse laugh – which he only uses when guffawing at one of his own dull remarks – ripped the air. 'Nice legs –what time do they open?' he smooth-talked one model. 'Is that a mirror on your belt? Because I can see myself in your pants!' he pandered to another. His scatter-gun laughter stopped abruptly at the sight of Marrakech. Extracting himself from the coagulation of guests, he circled her like carrion over roadkill. 'Hold my hand, will you? Then I can tell my friends I've been touched by an angel.' He gave my niece an oily wink and flashed his effulgent smile. Honestly, this bloke was slicker than the latest Exxon oil spill. 'You know, I could teach you all the supermodels' best-kept secrets . . .'

I scoffed. 'A supermodel's best-kept secret is how to stay alive on one pretzel a year, isn't it?' I said to an emaciated girl, sporting a pallid, ragged 'heroin-chic' look, who was perched precariously on a zebra-skin barstool directly above me.

Heroin Chic yawned elaborately. Obviously, models exhaust easily under the pressure to be interesting. But it didn't stop the prospective investors marvelling at her comeliness. I, too, felt amazed at the models' pulcritude – and just hoped they'd sashay close enough for me to trip them up with my handbag. 'We're So Young' segued into 'Maggie May' – obviously a compilation entitled, at a guess, *Top Hit Songs Guaranteed To Make Anyone Over 25 Feel Really Useless and Ugly*.

I was happily emitting invisible but deadly Acne and Fat rays at all the passing girls, when my sister sailed into view with an entourage of bimbae. She was taking great delight in sabotaging their prospects of modelling fame by dishing out pearls of wisdom, which were blatantly *paste*. 'Yes, a face pack mixed with kitty litter, especially if used by kitty first, just *eats away* dead skin. My real secret, darlings, is haemorrhoid cream around the eyes – especially if it's first been used on someone's bottom.'

I snagged the sleeve of her lacy Moschino cocktail dress with my little finger. 'Lock up your daughters, dogs and all house plants. Sven's back in town.'

'And your hostile, hateful point would *be . . . ?*' my sister said brusquely, flicking a long blonde frond of her silken hair into my face.

I hooked a thumb in Marrakech's direction. 'Some men love that new car smell, you know?'

'Sven's in love with *me*. He does *not* have sex with underage models,' she snapped.

'Victoria, that man's underpants could be inducted into the Hall of Infamy. He beds so many girls he needs a *placement* on his *pillows*.'

'He's just trying to help my daughter kick-start a career . . . Which is why I'm very pleased Marrakech wanted to come with me tonight.'

'Victoria, no model can get into his books until she's served the probationary two-year bulimia period.'

'Actually Marrakech could do with losing a few pounds.'

'Um . . . if Mother Nature had wanted our skeletons to be visible, I have a strong suspicion that she would have put them on the outside of our bodies. Look at them.' I gestured to the room full of surly-mouthed, sunken-eyed, slouch-shouldered, angular waifs. 'They're so weak with malnutrition it looks like they just escaped from a supermodel Mental Institution.

Speaking of the mentally challenged, what makes you so sure he's in love with you and not Britney?'

'He only got engaged to her to attract publicity for the clinic. It's a business thing. A publicity stunt.'

'It's only a business thing?' A thick stew of doubt began to simmer in my subconscience.

'Where *is* Hugo by the way? Gosh, I don't see *Britney* anywhere either,' Victoria added, in mock astonishment.

A spasm of anxiety darted raggedly through my skull as my eyes zigzagged around the party. 'Hugo is *not* having an affair with Britney Amore.'

My sister gave me a pitying look. She dug down the front of her low-cut dress, extracted two breast-shaped pieces of silicone and flopped them into my lap, nipple side up, where they quivered like old-fashioned 1950s beige jellies. 'Cleavage enhancers. That's what you need, darling. Then perhaps you could keep your husband and find a job.'

This was a sore point. I had now been out of work for five months. I wasn't being picky either – having rejected only pole-dancing and chicken-sexing as possible career paths. Flinching, I picked up the trembling blobs as though they were toxic, and stuffed them back down her *décolletage* in disgust. 'Women ask for bigger breasts, but what they really should be asking for is a personality. A life, maybe.'

My panic attack was interrupted by two gay, nude, male synchronized swimmers who disrobed and slithered into the pool. With all eyes in the grotto riveted in that direction, Britney Amore chose that moment to emerge from the adjacent Jacuzzi. And who was hovering nearby with a towel, but my very own husband, Hugo Frazer MBChB, FRCS, MD, FDSRCS.

'Oh, I see the Smut-o-gram's here,' Victoria hissed.

We watched as Britney's breasts heaved into sight through the foam. They seemed to have grown even bigger. It looked as though she was trying to shoplift a king-size Guinevere waterbed out of a store by hiding it down her bikini top. 'Oh, my God. Do you think she's had them enlarged *again*?' I asked, horrified.

'Noooo,' said my sister, with eye-rolling sarcasm. 'She's obviously a genetic mutation.'

Until then, the potential investors had adopted a convincingly professional 'it's-all-in-a-day's-work' façade of cheerful, slightly sweaty bonhomie. But at the sight of Britney's stupendous spheres they ogled, they gape-jawed, they drooled. Breast implants are like TV evangelists: you know they're fake but you can't stop watching them.

Britney Amore caught my gaze. She gave a sleek, self-satisfied smile before planting a kiss on the lips of my husband. Actually it was more than just a kiss. It was a lower-lip sandwich.

I felt a fist clench in my abdomen. Maybe I could drown her by putting a mirror on the bottom of the Jacuzzi? My deep existential cleavage crisis was interrupted by Victoria barrelling back over, dragging Marrakech.

'Do you know what my bloody daughter's doing *now*? She's writing to some *maniac* on Death *Row*. In *Florida*. That's why she's here. Not to sign up to be a model, but to get the rich and famous to sign her letter to the Governor of

Texas asking for clemency for this . . .' she seized a bystander's cigarette and sucked in a lungful of tar '*inmate*.'

'Aunty Liz,' Marrakech sighed, resignedly, struggling to free herself from her mother's ferocious grip, 'do you think it's too late to put myself up for adoption? Mum, you're just mad 'cause I'm not following in your footsteps down the catwalk.'

'I'm mad because I *believe* in capital punishment,' my sister fumed indignantly. 'Where would Christianity be today if Jesus had got seven to ten years with time off for good behaviour?'

Sven, who'd been eavesdropping, sidled up and checked the skirt label on the inside of Marrakech's waistband. 'Yep,' he schmoozed. ' "Made In Heaven".'

'My *daugh*ter has become a piece of *fly*-paper for *freaks*,' Victoria explained to Sven, through gritted teeth. 'We've decided to find it charming.'

Sven smiled in Marrakech's direction – the way a cobra would smile if a cobra could smile. 'How coincidental! I won't sign any girl who only wants to be a "face". We do insist on all our little girls developing a yen for human rights or at least showing an interest in Ecuadorian literacy projects or the Disabled Olympics. We have public-appearance days built into our contracts.'

'Really?' Marrakech drank in his words with open-mouthed amazement.

'It's so easy to morph from a model into a *spokes*model,' Sven elaborated, oozing sincerity. 'We have six UN goodwill ambassadors on our books. Tell me about this poor innocent man,' he sympathized, placing a ministerial arm around her shoulders.

'I've started a fighting fund for Bruce "The Tooth" Jackson.

He's in Gainsville Maximum Security Institution. He's been on Death Row for, like, nineteen years. Unless he gets an appeal he's going to the chair . . .' Marrakech shuddered. 'But I only earn, like, five quid an hour.'

'Jesus. Where are ya working? A *rice paddy*?'

'Um. No. Babysitting. For Aunty Liz mostly.'

'I could offer you a thousand quid an hour . . .' He looked at my niece. It was that calculated expression again – of a predator surveying his prey. '. . . to use your natural assets to make money to save the life of the innocent Mr Tooth – that way you can really "give back",' he said, employing the current buzz-phrase of the Bill Gates–Ted Turner super-rich.

'Yes I'm sure it must be fulfilling to know what comfort Britney's swimwear work has brought to men in maximum-security prisons.' But my catty remark was drowned out by a poolside melodrama involving the generously beloined synchronized male swimmers. The nude amphibians had an act that featured a substantial amount of backstroke but unfortunately Sven had turned off the heat in the pool for fear that the humidity would damage his African art works. The shrinkage factor in our pouting nautical supremos was greeted with dismay. Their duet suddenly included a lot of unscheduled front crawl to reach the pool's edge, where they flounced out to sulk in bathrobes. The ensuing kerfuffle ensured that it was five minutes before I noticed that Britney and my husband had disappeared from the grotto.

I darted my hand deep inside my sister's brassière, appropriated her plastic tits, shoved them down my own bra then dashed from room to room, trying to find Hugo, as fast as my idiotic stilettos would carry me. I flung open door after door, with my sister chasing me, until I finally, pantingly, located my husband in the ornately decorated upstairs drawing room. It was all leatherbound books (which nobody ever read) and bow-legged antique bureaux – (carved, of course, from the trees of endangered rainforests) tottering on legs so spindly they looked as if they might canter off across the Persian carpets.

But instead of finding Hugo *in flagrante*, I had caught him prostituting himself in an entirely new way.

A cluster of wide-eyed, angular models (we're talking Hail-a-Bimbo) and prospective investors were gathered respectfully around my husband.

'Let's face it,' Sven was saying, 'no one's gonna employ you if they've seen better heads on a pimple. Are they, Doc?'

Hugo frowned at my arrival and turned his back slightly, excluding me, before moving his heavy medical artillery into intellectual place. 'Personal appearance *is* a vital consideration at job interviews. In the chronically anxious future, people may feel they cannot afford *not* to be surgically restructured,' my husband essayed knowledgeably.

The audience hung on his every word, smiling radiantly at Hugo's genius. My husband glittered. He shone. He was like a deity. A Doc-o-crat. When did doctors get to rule the world like this? I wondered, hovering outside the circle. I listened, nauseated, as he went boldly where bad taste and banality had never gone before.

'Ageing is like a clock. At the Longevity Clinic we can't turn it back but we can stop it ticking.' His voice was sepulchrally deep, steeped in intellectual weight and authority.

'And when, ya know, should ya, like, start?' Despite the

automatic smile, Heroin Chic had a remote, taxidermied look in her eyes. Sven should have just whacked her up on the wall, really.

Sven touched her pale, fragile cheek. 'Angel, it's advisable to avoid all lines – except Cunard. You're so beautiful, babe, but breast implants could really bring out the woman in you, you know. Augmentation's no big deal. It's just like trimming your split ends.'

*A look of contemptuous sarcasm shrieked across my face. I hadn't realized that you needed an anaesthetic to have a hair-cut, followed by two weeks' bed rest. But, under strict instructions to 'blend in', I just radiated a numb silence.*

'J'know why the space between a woman's tits and hips is called a "waist"?.' Sven chortled. ''Cause you could fit another pair of boobs in there! . . . In and out. Home in one day. And it doesn't hurt, either. Not with the famous Hugo Frazer MD wielding the scalpel.'

*I gawked at Hugo. He'd obviously forgotten to pay his brain bill. It was clearly time to have my husband sectioned under the Mental Health Act.*

'I do aim for minimal discomfort.'

*'Minimal discomfort', 'quantum health', 'accelerated empow-erment', 'wellness technology', 'facial rejuvenation' – I listened distastefully, as Hugo and Sven dazzled the crowd with the obfuscatory jargon of cosmetic surgery.*

'Dr Frazer?' I blurted. 'Isn't "discomfort" the word plastic surgeons use to describe the excruciating agony of waking to find your tits all purple and oozing pus?' *Oh, when was I going to learn not to wear my heart on my sleeve? Hell, it's so hard to accessorize.*

My husband's eyebrows pyramided like a couple of copulating caterpillars. The select circle of cadaverously pale 'posh modelling totty' and prospective investors regarded me with sullen intensity. Sven scowled like a stage villain. I might as well have gone swimming in shark-infested waters while menstruating.

'If implants make a woman feel better about herself, why not?' Hugo preached, with evangelistic zeal. 'It's all about having control over your own life. Isn't that what feminists are always saying?'

'Here's the choice, gals,' Sven coaxed. 'You can rail at an imperfect, male-dominated world – or you can go get yourself a great pair of bazongas. So what's it gonna be?'

I realized then that it wasn't the models I hated (I mean, *modelling*, it could be learnt by an advanced rodent) but their vampiric manipulators.

'I'll have y'all know that Hugo Frazer is an artist.' Britney, still bikini-clad, wriggled next to Hugo and touched his arm in an overly familiar way. 'The doc here, well, he makes better boobs than God!'

I felt something tearing inside me. The extremely irascible wolverine was back, trying to claw its way out of my abdomen via my throat. I threw my eyes up to the ceiling. 'Actually you're on a waiting list for canonization, aren't you, Hugo?' I ridiculed. *(Oh, yes! Public humiliation. Now **that's** the way to win back one's husband. I was obviously depriving some poor village somewhere of its idiot.)*

When Hugo concluded his sales pitch, he came over and seized my upper arm. His mouth had pinched up like an irritated anus. 'It so happens,' he whispered, through gritted teeth, 'that since women already have fewer opportunities than men to get ahead professionally, an attractive body is a real asset.' Then my husband delivered the killer blow. 'Maybe then you wouldn't have lost your job, Elisabeth.'

It was a solar-plexus punch, which left me reeling. His words just cut me down. I had to escape. Oh, where was a pair of ejector knickers when I needed them? Teetering unsteadily in my unaccustomed footwear across the treacherous antique rugs, I tripped, stumbled, buckled at the knees, and splattered, spreadeagled, on to the floor. Did I know how to 'blend in' or what?

And just to drive home the fact that Britney Amore was the ingrown pube in the bikini wax of my life, I caught sight of her from my recumbent position, placing her arm proprietorially through my husband's. They looked, I realized dismally, the very image of a Power Couple.

Anger and indignation bubbled up inside me. Okay, models and actresses may be all gymmed and slimmed– but they need Personality Trainers to get their mental muscles into shape. You might be able to use my photo as a birth-control device, but I had a radiant personality. My personality was so radiant, I was positively giving myself melanomas.

Rehoicking my plastic tit-enhancers, I straightened up, shrugged off Victoria's consoling hand and marched back into the middle of the room to dazzle my husband with virtuosic wit and aerobic wordplay.

The very first person I ran into was Al Pacino.

'Hello, Al Apecia,' I said.

The shrill prattle of over-refreshed PR people fell silent. It was then that my plastic breast pouch flopped out of my fringed leather bra cup and landed at the movie star's feet, where it wobbled forlornly like a stranded jellyfish.

There was a hiss of amusement among the guests punctuated by a shriek of cruel laughter from Britney. Only Hugo was silent. His expression suggested a dawning realization that he'd married the only living brain donor in human history.

Obviously I'd been reading *The Sylvia Plath Guide to Love, Life and Living Happily Ever After*.

On my way home, alone in the taxi, I tore out my hair, gnawed my nails, downed a bottle of tequila . . . Stopped to buy a machete and combed the cabbie's *A to Z* to find out where She lived . . .

If only I hadn't gone to *The Vagina Monologues* that night, I wept. If only I hadn't taken Hugo with me. If only I hadn't found that grey pube and cropped my pudenda. If only I hadn't set fire to my own kitchen. If only I'd not gone to Sven's model awards ceremony. If only I'd worn flat shoes tonight with no breast enhancers. If only, if only, if only . . .

Of late, I had gambled with fate and lost so many times, I had roulette rash.

What's more, I had a terrible feeling there were a lot more spins left in that wheel . . .

# 16. With a Husband Like Mine, Who Needs Enemas?

One of life's great mysteries, apart from the fact that TV weathermen get a clothing allowance and still look the way they do, is why women continue to stand by their cheating husbands. I mean, *men* don't stay in a relationship when they don't think its working. Stephen Hawking walked out on *his* marriage and the man has no *legs*.

As I lay in bed later that night I tried to fathom when exactly Hugo had turned into the sort of person who insists on being seated in the first-class section of a lifeboat. I had met him shortly after he graduated with distinction from medical school. He would talk passionately, then, about making the world a better, kinder place. So why had my dedicated fountain-pen-pushing, poetry-quoting man taken to using expressions like 'multi-tasking' and 'out-sourcing' and other buzzwords, like, well, 'buzzwords'?

When did I first notice that he was turning into the sort of bloke who wore pinstriped condoms? I think it was about the time he became famous helping to reconstruct the faces of children injured in Sierra Leone and Sri Lanka. Princess Diana even came to watch him operate. She was so impressed that one of her charities funded his floating hospital which was moored off the West African coast, providing operations on deformities caused by landmines and machetes. Success had put him in danger of Taking Himself Too Seriously. He'd always been such a cautious man – passing scissors handle-first, not running with a glass in his hand, not getting out of his seat until the aircraft had come to a complete standstill. To be leaping into a business venture with these vultures, well, it was like Britain without a food scare, or I dunno, Britney without her hymen, just totally out of character.

At one a.m. I stopped pretending to read page 2789 of Cal's new manuscript, picked up the phone, which was still sticky with Jamie's breakfast Nutella, and dialled Hugo's mobile. He was at the hospital, he'd said – emergency brain-tumour op. I wanted to believe him. But after it clicked over to his messaging service, I placed the next call to Calim, begging baby-sitting favours.

Minutes later Cal, sockless and crumpled, was at the back door, tugging a tattered T-shirt over his tousled head. 'You're really leavin'?' he asked excitedly.

I looked at him, aghast. 'Leaving? No! I'm fighting.'

His sleep-creased face fell. 'Oh, Lizzie,' he said wearily. 'Tryin' to save your marriage is like tryin' to refloat the *Titanic*.'

'Hugo's the most brilliant, handsome man I've ever met. Can *he* help it if women hurl themselves at him? When he takes a woman's temperature, the nurses have to adjust it down a notch to compensate for the rush of excitement from his touch!'

'Come on, Liz, admit it. You only married Hugo because you have no da.'

'You think Hugo is my "father figure"? Of course he's a

father figure. *To my children,*' I said angrily, snatching the car keys off the peg.

Cal looked stricken. 'Hey, makin' shallow snap judgements is what I'm good at. It's important never ever to pay attention to anythin' I say,' he called after me apologetically.

It was a white-knuckled drive as I careered through Camden, dodging unmuffled mini-cabs, bat-out-of-helled around the Old Street roundabout and swerved on two wheels towards Shoreditch, deep into the grimy gullet of London's East End. The London Hospital, a decaying Victorian mausoleum, squatted, exhausted, to my right on the Mile End Road. I hung a suicide left into the filthy car-park, my heart sinking when I discover that his BMW was not in its allotted place.

Pushing into the overheated hospital was like opening an oven door to check a roast. A wave of stale heat hit me. The clapped-out lift responded with a grudging snarl. Too impatient to wait, I bounded upstairs to weave my way past the disgruntled trolleys, which were clattering over the warped hall floors. Rock-climbing over a mountain range of contaminated waste dumpsters, uncollected since the last world war, I rattled the handle of Hugo's office door. Locked. Heart palpitating, I peered through the oily glass. His briefcase was not on the desk. Where the hell was my husband?

What with eighty-hour working weeks, no sleep, financial cutbacks and waiting lists longer than the Great Wall of China, NHS doctors are a curiously uncommunicative lot.

'Have you seen Hugo?' I asked several I recognized. They grunted blearily and traipsed past me to their next emergency.

So I wandered the grim corridors down to Ward B, alone. The sticky linoleum sucked at the soles of my shoes, which squeaked defiantly as they pulled themselves free. Squeak. Squelch. Squeak. Squelch.

A nearby sign warned that if you contracted *Staphylococcus* from being too near contaminated people, well, it wasn't because you hadn't been warned. I cringed at the disclaimer. *Staphylococcus aureus* is a deadly bacterium that destroys you so swiftly you've barely got time to say 'Hey, I wish I'd paid more attention to that sign about the dangers of being near people contaminated with *Staphylococcus*.'

Radiators rattled asthmatically. Machines rasped. Septic yellow light filtered down from neon bulbs attached to flaky ceilings, which had dandruffed on to balding carpets. God, I thought. Was it any wonder Hugo wanted to rattle the bars of his prison gate?

Once in Ward B, I snatched back the flimsy, faded curtains inadequately separating old men from teenage girls. His patients lay there, in the regulation drab pyjamas of hospital inmates. But no Dr Hugo Frazer in evidence.

I plunged up the fire escape. It was littered with rags, a baby's bottle, a battered bong, a soiled sanitary towel. I took the steps two at a time, panic-stricken that Hugo was between the thighs of my nemesis. When I shoved through the swinging double doors to the theatre and found him scrubbing up at the urinal-shaped sinks, I thought at first I was having a hyperventilation-induced hallucination. Although kitted out in Listerine-green theatre pyjamas with his hair fetchingly bound in a blue paper shower cap and half his face shrouded in a surgical mask, he was still attractive. To me, he looked like a hero from a paperback romance. Relief washed through me.

'Elisabeth!' My husband addressed me formally.

'Are you fucking her or not?' I demanded in my best Bette Davis accent. The thick stench of disinfectant embalmed the room.

'Oh.' He groaned. 'Isn't there a statute of limitations on adulterous kissing guilt? Britney Amore was a temptation unsuccessfully resisted for two minutes. That's all.' A bright pink gloop squirted from the soap dispenser into his upturned palms.

'Well, what about MSB?'

'What, pray tell, is MSB?' he asked, scrubbing his hands with methodical precision.

'Maximum Sperm Build-up. When I was away at that stupid spa, well, you should have stored up loads of sperm and you hadn't. Just a trickle.' Tears pooled behind my eyes.

Hugo threw back his head and guffawed. 'Oh, well, *that*'s scientific. Which learned medical journal did you get *that* out of?'

'I base that statement on extensive scientific documentation in the form of something my sister told me.'

'Oh, your *sister*. Of course it would be your sister. The Brain of Britain. Sperm is like breast milk, Elisabeth. The more you use, the more you have. It's a supply and demand situation.' Water spumed from the taps, which he abruptly turned off with his elbows.

'Oh.' At first I felt consoled and comforted. But then a shopping list of evidence started chalking itself up in my mind – the lower-lip sandwich, his increasing absences, the chafe marks and unexplained bruises on his body, the new aerobic sexual repertoire, Britney's mysterious medical examination –

and I felt the acid of doubt bite into my skin once more. I envisaged Britney Amore in his arms, all lithe and light and lean. Next to her I was lumpen and small, weighted down with worries. A sob choked out of me. My voice emerged in a croak. 'Don't deceive me, Hugo. I'm beginning to question my own bloody sanity.'

My husband ripped off his mask, took me in his arms and pressed my head to his familiar chest. He smoothed me down as though I were a crumpled bedspread.

'What *was* it about her?' I searched his face. 'Just because she's in a famous medical drama, did you think that made it okay to play doctors-and-nurses?'

Hugo chuckled into my neck. I inhaled the clean, masculine smell of him. The aroma filled me with a hot, empty ache; I closed my eyes and held on to him for as long as his patience would allow.

'Was it her body?' I asked, when he pulled away. 'But, for God's sake, Hugo, the woman did a *Playboy* spread. That's not a vagina between her legs. That's a sperm Jacuzzi.'

Hugo affectionately chucked me under my chin.

'I mean it can't have been her *brain*. While signing autographs she has to stop and say to her fans '*What*'s my name again?' He laughed.

'Was it . . .' I didn't want to say it. 'Was it her breasts? Are you a "breast man"?'

'Once and for all, I'm not a "breast man" . . . I'm a "breast *person*",' my husband teased.

I raised my eyes to his, searching for a clue. I looked long and hard into his face. The face I knew so well and adored so much. 'Well, if you look at her again, I'm going to wash your eyes out with soap. Is that clear?"

'Elisabeth, she's the future wife of my new business partner,' he said, in a wearily patient tone. 'I can't just ignore her.'

'Then don't go into business with them.'

'Lizzie, look around you!' He gestured to the swinging, naked light bulbs. Their watery greyish light illuminated the blemished plasterwork and blistering paint. 'This is *not ER*. There's no glamour. Only exhaustion. My talents are wasted here. All I want to do is operate.' His voice sounded so sentimental, so sincere, it could have been a film trailer. 'Yet there's no money for surgery. My cancer patients die before I can save them and all because of the inefficiency of the National Health Service.'

'But it's intellectual emasculation, Hugo. Sven and his girlfriend are low-lifes. They're the Illiterati . . .'

'I've done enough heroic self-sacrifice. I've worked the four-day shifts.' He sighed discontentedly. 'I've done the thirty-hour operations . . . Darling, do you realize how much money there is gushing out of the Fountain of Youth?'

'Fountain? It's not a fountain, Hugo, it's a sewer.' I dropped my hands away from his shoulders.

'The world's best Longevity Clinic. Not only cosmetic surgery, but egg-freezing to help women beat the biological clock, embryo research into the causes of Alzheimer's . . . useful as well as lucrative. We could be set up for life. Let's face it, now that you're unemployed, how are we going to pay the school fees? And the cleaning lady. Not to mention our annual skiing holidays. We can't afford to be poor! I'm doing this for *you* too, you know. Money isn't everything, but it's right up there with *oxygen*!'

In the sudden lull, I became aware of the thundering of hospital trolleys in the corridor outside. It seemed symbolic of all the routine chaos waiting to engulf him.

'And if *I* don't take this opportunity, some other surgeon will.'

'But operating on underage models? Girls we don't consider old enough to vote or buy a drink? And for what? To cater to some pathetic male fantasy? Hugo – I just don't know what you stand for any more.'

'At the moment, I stand for whatever the general public will fall for,' he said dolefully, as the naked lightbulb above us sputtered and died. 'Now, if you'll excuse me, I need to scrub up again.'

There was a thin, bare silence between us.

'I'll give up the cleaning lady. The kids can go to the state school—'

Hugo took hold of me one more time. 'I am going ahead with the business Lizzie.'

I stiffened in his arms. 'Why don't you travel light, Hugo, and leave your hypocrisy at home?'

'And I expect your support,' he added, sternly.

'Then you're going to have to choose,' I replied, with grim finality, shrugging him off, 'between me and Sven's wretched clinic.'

'How can you ask me to make such a decision?'

I turned crisply for the door. 'Just ask yourself what Dr Jekyll would do.'

138

# 17. I Can't Believe It's Not Marriage! It Smells, Tastes, Looks and Spreads Like Marriage, but It Just *Isn't*

It's not only doctors' handwriting that is indecipherable. Their language is equally cryptic. When a physician is examining you and says, for example, 'Hmmmmm,' what that really means is that he has no bloody idea what the hell is wrong with you but whatever it is it's *disgusting*.

'That really is an interesting skin complaint' decodes as 'Excuse me while I go throw up my lunch.'

'Nothing to worry about' means you'll be dead in two weeks.

And the old favourite, 'There's good news and there's bad news'? Well, in Hugo's case, the good news had to be that he was having an affair with a famous daytime TV soap diva. (Well, the symptoms were definitely pointing to that dismal diagnosis.) The bad news was that *I* was the one who was going to have to suffer for it.

Christmas and New Year I spent boldly going nowhere. Life had put me on hold. I know I vowed to give Hugh some emotional distance. But nobody had said anything about physical distance. As out of sight can be out of mind, I found a million reasons to discuss children, household insurance, storm gutters. I determined to make each contact pleasant. (Valium helped.) By smiling, laughing at his jokes and looking my most seductive (although, believe me, wearing a Wonderbra is like volunteering for a car crash – it strangles your breath and crushes your ribcage), I hoped that he wouldn't remember only the God-awful moments – and compare them unfavourably to the fabulous times he was having with *her*.

I was like Doris Day on acid. One morning I toasted my hand, spread strawberry jam on it and placed it on Julia's plate. My bewildered nine-year-old suggested that perhaps it was time that I went back to work.

'Oh, good idea, Julia,' I said sarcastically. 'So, tell me, do you think I'm too old for a paper round?'

Jamie provided the answer after serious consideration. 'Yeah, I think so.'

'Do you really want to spend your entire childhood locked in your bedroom with only green vegetables to eat and educational TV?' I snapped, as if competing for the Dysfunctional Mum of the Year award.

But as the winter squalls battered our Hampstead home, I convinced myself that we would weather the Britney storm. The clinic had been important to Hugo, sure, but he would soon realize that it wasn't worth losing his marriage over.

When my spirits flagged, I reminded myself that I was making all this effort for the greater good – getting my man back where he belonged. I made an inventory of all the things I loved about him and recited them daily as a matrimonial mantra. We'd got each other through chickenpox, lost luggage, the death of relatives, the guinea-pig's pneumonia, flat

tyres, a brush with salmonella and a bomb scare. Yes, we'd
been bacteria to each other, but also penicillin.

When Hugo didn't make it for Christmas lunch (a surgical
SOS as usual), Cal and Victoria began to lecture me stereo-
phonically about the joys of living alone.

'Why won't you leave him, Lizzie? I mean, think of the
money you could save on anti-depressants,' Cal insisted.

'I love him.'

'But how do you know?' Cal flumped down beside me on
the wooden bench in the hall, from where we could watch the
children disappearing up the stairs with the babysitter between
their teeth.

'Well . . . when he cuts his finger while grating the truffles,
I wish it were me, you know?'

'Oh, that's gotta be love,' Cal mocked, firing up a fag. 'The
point is, if your husband gets any more selfish, he'll make a
footnote of himself in a medical journal.'

'We've been through so much . . . I didn't even kill him
during flat-pack furniture erection when we were first married
– grounds for homicide normally.' I tried to make light of
things. 'And, there's the suntan lotion, there are parts of my
back I just can't reach . . . And we've just landscaped the
garden . . .'

Victoria emerged from the kitchen, her crocodile-skin heels
castaneting on the pine floors, her sharply tailored satin pant
suit shimmering. 'So, are you kicking the creep out?'

'No,' replied Cal, on my behalf. 'They're stayin' together
for the sake of the plants *apparently*.'

They both looked at me quizzically. It hadn't come out

right. Love is complicated. Even Einstein had never managed to explain it. 'Look, I've saved my marriage. Aren't you even going to look happy for me?'

'Aren't I looking happy?' My sister prodded her frozen forehead, benumbed with botox.

'Hello, I'm your sister,' I extended my hand. 'Lizzie McPhee. I don't believe we've met. If you have any more "procedures", Victoria, I'm no longer going to be able to pick you out in a crowd!'

'Sven likes it . . . Where *is* he?' She checked her watch. 'He was supposed to pick me up hours ago.'

'Why on earth do you want him so badly? Everyone he's ever dated has ended up in rehab or a nunnery.'

'Because the only job offer I've had this month is to advertise a cream for *yeast* infections on daytime TV. The chance of brokering this gig into a movie career looks as slim as Britney bloody Amore. Have you any idea what I've been *reduced* to? Belgrade catwalks, where some mor*onic* designer whose collection is inspired by "negative space" and "airports" tells me to "be manly, butch, hot. It's a jungle out there – but also lesbian". The *next* day I'm told to walk a third of the way down the catwalk and then stop. Whinny. Stare at everyone, then go backstage. Ten years ago I was arriving at premières with Mick Jagger on one arm and a panther on a gold lead on the other. And *now* look at me!!!'. She shook me violently by the shoulders. 'If he doesn't marry me soon I am going to *shoot* myself, do-you-understand-me?'

My sister slid her pale arms into the satin lining of her raspberry coat sleeves. 'Since Sven is obviously not planning to grace us with his presence, I'm leaving. Today has just been a total waste of makeup.' She gave an elaborate sigh and then wove a sinuous trajectory around the kids' bikes, skates and scooters to the front door.

I scanned Cal's face for a flicker of tell-tale emotion. 'How goes *your* love life?' I probed.

'On my good days I pray for death. Speaking of which, how tall are you, shug? I just need to know so that I can order *your* body-bag.' Cal ground his butt into a pot plant. ''Cause this marriage is gonna kill you.'

'Well, then, bury me in a herbaceous border somewhere. And, at the funeral, don't let 'em play "My Heart Will Go On" by Celine Dion.'

'Good God, if only that woman had gone down with the *Titanic*.' He sighed.

*

On New Year's Day, when Hugo called my mobile to say he couldn't make the family lunch at Richoux's restaurant because of another emergency surgical procedure, my sister raised her crayoned brow like a dominatrix's whip.

'That just shows what a noble and good person he is,' I said, defensively, 'performing all this emergency surgery through the holidays.'

'I've never heard butt-sag called an "emergency" before. Still, thank God all those self-sacrificing, philanthropic doctors who work in plastic surgery are there to help we women in our decade of need.'

I blinked neutrally. 'He's abandoning the Longevity Clinic.'

'The clinic, you idiot, is a big success. Where do you think I've been getting all my procedures done recently?' she announced.

Dismay skittered through my belly. 'But . . . but I told him to choose between me and the clinic.' A tiara of sweat beads adorned my brow. 'In the end, I presumed he chose *me*.'

I was a glutton for punishment, I really was. I needed to join a psychological Weight-watchers to weigh up my excess emotions – yesterday two tantrums, the day before, three sulks; today, one nervous bloody breakdown.

With trembling hands, I lit up one of Victoria's cigarettes. I hadn't needed a smoke since my days as a foreign correspondent. Being married to Hugo Frazer MD I had, of late, found myself craving the peace and tranquillity I'd known caught in crossfire on the Gaza Strip. A French waiter swooped upon us. 'Good afternoon. Would Madam prefer the smoking section?' he asked, pointedly.

'Actually, do you have a heroin-injecting, nervous-breakdown-having, suicide-while-you-wait section? Because that would do quite nicely thank you!' I blurted, before shattering into hot, humiliated tears.

'The Patient has no past history of attempted suicides but is constantly tearful. The patient refused a lobotomy . . . though suggested some serious drugs might help.' Of course, the reason I didn't need a lobotomy was that I already had one. It's called a marriage certificate.

# 18. The Night Is Young, but You Are Not

How many roads must a man walk down before he admits he is lost?

Stepping into the clinic was like stepping into *Austin Powers III*. An elaborate ziggurat of glass and marble behind a traditional Harley Street façade, it featured bleached walls, plinky-plonky Enya soundtracks and white-coated pod-people moving around efficiently with clipboards. Perhaps Sven was really Dr Evil. And Britney Amore his beautiful but deadly assistant. Perhaps they were secretly manufacturing giant hair-sprays in their subterranean caverns to rip the ozone layer and melt the poles so as to drown all the ugly people?

I pushed through the gilt-edged gates, macheted through the flowered vines tendrilling from the towering atrium and trekked for a mile or two around the ornamental lake in the foyer. It struck me how much the place *didn't* look like the London Hospital. It gleamed with designer confidence. The windows sparkled. The Muzak pumped hypnotically. No dilapidated chairs, no corroded pipes, no shabby carpets, no despairing, overstretched nursing staff, no bacteria the size of mature elk. Here, beaming secretaries buzzed between filing cabinets and phone calls. Vibrant Christmas decorations were still strung festively in the foyer between sets of Corinthian columns and marble cloisters that would not have looked out of place in the late Caligula's pleasure palace.

I'd come with Victoria, who was to feature in the 'before' and 'after' segment of a promotional video. The star presenter was Britney Amore. At the sight of me, Britney made a face like the heroine in a horror movie who has just seen the Creature.

'Nice to see you too,' I mumbled. It may have been my imagination, but her breasts seemed more gigantic than ever. It looked as though she'd just dragged her buttocks through her legs and strapped them into her bra cups. 'When you're eighty those thirty-two double D-cup silicone jobs are going to cramp your swing in the Seniors' Golf Tournament, you know.'

'This is a private shoot,' Britney barked brusquely. 'PR people only.'

A loving kiss on my hot cheek distracted me. 'Marrakech! What dark satanic forces brought *you* here?'

'Um . . . I came with Sven.'

Enough said.

Sven was busy beguiling the young, overawed models, including Heroin Chic, in the waiting room. 'Can I take your picture? That way Santa will know *exactly* what I want next Christmas!'

'An obsession with teenagers just proves how truly ignorant you are.'

Turning, Sven bestowed on me a warm and pleasant smile; the sort of smile that immediately put me on guard. It was disarming – like a cat toying with a canary before devouring it.

'Women don't even reach their sexual prime until their forties.'

'Yeah,' he responded casually, 'but who'd wanna fuck 'em?'

'Really? Have you pointed this out to my *sister*?' I said coldly.

Smiling with sinister obsequiousness, Sven moved out of earshot of the others, beckoning for me to follow. 'Oh, look,' he boasted, as I approached, 'I just made you come with one finger . . . Now, piss off out of my clinic.' He clamped me on the shoulder. (Whenever he did this, I was always surprised to discover it wasn't a knife blade.) He then steered me – propelled me, really – towards the outer marble corridor. 'This place is for babes only. Babia Majora.'

'Marrakech!' I called her, my blood boiling. 'Come on.'

Sven's left arm snaked around my niece's waist.

'I think I'll stay,' she said. 'Sven promises that beautiful egg donors can sell their eggs to, like, the highest bidder.'

'That's enough, babe,' he ordered, placing a finger to her lips.

But she kept trotting along beside me. 'He's auctioning our ova on the Internet. You know. To parents who want a beautiful child.'

My niece had just taken an IQ test . . . and failed . . . 'What?'

'One model got a bid for fifteen thousand squids! It's kinda off, but do you know what that sort of dosh could do for my Bruce? It's going to pay for the lawyers who can help get him off Death Row.'

So Sven really *was* Dr Evil. And his twisted mind wasn't

just hatching plots, but also the eggs of supermodels to breed Beautiful People. 'You're selling your eggs?' I asked Marrakech, horrified. 'What are you? A *chicken*?'

'Yeah. Free-range,' triumphed Sven. 'Meaning she's free to make up her own mind.' He strong-armed me towards the glass door leading to Harley Street.

And that bastard would have bounced me too, except that Britney Amore was busy ushering in the camera crew and public-relations people who were making the promotional video. Sven immediately turned his strong-arming into a friendly, affectionate embrace.

'Welcome!' he said expansively. 'Refreshments, anyone? A little New Year cheer?'

After all the deafening mwah-mwah cheek kissing synonymous with PR execs, I watched Britney do her opening scene to camera. 'Welcome to our Longevity Clinic. Soon, we'll be known all over the world – and other places. We're gonna sweep the country like wild flowers!'

Jesus Christ. One more neurone and Ms Amore would have a synapse.

'All women are unique, just like all other women.'

It was clear that *this* woman had spent her Texan childhood playing with the plutonium. The lieutenant of the Space Cadet Academy then introduced her partner, 'in business and plea-s*urrrrrre*' she rolled the R in her mouth, positively fellating it.

Sven took the cue and, helped by a large idiot board, lapsed into one of those 'I really do *care* about women' monologues to which the modern man is distressingly prone. His smile was greasy enough to fry kebabs.

'Tell them about the eggs,' I heckled. 'And the underage models.'

Britney, seated on a makeshift podium next to Sven, crossed her legs in an effort to distract. Her skirt hem disappeared underneath her armpits – along with the investigative brain capacity of every man present.

Two henchmen materialized. I pushed into the ladies' loos and splashed my face with cold water. Why was Hugo involved with these charlatans, I wondered, as a malfunctioning hand-dryer sucked my arm in up to the elbow. And why hadn't he told me he'd chosen them above his marriage? My husband was treating me like a side dish he hadn't ordered.

Flummoxed, I collapsed on to the loo. I was sniffing back tears when Britney Amore shoved her way into my cubicle. 'Hey!'

'God*damn* it to hell. How many times do I have to flush before you'll go away?' she demanded, in a voice like acid.

'Haven't you got any fan-mail to go forge?' I managed to retort.

'Stop trying to sabotage our project.' She loomed over me.

'I don't know what you mean.'

'Don't play dumb with me.' She raised her tangerine-coloured brows, ruthlessly plucked into two cynical arches. 'I'm much better at it.'

'Who *are* you?' I asked the not-quite-as-famous-as-she-used-to-be actress, who was not quite as stupid as I'd imagined.

She levelled a chilling stare on me. 'I'm a share-holder in this clinic. And so is your hubby. There's no way the Longevity

Clinic will work without Britain's leading facial surgeon.' She lazily half closed her lids, an insolent set to her lower lip.

Had she deliberately seduced my husband? In that case my mistake had been to think she was a bimbo. She wasn't. She was a praying mantis in Prada. Let's face it, it takes a lot of intelligence to look that stupid. I took aim with the best ammunition I had. 'Do you know Sven's sleeping with my sister? And has been since before you got engaged?' I revealed, triumphantly.

She shrugged. 'So what? It helped Sven persuade your sister's little bunny to sell her eggs in time for Easter. Once Marrakech is signed, he'll have her flashin' her gash for a men's mag in no time.' I felt momentarily unable to contribute to the conversation.

'Well, one thing's clear,' I finally responded. 'You're definitely never going to be a character actor – because YOU DON'T HAVE ANY. I don't know what my husband sees in you.'

'Well, he'll be seein' it more regularly, hon, unless you get with the programme.'

Curiously, I began to feel sorry for Hugo and his entanglement with this woman. Enter Britney's vaginal zone and you could just vanish; never to be heard from again. She was the Bermuda pubic triangle.

As Britney Amore sashayed her way out of my toilet cubicle, pausing only to reapply a slick of magenta lip-gloss, I tried to steady myself against the basin. Moments later, as I hurtled, pell-mell, in a toe-stubbing flurry down the hall, I realized that the only difference between a Hollywood actress and a piranha is the silicone implant.

# 19. A Stitch in Time – Now That Really **Would** Have Confused Einstein

There is no law of gravity in Harley Street. Skin sags upwards. You know how they do cosmetic surgery? Basically they just drag everything up: the ankle becomes the knee, the knee becomes the navel, the clitoris becomes the chin. The way to spot a recipient of cosmetic surgery is to look for a woman who's rubbing her jaw a little bit too vigorously.

When I found my sister she was on the fourth floor, surrounded by the film crew, stretched out on a hospital trolley, clad in a white surgical gown and shower cap rehearsing for the 'before' segment of the promotional video. Standing over her was the new potentate of plastic surgery, Hugo Frazer, who was skilfully marking up her face and neck in black felt-tip pen, like a designer's instructions for a tailor. Carnationed button-hole, bow-tie, black jacket, pin-striped trousers. Really, the man should have been struck off for serious sartorial misconduct, i.e. impersonating a prat doctor.

Hugo rustled up a defiant smile. 'So, oh . . . what do you think of the clinic?'

'Well, it's, um . . .' catching him in the act like this had left me dumbfounded '. . . clean, isn't it?' I said, proving that little escapes me in architectural matters.

Hugo moved around the bed taking Victoria's pulse and temperature with cool efficiency.

'God, all that medical training, all that expertise, and here you are staple-gunning excess facial flesh to the back of brainless heads. Vick, instead of having bits of your body cut off, hey, why not add bits *on*?' I suggested, desperate to make her see the surreality of the scenario. 'Another nose for when the first one gets sinusitis? A spare vagina to use after child-birth? Why not just have all your body parts attached to Velcro so you can take them on and off as they go in and out of fashion?'

'Don't start, Lizzie. Roll tape!' My sister cued the camera man. 'I'm only having a little bit of Restylane and Hylaform to fill in all these little grooves and hollows.' She ran her fingers over her beautiful face. 'Plus a chin implant . . . My chin is too far back. It should be in line with my upper lip.' The camera man moved in for a close-up. 'They make an incision by the lower teeth, saw open the jaw then move the chin forward and pin it into place. So I might as well have the cheek implants at the same time, to make them higher.'

'Is that *it*?' I asked, with flabbergasted sarcasm. 'Or is there some other *little* thing?'

'Well, while I'm under, I might as well have some abdominal lipo.' She slapped her taut tummy. 'To get rid of some of this beastly fat.'

Beastly? She made it sound as though she needed a whip and a chair to tame it. A line-tamer. Hugo would have that fat jumping through hoops and standing on its hind legs in no time.

'It hurts a bit, 'cause of the bruising on your muscles,' she said to the camera. 'But it's quite economical because I can freeze the unwanted fat for reinjection into my cheeks later on. All minimally invasive.'

I was staring at her, dismayed. At least I now knew that blondes don't always have more fun.

'God, if that's minimal I'd hate to see maximal. Soon only about one per cent of you will actually be *you*. Just a pube or two and the odd eyeball. You'll be silicone from tits to toenails.'

'Sven suggested that it might be time for a little remodelling.'

God, how I longed for a semi-automatic weapon or perhaps a small nuclear device to blow the whole hideous Longevity Clinic sky high.

'Sven's only using you to get at Marrakech. Britney admitted it.'

'Of *course* she'd say that. She's jealous of me.'

'He's convinced Marrakech to sell her eggs. Designer genes. Did you know about this, Hugo?' I dogged his steps from one side of the bed to the other.

My husband shrugged imperiously. 'It's a celebrity-obsessed world, Elisabeth. If we can help increase the chance of reproducing beautiful children, giving them a huge advantage in society, why should I feel guilty about that?'

'Because it's unethical. *Doktor Mengele*.'

'It's Darwin's natural selection at its very best. The highest bidder gets youth and beauty.' The nurses and PR reps were listening to him with grave courtesy, nodding heads bent

153

respectfully. 'People are only interested in looking at the beautiful. Just turn on your television any night and see for yourself.'

If he'd meant to wound me, he'd succeeded. 'I *know*,' I said bitterly.

Hugo tapped his wristwatch. 'Well, if you good people would excuse me, I have a surgery to run.' He turned and paced swiftly down the corridor.

I ran after him. Alone with Hugo at the lift well, I grabbed his sleeve and looked at him imploringly, 'Have you lost all respect for yourself?'

'Elisabeth, for the first time I actually *have* respect. For the first time, I have the surgical support I need. For the first time I'm going to be properly paid for what I do. Stop asking so much of me, Lizzie.'

'So *much*? It's not like I'm asking you to slay a dragon or pull a sword out of a stone. All I'm asking is that you don't throw away your reputation.' This had the same deterrent effect as an activist on a tank in Tiananmen Square. 'They're nothing without you,' I persevered. 'Just a cowboy clinic. Did you ever think that Britney may have come on to you just to entice you into business?'

His stethoscope, I noted, was now looped around his neck like a noose. But, when my husband turned disdainfully on his heel and strode off to scrub up, I realized that *I* was the highly strung one – strung out to dry.

Staggering in a half-stupor towards the fire exit, the cold blade of reality sliced into me: my husband no longer loved me. It was as obvious as a pre-1990 nose job.

# 20. All Stressed Out With No One To Kill

·····································································································

Think negative and you have nothing to lose. It was my New Year resolution. I made it a week late, all alone, crying in my bathroom, the kids tucked up asleep in my bed – while the cave-like echo of the empty house sent a chill through my heart. Hugo was always working now. He was doing so many operations, it must be like drive-through breast augmentations over there at the Longevity Clinic – McBoob and Co.

What happened to the tender, sensuous man I'd married? The closest I got to sex now was a nice pat-down from a security guard when I went for job interviews at television stations. My favourite sexual fantasy was – *a partner*. I was so lonely I'd taken to sexually harassing myself. With Hugo's transformation. I lost the star I was following and, with it, my sense of immunity. I felt imprisoned by inferiority and the plain, cold fear that I was about to forfeit my family life. My husband's love was simply fading away, like the end of a pop song on the radio.

I became short-tempered with the children. 'I want you to come down for breakfast in five minutes or before your mother is institutionalized, whichever comes first!'

I became short-tempered with my husband on the odd evening Hugo actually turned up in time for dinner. 'We are going to be a happy, close-knit family unit, even if I have to hog-tie each and every one of you to this damn table.'

Not that my domestic skills were worth coming home for. I developed a tendency to soak baking trays instead of scrubbing them. I soaked them for up to two weeks at a time. Every sponge cake I made had to be rebuilt with toothpicks. In fact, the kids were often left to forage for food while I took to zigzagging around Harvey Nix buying leopardskin hot-pants I was way too old for. My employment prospects were equally forlorn. I was short-listed for a few presenters' positions but unless you're a country-and-western singer, crying when drunk doesn't seem to improve your image. My Prozac prescription refill was programmed into Hugo's secretary's speed dial. Taken with alcohol it soothed my stretched nerves, but then I became paralysed by the boredom. I was the Monarch of Ennui – Ennui the Eighth I am, I am.

I tried to turn to my sister for emotional support, but she was preoccupied with her recovery. My sibling now had a body more preserved than Lenin's. Her livid purple neck and the mouldy rainbows of her eyes gave her a Bride of Frankenstein countenance. The first time I saw her without bandages, her face like overworked play-doh, my jaw hit my chest. 'Um, was anybody else hurt in the accident?'

'So, what do you think?' she asked, tilting her head. Her eyes seemed to be on the sides of her head, like a fly. She also looked perpetually amazed. Basically my sister's face-lift had given her the look of an insect who'd just seen a very big dick.

'What am I lookin' at exactly?' Cal quizzed, perplexed, leaning against my kitchen door, sipping Earl Grey.

'Marrakech's university fees, right there, on her stupid face,'

I explained, pointing to Victoria's uplifted cheeks and chiselled chin.

I tried turning to Cal, but he had also changed. He'd left university and gone back to working on a building site. It was nihilism by numbers.

'Labouring?' I screwed up my nose when he'd told me.

'Yes. Just imagine,' he said flippantly, 'soon that island in the Aegean will be mine!'

One frosty winter's morning I caught him at the back of my garden, about to barbecue his novel. I galloped down the path in my pyjamas and knocked the match out of his hand. 'Calim! Don't you dare! Okay, when you started writing you stunk. But now you stink much better!' I hazarded a smile.

'Lizzie, I have raised writing to a new low.'

'That's not true! Your novel is excellent . . . though you may need to trim a few thousand pages. You're the best writer on the planet – now that Tolstoy has kicked the bucket.' I punched his arm.

'You're living in a fantasy world.'

'I do *not* live in a fantasy world. If I lived in a fantasy world, I wouldn't get cystitis . . . And my lovely husband, my darling Hugo, wouldn't be leaving me,' I shivered.

'You've got him on a pedestal, Lizzie. The only time a man should be put on a pedestal is when he's too short to change the lightbulbs.'

'Well, the woman *you* love has obviously got you *under* a pedestal. Hugo has promised me he isn't cheating and—'

'With a mind like a steel sieve, you believe him. I didn't realize you had such a rugged determination to lose, Lizzie. That's *my* job.'

'I *won't* lose. I will not let it happen. It wouldn't be fair on the children.'

'Who said anythin' about life bein' fair? Was it fair the way you got the sack? Is it fair that your husband is off ridin' some actress? Is it fair that the woman I adore more than my own life won't love me back?'

My best friend had bought a one-way ticket on the Disorient Express and it was all my fault. If it weren't for me, he would never have become infatuated with my superficial sister.

He struck another match across the box.

'Listen, Calim Keane, I know you better than anyone. I've known you at least since the Palaeolithic period. You are not a shallow, cynical person. Don't do this.'

He paused. 'Hmmm. You say "shallow" as though that's a *bad* thing. As for "cynical", you go round pretendin' to be happily married . . . yet spend all your time moanin' about him. You simply *must* pop down the shop and pick up some more salt for that wound, Lizzie!'

'Excuse me. But *I*'m not the one who's burning my bridges before I even *get* to them. I don't want to be judgemental, but destroying two years' work? It's obscene, it's sick and it's wrong!'

'*Now go to your room young man and think about what you've done!*' Cal said, imitating my voice, before tossing a lit match on to the pile of coffee-stained pages.

'I'm pretty sure you could put the teeming fecundity of your imagination to better use than falling in lust with my sister. A living example of artificial intelligence – Brains by Mattel.' Cal looked at me with surprise as the burning paper flared. 'Oh, yes, I've known about your feelings for Victoria for ages.'

'Have you now?'

'Yes. And I hope you work out as a couple. Because you really deserve each other, do you know that? You're just as full of bullshit as she is!'

'Oh, really? It seems to me that *you're* the one who's living a lie.'

A huge Grand Canyon rift erupted in our friendship. We stood on either side peering into the dark chasm.

Just to put the cherry on the *Angst* Sundae, it was then I found the pair of scanty lace panties at the bottom of our bed. *Worn* scanty lace panties – crotchless.

Despite the mounting evidence (literally), Hugo promised that he wasn't seeing the winner of the Pants Open. I kept calm. I didn't pry. I didn't spy . . . The fact that I had to call the ambulance on my mobile phone to free my facial protuberances from the glass of the car window where they'd frozen during a midnight surveillance of Britney's Holland Park apartment was purely coincidental. But I was gripped by an even icier terror that I might really lose my beloved. This was a Romantic 999.

If I could just extract him from her clutches . . . Stalling seemed the best option because, surely, soon he would tire of her. Like key-hole surgery, I would have to carry out the operation delicately, from the surface. I practised what I'd say in the mirror. 'There's so much at stake, Hugo. The very least you can do is to give our marriage another try.' Or 'Perspectives shift dramatically with time. What may seem like insurmountable differences today often shrink to nothing with a little distance.' It occurred to me that I should make sure that distance happened – all two thousand kilometres of it.

*

'Holidays are like men – never long enough,' sighed my sister, when I asked her to mind the kids for a week. 'Hey! Why don't I come with you? I need a place to recover from my lipo. Somewhere Sven can't see me. He hasn't rung for weeks. I'm getting desperate, darling. I have to make myself more attractive to him. Look.' She hoicked up her Armani skirt and turned to reveal a sculptured buttock. 'I ran out of money after one butt cheek. I have to save up for the other side.'

'Oh, God, Victoria. Liposuction is so dangerous! What if they accidentally vacuum out internal organs you're still using? A liver or a kidney or an ovary or something.'

'You should try a little yourself, sweetie,' she huffed.

'Um . . . everything in my body seems to have a specific working function, you know?' I scorned. 'I don't think there's anything *spare*. And what are you gonna do with all the fat they've sucked out? Maybe you could have it sculpted into a statuette for Sven? Maybe that explains "The Blob"!? It's escaped liposuctioned fat, running free!'

'It's not funny, Elisabeth. I've lost my only asset – my looks. I used to sow wild oats. *Now* I'm just going to seed. Unless Sven marries me, my residential address will soon be a cardboard household-appliance carton,' she moaned, trying to make me feel sorry for her. 'Last *year*'s household-appliance carton!'

'You are not coming, Victoria. And that's final.'

160

'But it's my birthday,' she pleaded.

'I know. How old *aren't* you today?'

She opened the book I'd bought her, *The Portrait of Dorian Gray*.

'Okay, your husband's leaving you,' she stropped, 'but *what am I going to do about my vagina*? I think it's moving sideways. Because of all the lipo!'

'Then you really will be Sven's "little bit on the side",' I laughed lamely, but the laugh mutated into tears. That morning I'd noticed that Hugo's blackheads had been freshly squeezed. On his *back*.

I told Hugo that we needed to have some time together, to revive our marriage. 'Let's go somewhere and get sun cancer!' I fingered the heart-shaped locket in which I kept photos of our children – he'd given it to me on our tenth wedding anniversary – hoping to remind him of our shared history.

Julia and Jamie tumbled into the house then, back from their Little 'Uns' Feng Shui or anatomically correct gingerbread-men cooking class – I'd lost track of what particular Hampsteady after-school activity it was that day. But, oh, the miraculous comfort of your children's hugs and kisses, warm and wet as bath water. Hugo smiled, then agreed to book. And for once the Fuck-up Fairy was not waving her evil little wand, because he added three beautiful words as he stroked my hair: 'Somewhere really romantic.'

\*

'*A medical conference*? Does it get more romantic than *this*?' I clutched the plane ticket for Antigua in disbelief. Oh, thank you, Fuck-up Fairy. Have wand, will wave.

We were in a queue at Heathrow behind a heavily bearded Arab man who was rummaging through his bags looking for his ticket, or perhaps a bomb. All the check-in staff were away on a three-hour brunch break and our plane was leaving in twenty-five minutes.

'But, Lizzie, you know I always have to go home two hours into a holiday because I can't bear the tension of taking it easy. I thought with a bit of work to do every day I might be more relaxed about the vacation.' Hugo beamed.

'Yes, but I won't.' All those sloshed surgeons in the hospitality suite, stabbing me in the boob with their nametag pins; a whole week of conversing with chests that read 'Illegible' and 'Indecipherable'. Ugh.

I thought I couldn't be more disappointed until we boarded the plane to discover that Hugo had been upgraded to business class and I hadn't. No. I was to spend the next eight hours squished next to a guy with a lawnmower in his cabin luggage which he couldn't quite fit in the overhead compartment because his mini jet-ski was already crammed in up there, meaning that he was going to fly the whole way with a major horticultural appliance on his lap. On the other side of me was a man who introduced himself as 'Glen, from the Margarine and Spreads Association. We deal with twenty-six per cent of the yellow fats industry. Spreading the word . . .' He winked.

And it was then that my sister wafted by.

'What the hell . . . Get off this plane immediately! You're supposed to be looking after my children!'

'You know I have an allergy to children. Aren't I always frisking you on arrival for fingerpaintings or photographs?' She shuddered. 'They're with Cal. They're in the garden practising their gross motor skills as we speak, darling,' she said, fluttering goodbye with bejewelled fingers, as her uneven butt cheeks, matchstick legs and askew vagina disappeared down the aisle.

Things were turning out to be romantic all right – about as romantic as a herpes underneath a mistletoe. But at least I'd pulled Hugo away from Britney Amore.

*

The best time to go on holidays was probably 1922. No Club Meds, no crowds, no oil spills, no karaoke, no jet-skis, no matching his-and-her genital thongs, no condominiums, no leisure co-ordinators, no flotsam and jet-set and no medical conferences.

The hotel comprised a necklace of hairy huts ringing a large thatched cabaña, which housed the bar, restaurant and dance floor. Beyond the hammocks, lazily laced between palm trees, lay the lagoon, a turquoise sea distantly semi-circled by foamy breakers on the coral reef. If it had been any more perfect, it would have been a Coca-Cola advertisement.

The view was only spoilt by the cosmetic surgeons. Most were of the comical-shorts-wearing variety. Over-exercised coffin-dodgers in phlegm yellow fitness-orientated clothing, with starved bodies and decrepit faces, trying to extend their lives with enemas and sunshine. Their wives had obviously succumbed to an excess of plastic surgery which accounted for their painful, pinched, expressionless expressions – as though tortured by secret cystitis. They oozed been-there-and-bought-that apathy.

The three of us stepped out of the taxi into air that was steamier than Jennifer Lopez. It was four-to-five-T-shirts-a-day weather. As the wall of heat hit me I thought it might be drier in the sea. But that heat was nothing compared to the thermo-nuclear meltdown I was about to have as I glanced up from my 'Welcome!' rum punch to see Britney Amore sashaying towards me, a frangipani in her flame orange hair.

'Well, hi, y'all!'

# 21. Say Goodbye To Childhood, Hello To Adultery

The Sabre-toothed Husband Hunter flung her arms around Hugo, throwing her weight forward on to a set of perfectly pedicured toes, one waxed leg folding up flamingo-like behind her pertly rounded posterior.

'You knew *she*'d be here?' I fumed at Hugo, once my heart had started beating again.

'No. I knew Sven was coming to drum up some business . . .' he mumbled.

'*Sven*'s here?' As this was her first time in direct sunlight in her entire life, my sister was stumbling around like a newborn field mouse. 'Oh, God! Hide me! Oh, God!'

'Ain't this gonna be *fun*?' Britney crooned, pinching my husband's bottom – her way of firing a warning shot across my marital bows; this conference was important for the clinic's credibility and I wasn't to make waves.

'Ah-huh!' I replied. About as much fun as having a personalized lap dance from Ian Paisley. My marital waters were calm, all right – *calm as Lake Placid*.

'W-where is Sven?' Victoria asked, turtling her neck further into her collar and peering nervously over the tops of her shades.

'Attending the birth of his next wife, probably,' I replied, under my breath.

'Get changed, y'all, and come down to *our* beach over yonder.' Britney indicated the direction with a flick of an orange talon. Her smile was sewn on like a sequin. And it was practically all she was wearing, apart from a pint or two of cooking oil.

While we waited for our room to be made ready, Britney lay supine on a banana chair in her leopardskin bikini. She stretched out her honeyed legs, which ended in gold sandals about a mile away from her hips. As she giggled with Hugo, Victoria and I made totally unnecessary trips to the loo to gawp at her chest on the way.

'She's had them Done again, hasn't she?' I whispered, in awe.

'Wait, let me have one more look . . .' Victoria replied, making a quick saunter loo-wards. 'Jesus. She could use her bikini top as a slingshot and fire Exocet missiles at Iraq!' she reported back.

'Iraq?' I murmured. 'Those tits could deflect meteors from outer space!'

Britney uncoiled to standing position, diamond ankle chain glistening in the sun. 'So, come *on*, happy campers. Let's go swimming!'

'No thanks. We're tired, *aren't we?*' I glared at my husband pointedly.

Britney Amore's eyes slid down to my abdomen. 'Course ya are, hon. I mean, in your condition . . .'

I sucked in my stomach so violently my neck got thicker.

Hugo cleared his throat. 'No, um, actually we're not having any more children.'

'Well, then, waddle on over to the beach, gal, and get fit,' she chided.

Clearly Britney Amore had been separated from Eva Braun at birth. 'I'm not overweight, you know,' I sputtered defensively. 'I mean, for my height . . .' Why did this woman have the ability to make me sound like a Mormon elder? 'Am I, Hugo?'

'Well, maybe you could do with a little suction round the saddlebags . . .'

'I *was* on a diet, but I'm in remission,' I said, tartly – a pretty Mae West-esque reply, seeing as I was halfway through a heart-attack. Of course, what I wanted to do was book my husband on an all-expenses-paid trip on a Russian submarine – but, determined to win him back, I merely smiled. Not much of a smile, really, more like open-face surgery.

As Hugo rummaged through his suitcase for his swimmers, I begged my sun-hating sister to put on her asbestos sun suit. 'I cannot go to the beach with *Her*, alone.' I shuddered.

Victoria pooched her lips defiantly. 'I can't let him see me like *this*! Have you seen my waist? If I'd known Sven was bloody well going to be here I'd have only drunk water for four days. Or maybe just had a bottom rib removed.'

I looked at my svelte sister and shook my head in disbelief. It was clear she was following the 'Fabulous Karen Carpenter Dietary Secrets To A Thinner You'.

One of us had been adopted, definitely.

*

Cresting the hill behind Hugo and Britney Amore, I tried to put a positive spin on things. There are, after all, some good things about nudist beaches. First off, you never have to buy anyone a drink – 'I'm sorry. But my money's in my jeans' pocket.' Nor is it likely anyone will *ever* steal your vinyl sun-lounger. What's more, it does away with the usual am-I-too-old-to-wear-a-bikini? trauma.

Britney Amore immediately peeled off her G-string to reveal a red patch of pubic hair topiaried into a heart shape, an all-over tan, and those pneumatic breasts. When she got out a mosquito coil, so many male conventioneers lunged towards her with their lighters ablaze that she was practically flambéd.

'Come on, ol' son.' Sven playfully yanked my husband's shorts down to his knees. 'Don't be shy.'

'Oh, is *that* how the prison guards did it?' I asked, clutching my clothes tightly to my sweating torso.

Gritting my teeth, I tried to shed my Speedos and dive-bomb face down on to the towel in one deft movement – which merely resulted in a grazed nose, a cracked rib and a bit of seaweed up my fanny. The next hour was agonizing. I lay on the sand, fantasizing about putting my clothes back on. Then, just to be really kinky, I fantasized about *other* people putting their clothes back on as well. After another hour I hissed at my naked husband. 'Um, it's a hundred and ninety degrees. What exactly is the point of this? Must we give third degree burns to *everything*?'

'You're just angry because Britney's here,' he whispered. 'I didn't know she was coming, darling. Honestly.'

'Who cares about *her*?' I feigned nonchalance. 'Being in the presence of perfection wears off after a while, you know?'

Britney, on cue, rolled towards us on her beach towel. 'So, what shall we do now, y'all?' Judging by her muscled physique,

Britney was one of those 'Excuse me while I do the six hundred-metre butterfly, climb two Alps and abseil back down for some dressage and parachute formation before lunch' types.

*My* only rules about sport are – nothing involving water, balls, my feet leaving the earth, or sweat. My preferred activity is reading, in which there is not much potential for death. And I would have kept it that way too, except for Britney's next utterance.

'You really *do* have the kind of figure that looks better in clothes, don't you, sweetie?'

Now, all I'd planned to do on this holiday was loll about reading inferior fiction and making love to my husband. But if Hugo was going anywhere with Her then, by God, I was going too, come hell or high water . . . Oh, hang on, I'd forgotten, high water *is* hell.

*

'Skin-diving? Yeah. Sure. I can skin-dive,' I lied, as Britney doled out flippers and goggles. A clammy sense of dread filled my being. Did I mention that I'm one of those people who won't even go into the bath without a life-jacket and a distress flare? In my view, if God had meant us to swim in the ocean, he would have given us shark-proof metal cages. I mean, there must be a reason fish never look truly relaxed – *because something much, much bigger is always trying to devour them.*

'Um . . . what about sharks?' I queried, as I attempted to jack-knife a foot into a flipper.

Britney was already wading backwards into the sea. 'Sharks?' she scoffed, her goggles perched expertly atop her glossy locks. 'Y'all got more chance of being hit by a car.'

'I have been hit by a car!' I wailed miserably. 'Um . . . really, Hugo, let's rethink this . . .'

Too late. His naked buttocks were already cresting the foam like two scoops of vanilla ice cream in a zabaglione froth. In the list of 'Ways To Win Back Your Hubby', letting him go nude snorkelling with his mistress is curiously absent. He was treading water now, by her side.

Britney executed a back flip, offering a view to which only a midwife should be privy. 'We'll swim over to the reef. If y'all get into any trouble, this is the International Sign for Rescue.' She demonstrated, one hand raised in the balmy air. 'Okay?' And she was off.

'The reef?' I gave an apprehensive glance towards the white lace on the water – way over near Cuba.

'Do I have to keep my feet off the bottom the whole way?' But when I turned to Hugo for an answer, he was already swimming in hot pursuit. Sven, busily working on his tan, dozed on the beach, oblivious.

I started gingerly, flapping my arms in a windmill motion, while groping in vain with my foot for the ocean floor. Then I felt something brush my legs. Horror coiled its fingers around my abdomen. As my eyes frantically searched the water around me, a black fin sliced the surface with knife-through-butter ease. Panicking on dry land is uncomfortable enough, but in water what ensues is a surprisingly rapid decrease in buoyancy. I bobbed up and down like some deranged species of pelican. What was the International Sign of Rescue, I wondered, for 'My Aorta Has Ruptured 'Cause I'm Being Eaten by A Tiger Shark'? I started taking in a lot of water. As I went down for the fifth time, I was just picturing myself as a legless intensive-care patient in a semi–vegetative state, blinking out coded requests to have my chin wiped or the channel changed when, flailing one arm desperately behind me, I hit something solid.

It was a shark all right. Not a tiger shark, though, a leopard shark. Shedding her leopardskin bikini hadn't made Britney any less carnivorous. The athletic actress flipped me on to my back, hooked an arm around my neck and launched into a strong breaststroke towards the sandbar. The great green surly mouth of the sea spat me back on to the shore in disgust.

'A shark – I felt a . . .' I tried to explain to Hugo, who shone admiring eyes on Britney Amore.

'You were amazing!' he praised her.

'Hugo!' I spluttered. 'Don't you care that I was nearly eaten by a prehistoric predator?'

'Probably a harmless reef shark,' dismissed Britney.

'Hey,' I protested. 'No creature gets to be that size by eating seaweed.'

About this romantic holiday with my husband? I was beginning to think I could have experienced the same level of enjoyment on a blind date with a bloke named Lector, first name – *Hannibal*.

\*

'Are ya sure you won't be a scaredy-cat?' Britney Amore teased, strapping herself into the harness with practised efficiency.

Day Two found me parasailing. Don't ask. That's how desperate I had become for Hugo's approval.

'Scaredy-cat? What's there to be scared of?'

Catapulting to the upper stratosphere into the flight path of a jumbo jet in total defiance of the laws of gravity, physics and logic . . . 'Of course I'm not scared,' I said, praying that someone had the number of the Emergency Airlift Rescue Service. 'But, Hugo,' I desperately consulted the conference schedule, 'aren't you supposed to be chairing a session on Hylaform Filler in the Promenade Room?'

'Hyla-*what*?' Britney demanded.

'It's a protein that makes lips look fuller,' Hugo explained. 'Obtained from a rooster's comb.'

Britney gave a bored sigh. The woman's attention span was obviously limited. Or perhaps she just felt she'd had enough cock in her mouth for one lifetime. 'Your wife's too chicken, won't *you* come with me instead, Hughie?'

'You *do* look a little nervous, Liz.'

'Nervous? Nah. Me? One hair is maybe raised somewhere on my neck,' I lied insouciantly, as the instructor strapped me on behind Britney, '*Hughie*.'

We arced up into the sky, the air whooshing by us at a terrifying speed. As Mother Earth sped away below, at about warp-factor 1,000,000, Britney whooped with delight. I, however, was overcome by the surprise fact that nuclear fusion can actually take place in one's bowel.

Back on deck, once I had stopped screaming long enough for the captain to establish that I could breathe unassisted, I notified my humiliated husband that I never ever wanted to fly over the Caribbean sea again unless accompanied by a *lot* of aviation fuel.

*

On Day Three when Britney asked, 'How 'bout some jet-skiing?' I replied, 'What, as an alternative to suicide?'

It is my opinion that people only jet-ski because it is illegal to masturbate in public. We were attending a lunch for Gore-Tex Facial Implant salesmen on the mezzanine floor. Britney had playfully swapped nametags with Hugo. What a kidder that gal is!

*My* nametag had fallen off and I couldn't remember who the hell I was any more.

An hour later Britney had gone twice around the bay, executing wheelie spins, front-wheel stands and double back flips while my husband applauded. Then it was my turn. I wish I could have made him proud. But, five minutes into my ride, terror of capsizing in that shark-infested lagoon had frozen me into a seated position, gripping the handlebars. Hugo could only remove me from the motorcycle seat by prising my fingers free one at a time. Shaking his head with disappointment, he then carried me horizontally under one arm and parked me on a bar stool, where I could stay, inconspicuously, hands gripping the bar rail, until I thawed out. About ten hours later.

\*

Day Four already! Doesn't time fly when Ms Amore keeps coming up with more fun activities, like windsurfing? I considered suggesting that we save time and just call the paramedics in advance. But a viperish riddle from Britney – 'Why are flat-chested gals like rocks? 'Cause they're so much better to *skip*' – had me strapped into my wet suit faster than you can say 'mouth-to-mouth resuscitation'.

Hugo trained his video camera on Britney, who was soon tacking her surfboard expertly for his benefit.

'Have you windsurfed before?' the instructor asked, preparing to launch me out across the sea directly into gale-force winds.

'Well, technically no, but I've read the instruction manual.'

Where the manual let me down was its failure to explain how to change your surfboard's direction while you're balled up like a petrified armadillo. Half an hour later I was rescued two miles out to sea by the water police.

'Glad to be back?' Britney, ensconced in her nice dry hammock, purred between sips of piña colada.

'No. I always tongue-kiss the beach like this,' I replied. My husband merely shook his head wearily. That's when I noticed she was holding the cam-recorder in her lap. Not content to be an eye-witness to my profound humiliation, she had determined to capture it for posterity.

Now *that*'s what I call a costume drama.

*

Day Five. Victoria was beautifying in the spa – she'd moved in there, basically – and Sven was giving his keynote speech, 'From Detox to Botox: Ageing in the Modelling Industry', which left just Britney, Hugo and me, *as per usual*.

'Game for a spot of water-skiing?' Hugo grinned over breakfast. The warm wind was blowing his hair into a rakish halo. His sun-kissed skin had turned caramel, making him more delicious than ever.

'Water-skiing?' I resisted the temptation to point out that water-skiing is merely the art of drowning with planks of wood on your feet. 'Ah-huh!' I enthused.

Britney and Hugo, of course, were both 'naturals'. They took turns to videotape each other's spectacular stunts in hours and hours of fabulous footage.

'Sure! I'd love to have a turn!' I thrilled from the dock when the speedboat skidded to a foamy halt. But unfortunately, once aboard, I so dreaded going over the side that Hugo warned me he'd have to use an oxyacetylene torch if I didn't unfetter my fingers from his leg.

\*

By Day Six Hugo no longer invited me to join him and Britney for water sports. At the conference dinner-dance that evening, he brushed my hand off his shoulder as though it were lint. My husband had lost all respect for me. Which is not the greatest foreplay in the world. In bed later that night, after I'd sucked and licked him for an hour or two, he reciprocated with some perfunctory cunnilingus. He was like a cow chewing methodically upon a bale of hay.

Afterwards I fell into a deep, despairing sleep. Woken later in the dead of night by a mosquito with a head cold, I stretched out a hand only to find the other side of the bed was empty. Apprehension swamped me. I floundered to my feet in an instant. Outside our hut, standing in the anaemic moonlight I decided, on a hunch, to walk towards the pool. The grass felt chilly and slick beneath my bare feet. Then I heard it: soft murmuring from one of the hammocks strung between the poolside palm trees. Dreading what I might discover, I tiptoed closer.

The best way to catch a cheating husband is with his pants down. Far more effective than a private eye or a Xerox of his bank statement. But as I got closer to the tilting hammock, I felt I was about to risk the same brush with danger as when the shark swept too close to my legs in the lagoon. I re-experienced that terror and, suddenly disoriented, stumbled. My vision blurred and swam – the only part of me that could, I remembered, as I stubbed my toe on a sun-lounger, hopped on one foot, cursing loudly, crashed into a sun umbrella, which had failed to take evasive action, and fell, head first, into the pool.

I probably owe my life to my sister, who fished me out of the drink, coughing and spluttering. 'Were you following me?' I spluttered. 'I mean, what are you doing up at this hour?' I asked, momentarily forgetting that the modelling species is primarily nocturnal.

'Oh, just working on my tan,' she replied, coolly.

Red-eyed, mucus streaming from my nose, I regarded my saviour. She didn't look at her best either. Her lips were all smushed from kissing, mascara smudged, clothes rumpled. 'It was you and the Slimeball in the hammock, wasn't it?'

'Do you think you could ever have a good word to say about Sven?'

'I dunno. Is there a nice way to say 'nauseate'? I'm just relieved it wasn't Hugo and the Penis-hogging Prom Queen.'

When I staggered back into bed, exhausted, Hugo was cosily coiled around a pillow. He'd been out for ice, he explained innocently. Seems to me that he could have just taken some from around his own heart. 'Just relax, Lizzie.

Look outside the window, darling,' he said softly, slipping his arm around my shoulders. 'This is paradise.'

'Yes, paradise.' Or, possibly, Rwanda.

*

On the last evening of our 'romantic' vacation, Britney Amore insisted on screening the week's video footage. And so, after the conference farewell dinner, five of us sprawled across my cabaña – Britney, Sven, Victoria (as close to Sven as she could get while avoiding direct lamplight), Hugo and me. Hugo was in Host Mode, handing round vodkas and crisps. We were in the midst of the apparently *hugely* entertaining spectacle of *my* sporting failings compared to *Britney*'s athletic triumphs, when the TV screen flickered and blurred. Everyone groaned, there was a grainy hiatus and then two thrusting buttocks came into full view. At first I think we all just presumed Hugo had taped over some routine programme on Channel 5. Then I looked closer at the screen. There was something familiar about the sofa. It was *my* sofa in Hampstead. Then I made out something else familiar: my naked husband, on my sofa. Then something else. My naked sister, came into focus, on my naked husband, on my sofa. And my living room sofa was not Scotchgarded! Until this moment, the thought had never crossed my mind that my sister had got a new face just so my husband would sit on it. In the next split second I got so hot it was as though the Gestapo were trying to sweat a confession out of me. Then I became as cold, dark and hard as a stone. I squinched my eyes shut tight. Hugo, who'd been fetching more vodka from the bar, stopped dead still in the doorway, a fixed moronic grin on his face.

'What's that on your penis, Hugo?' I asked. 'Oh, look! It's my sister's mouth. Let me guess,' I wailed at my half-sibling, 'you were just launching your new face. A face-warming party.'

'Liz,' blurted Victoria, ashen-hued, 'I'm . . . oh, God . . . It's . . .'

On the screen their bodies shifted once more in a blurry jump-cut so that we could clearly see my husband's hand between Victoria's legs. Snatching the remote, I freeze-framed the image. The realization of their betrayal was like a sudden photographic flash – the negative image imprinted on the backs of my eyelids and seared into my brain

'Um . . . would you believe I was taking her temperature?'

'With your finger? Um . . . no.'

Something cracked open inside me then – open heart surgery, a gaping wound. I'd thought we were just going to watch a holiday video. But *this* was a disaster movie.

'We need to talk,' Hugo mumbled, diving for the remote control, and fizzing the television screen into silence.

'Sure,' I replied, in a high-pitched voice I didn't recognize, 'if you can manage to extricate your tongue from my sister's twat.' I turned to Sven and Britney. 'Would you mind leaving now, because I seem to be in a Greek play all of a sudden?' Inside I was wailing, screaming, sobbing, to the accompaniment of wrists being cut, but outside I was all crass sarcasm.

Britney tittered maliciously as I shoved them outside. The door to our room clicked shut behind their snickering forms. And then we turned, we three, to stare, in horror, at each other.

'If you weren't father to my two children and a brilliant surgeon, you'd be nothing but a philandering bastard, do you know that?'

'Look,' my husband busked, in his most authoritative, diagnostic voice, running his hands through his thick mane, 'I . . . um . . . I was just helping your sister with some intimacy issues and things got a little out of hand . . .'

But I wasn't interested in any of *his* feeble explanations. Instead, I rounded on my sister, who had taken up the foetal position in the corner of the couch.

'It's your fault!' my sister sobbed. 'You threw us together. That night you got Hugo to drive me home after the dinner party from hell. You ordered us to kiss and make up! We got talking and—'

I gasped. 'All this time I've been accusing you of sneaking around with Britney, you were sneaking around with my own sister?'

'I'm sorry, Lizzie,' he grovelled. 'I was thinking about *you* the whole time. It's just . . . she's so like you. You without the worry lines and leg stubble . . . A more glamorous version of you.'

I glared at him. 'Glamorous? Victoria? You've turned her into a bloody patchwork quilt. There are bits of her body that you've operated on that don't go with the bits which *haven't* been. Her arms are over four decades old and her lips, two

179

weeks. She's sitting on one brand new butt cheek while the other half of her arse is forty-two.'

'It's just so unfair,' Victoria bawled, in an attempt to get me to feel sorry for her. 'At twenty I looked younger than I was. And at forty I look older.'

'Oh, yes, it's on a par with ethnic cleansing on the scale of unfairness,' I shouted back.

'I don't want to be too old to die young!'

'That's good because I am going to kill you!' I lunged at her.

'You don't know what it's like!' She swatted at me. 'I'm slowly becoming invisible. I'm slowly being airbrushed out of life – like an ex-chum of Stalin's.'

My voice wavered. 'You've never had to try, Victoria. Life has just fallen into your lap. Since we were kids there's been a two-year waiting list to get into your address book. While I've had to juggle and struggle and learn Latin roots and trigonometry and new languages to get noticed, all you've ever had to do is enter a bloody room.' I got hold of my voice again. 'You've had everything just handed to you on a plate. But that wasn't enough. You had to have my husband too!' My voice gave way again.

'Oh, go comb your eyebrow, Elisabeth. *You*'re the one who's had Life fall into her lap. You were Mother's favourite. The intellectual of the family. You'd swot all night for a cervical-smear test! And yes! I was jealous of you and your happy marriage. I always have been!' She coughed this confession up like a fur ball. 'Plus, I got fifteen thousand pounds' worth of surgery for nothing.'

I stared at her, uncomprehendingly. 'You have no heart, Victoria. Do you know that? If Hugo X-rayed your chest cavity he'd find nothing. Just a hunk of lung. All this bloody time you've spent changing your exterior but your interior's still the same. Inside you're the ugly, spoiled, cruel little girl you always were.'

'Well, *you* spent all that time changing your interior – reading books, getting degrees – while neglecting your exterior. You can't blame me that you lost your husband!' Victoria retorted, stomping her foot.

I buckled at the knees. A gushing, roaring pain flash-flooded through my body. Hugo took my arm and lowered me on to the couch.

I looked up at my husband in dismay. Some men play hard to get. Well, Hugo played hard to *want*. But damn it all! He was the man I loved. I know what you're thinking. Why, in God's name, did I continue to adore him? Why was I so determined to be a member of the UK Married Women's Drowning Team? I dunno. Maybe my solar panels were directed at the moon.

'Do you want me to leave?' asked my husband, sombrely.

'We have a loving, contented, supportive family, Hugo Frazer, and you, you cheating, moronic ratbag, are not going to fuck it up!'

'Look, we can sort this out,' my half-sister placated.

'Chaos, tragedy, heartbreak.' I opened the door for her. 'I'd say your work here is done.'

'Lizzie—'

'Shut up. I never, ever want to see you again.' I slammed

the door in her face, and collapsed on the floral settee in the middle of paradise. As I sobbed I realized I had learnt a very important lesson: it's a good idea to love your enemies. Just in case your friends and family turn out to be two-faced, low-down, rotten, lying mongrels.

# 22. Sigmund Freud Floor – Neurosis, Psychosis, Paranoid Schizophrenia, Delusions of Normality And Ladies' Lingerie, All Exit, Please

To be a successful wife you need a degree in Animal Behavioural Psychology. Without this education, the only possible way to put a husband's affair into perspective is to consume boxes of chocolates, pints of vodka and pass out on the next available plane back to London, squashed up at the back near the economy toilets.

When I came to, eight hours later, the scene from the plane window as we circled Heathrow resembled a page from *Where's Wally?* only I was more lost than Wally ever was.

If there were a Self-loathing Chart for wives, then seeing your husband between the thighs of a much prettier woman with huge bazookas who also just happens to be your older sister would have to be at the top. At the bottom of the chart, it would say in small print, 'Expect crying, total insecurity and talk of breast implants for about, oh, the next decade.'

I hadn't felt old until my husband started having an affair. Then, suddenly, it was as if the warranties had simultaneously expired on all of my internal organs. By the time I staggered down the gangway, there were a few give-away signs that I was becoming slightly deranged. In the immigration queue, I noticed that the date stamped on my passport was 14 February. I composed a Valentine's Day message for my husband. 'Hugo, please be so kind as to pick up your scalpel, turn it on your own chest and plunge it in and out repeatedly until dead. Love from your wife, Lizzie.' When the officer took too long inspecting my passport, I snapped at him to hurry up. 'I've got a lot to do – children to raise, dry-cleaning to pick up, husbands to kill . . .'

I fantasized about replacing Hugo's KY-jelly with a tube of superglue – that would fix them – but in reality there was no fight in me. Wrestling my club-wheeled baggage trolley through Customs, I felt as stale as the aeroplane odour emanating from my clothes.

'I got your message,' said a voice in my ear. Cal whistled through his teeth and shook his head sympathetically. 'Did a gypsy put a curse on you at birth, Lizzie, or what? You must have been gutted.'

'Put it this way, a paramedic and a defibrillator would not have gone amiss. Who's got the kids? And why are you wearing a tie? What? Are you on *trial* for something?' I was still angry at him. Hell, I was angry with all men. I was in that if-you-can't-say-something-bad-about-men-then-don't-say-anything-at-*all* phase.

'Um . . . I believe "nice to see you" is the internationally accepted formal welcome of choice.' He smiled. 'The kids are with Marrakech.' He commandeered the stroppy trolley and pushed it through the revolving door into the Arctic air. After Antigua, London was as cold as a giant meat locker. 'You've *got* to get rid of him, now,' Cal advised. 'This is more proof, not that you needed more, that marriage should go the way of other archaic traditions, like human sacrifice – which, interestingly enough, also takes place on an *altar*.'

'Calim, I am only leaving this marriage at gunpoint.'

'Your man has proven himself to be a pig, a total snake, a rat. If you're so in love with animals, you should go open a sanctuary someplace and, I dunno, suckle a wombat.'

'Why is it that everybody has a marriage-guidance book within them? And why are they so keen to Let It Out?'

'He's a greedy, opportunistic liar. Apart from those few shortcomings, your man's a prince.'

'He's also my husband,' I was practically screaming as we rattled over the faded zebra crossing, into the car-park lifts, 'so do you mind if I delude myself just a little longer?'

Cal backed off. 'That's my moral position. But, hey, don't worry. If you don't like it, I have plenty of others,' he joshed, fidgeting for a fag.

'Let's face facts. A thirty-nine-and-three-quarter-year-old divorcee with two children and no job. Who'd want me? I'll end up choking to death on people's leftovers in some tacky little eatery in King's Cross where nobody knows the Heimlich manoeuvre.'

Cal fed a five-pound note into the surly mouth of the automatic parking machine. 'You're a sound woman, Lizzie,' he said earnestly. 'Loads of men would want you.'

'Yeah, right.' I trailed leadenly after him. 'All my life I've been second best to Victoria. All my life I've had her hand-me-downs. Everything I ever wore she'd already sweated in. Including my husband, now!'

'Relative humidity,' Cal quipped, in an effort to cheer me up.

I flung myself into the V Dub and slammed the door against the gnawing cold. 'The worst thing is she's right. If only I hadn't "let myself go". I mean, look at me! I'm rusting. I'm corroding.' I slapped the dashboard. 'If I were a car, you'd trade me in, you'd strip me down for parts. Hell, you'd scrap me. And yet the only mechanics who can fix me cost a thousand bloody bucks an hour.'

'*Fix* you?' Cal queried, contorting behind the wheel.

'Yes, starting with breast implants.'

Cal's hands fell off the steering-wheel as though it was scalding hot. He scrutinized me with such intensity I wondered if I'd forgotten to take off my airline socks or something.

'Lizzie, implants eat away at your immune system. They cause neurological problems and memory loss – although, hey, you're obviously sufferin' from that already 'cause you seem to have forgotten you're a feminist.'

'Hey, walk a mile in my Wonder-bra and then we'll talk.' My seat-belt buckle made an irritated click as it snapped across my puny chest.

Cal looked at me dubiously. 'That is *you* in there, isn't it, Lizzie?'

'As long as a woman's pretty, that's enough for most men. A brain is optional.' I thumped the heater without success. Despite the freezing chill, I had to wind down the window to get some respite from Cal's cigarette fumes. 'In some languages, German, Hungarian, Spanish, Swahili and Zulu, beautiful actually means "good". Which is why I'm also going to have a face lift,' I said, gulping oxygen.

Pulling out of the car-park, my best friend's forehead was corduroyed with concern. 'Lizzie! No. You're a beautiful-lookin' woman – in a lovely, natural way.'

'Calim, after a certain age a woman realizes that "natural" is a euphemism for "haggard and old and not getting laid any more".'

'No! You're grand just as you are – with your life's experiences there on your gorgeous face. People can read between your lines.' Cars lurched backwards and forwards in a hoe-down of sixteen-point turns as we all manoeuvred our way out of the airport. 'What about *je ne sais quoi*?'

'French for crêpy necks and crows' feet.'

'Wit and wisdom are just as important as beauty in a woman. Actually more important. Beauty comes from within.'

'Yeah. Within a jar marked "Estee Lauder". Women are as close to being appreciated for our personalities as Myra Hindley is of getting a job in a school nursery.'

We merged into the bobbing black sea of taxis ebbing towards central London.

'Well, speaking for your family and friends, we love you as you are. And to have anything removed certainly makes you less than we bargained for.'

'Same goes for you when you lose a lung.' I took the cigarette from between his lips and stubbed it out in an ashtray already submerged in butts.

'I am not smokin' too much,' Cal insisted, fishing in his pocket for another fag.

'You are too. In the middle of smoking a cigarette, you stop for a cigarette break. What are you so nervous about?'

'Imagine it. If I had a tracheotomy, I could smoke two fags

simultaneously!' he said, igniting another. 'One thing I've learnt about Life, Lizzie. None of us get out of it alive. And happiness – well, it's unexpected. It's the cigarette you shouldn't smoke. It's the cold Guinness you forgot was in the back of your fridge on a hot day. It's the book of your enemy bein' remaindered. It's realizin' that the love of your life is right under your nose.'

'Yeah, yeah,' I said, dismissively, fiddling with the radio dial. I'd just found an appropriate song, Whitney Houston's 'I—*I*— I Will Always Love Youuuuuuuuuuuuuuuu', and was madly emoting to it, when Cal unexpectedly pulled off the motorway.

He took a deep breath. 'To *fall* in love, you actually have to take a *step* first.' Cal turned the car into a quiet cul-de-sac. 'And I'm kinda crippled that way. In fact I'm a foundin' member of the Fear of Intimacy Support Group.' He cut the ignition.

I protested as he turned off the radio. 'Hey! I was wallowing in self-pity to that.'

He swivelled to face me. 'But I think you might be the cure.'

'Me?'

His eyes were opaque, and every muscle in his body was tensed taut, about to snap. 'Liz, please suspend your disbelief for the duration of this next sentence. It's you I love, Lizzie.'

There was a beat of stunned silence while I took in this information. The thin smoke of our breath evaporated before us.

'I wanted to wait till things were over with you and Hugo

before I told you. Liz, look, I know I'm a chain-smokin' failed novelist. I'm an amoral piece of lapsed vegetarian scum. I'm guilty as charged. But I adore you. I always have and always will. You are the warmest, wittiest and most sexy woman in the world.'

I tried to speak but my uvula seemed to be in spasm.

'On my organ donor card, it says, "For Lizzie Only".'

My face in the visor mirror was a stupefied mask.

'Um . . . Now would be a good time for you to say somethin' nice about me.' He smiled shyly.

I just looked at him, flummoxed. 'You mean, the whole time you've been telling me to leave Hugo, to give up on my marriage, you've – you've had this other agenda?'

'All right, maybe I tried to influence you a wee bit – that doesn't make me a Serbian war criminal, does it? Can't you forgive me?'

'A *wee* bit? I thought you had my best interests at heart. I mean, you're my best friend. Yet all that time, you had this . . . this . . . ulterior motive.'

'Lizzie, I'm sorry. I'm gonna move into a geodesic dome, say, someplace in the Lake District, where I can take up an obscure religion and try to forget that I wasn't honest with the woman I adore. But the truth is, I would have encouraged you to leave Hugo whether I adored you or not. Because he doesn't deserve you, shug.'

'But *you* do?' I kept my expression neutral – as though trying to remember whether or not I'd left the iron on – while desperately concentrating on not rupturing a neck vein. 'Isn't the truth of the matter that you couldn't get Victoria so why not go for second best?' This was a pain too far.

'You're not second best! Though Hugo has made you feel that way. Your man doesn't get you at all. And I've never fancied Victoria! The woman only has sex because she looks thinner lying down! My "mystery woman" has always been *you*. Can't you see it, Lizzie? We're so alike. We make the same jokes. We know each other inside out, Liz. We even finish each other's—'

'No, we don't!'

'I know what you're thinkin' before you even say it!'

'Well, then, I'm sorry you had to hear that,' I blurted. 'Please take me home. I just can't talk about this. It's too much right now.'

'Liz . . .' His eyebrows collided on his forehead.

'No. Just take me home, okay?' I said, in a voice as flat as Holland.

We drove in silence, finally twisting our way through the cobbled, claustrophobic lanes of Hampstead. At the door of my house I clambered out of the car. 'I'll be in touch soon, okay? I promise, by tomorrow – or maybe next millennium.'

*

For the first time I felt the true vertiginous terror of losing my foundation, my rock, my husband, my Hugo. As an abandoned, unemployed mother of two, there was only one course of action. It was lit up with runway lights to guide my approach and I was on auto-pilot.

*

Entering the cosmetic-surgery clinic in Knightsbridge, a surge of exhilaration flooded my chest. I felt ethereal, airborne. The brittle, helmet-hairdo-ed nurse talked me through the procedures.

'Insertion through the armpits or belly button reduces scarring. Pre-filled devices reduce leakage. Of course, implants have to be removed if there are ruptures. Or if a tough capsule of body tissue forms around the . . .' she searched for the right euphemism '. . . device. It's my duty to warn you that about one in ten implant patients needs a second operation within five years.'

You might be thinking that the only rational response at this moment was to run screaming into the streets. But I was no longer a rational person. I was on the brink of forty and my husband was fucking my sister. 'Book me in,' I said.

\*

The day of my operation, I awoke with one thought in my head, that inside every older person is a younger person screaming, *'Get me the hell outta here!'* Why is it, I ask you, that just when a girl starts getting her head together, her body falls apart? That Mother Nature sure is one bitter, cynical 'n' twisted, monumentally fucked-up, pre-menstrual malicious psycho.

'Have you suffered from raised blood pressure, rheumatic fever or heart trouble?' asked another coolly efficient nurse – this one seemed to have a Danish pastry on her head.

A *broken* heart – yes. 'No,' I said automatically.

'Any other diseases or illnesses?' the pastry asked, ticking off black boxes.

What about addiction to a certain medic? Did that count? 'No.'

Stop! I told myself, as she stripped me down to a pair of paper panties and the surgeon drew dots and dashes all over my chest with a felt-tip. Run! This is ridiculous. Did I really want to become a graduate of the Inferiority Complex Institute? What the hell happens to women once they hit forty? It was a question worth repeating. What the hell happens to women once they hit forty? I had read Proust – well, a couple of pages. I could sight-read Puccini. I'd interviewed Putin, Pinochet, Steinam, Mandela . . . I gazed agog at the doctor's blue geometry. Yet in ten minutes I would be out cold on the slab. And this man would be slicing off my nipples with a carving knife. You know that bridge you're always going to cross when you come to it? Well, I was at that bridge. At the doors of the operating theatre, the doctor paused, smiled, then led the way in to surgery.

And I meekly shadowed him.

Going over the Niagara Falls of forty – there really is no choice but to get a bloody barrel.

# 23. Shopping and Tucking

A woman planning to have breast implants is advised to follow a few simple procedures. By taking a couple of minutes the day before the operation to do these practical exercises you will be totally prepared for the surgery.

First, remove top and bra. Next lie down upon the street, placing your breasts directly behind the back wheels of a ten-ton lorry. Shout, 'Reverse.' Or simply detach the safety guard from a household electric fan and hurl yourself chest forward into the rotating blades. To complete the preparation process, locate nearest boxing ring. Remove upper garments, and permit the use of your breasts as punch-bags until they are black and blue and bruised all over.

You are now prepared for the augmentation experience. Enjoy!

*

Motes of darkness swarmed around me as I came to. The first thing that hit me was the pain. Giving birth without an epidural did not come close. My lungs scrambled for air. I made a groggy reconnoitre of my ribcage, which was tightly strapped in bandages. Two clear tubes ran out from the sides of my chest and dripped into buckets. This cocktail of yellow slime and blood would have had me fainting in revulsion, except I could not at this stage crane my head to look into the bucket. Even minuscule movement sent me screaming for morphine.

The doctor had ordered me to keep the bandages on for a week. But as soon as I got home the next day curiosity got the better of me. I stood before the mirror. The trembling weakness in my limbs made every movement an aching effort. But little by little I peeled away the dressings. In horrified fascination, I examined the puffy, weeping red skin, mottled in technicolour bruises and the angry, throbbing stitches carved beneath each nipple. I'd been warned that I wouldn't be able to shower or sleep on my stomach or fit into any of my clothes. But no one had ever mentioned the cruellest restriction; that I wouldn't be able to cuddle my kids. The children were unsettled and anxious because Hugo had moved out – he'd been sleeping at the clinic since Antigua. On my return from surgery Jamie and Julia ran down the front path to me with open arms – and I had to push them away. I had never felt so sick, so sorry and so, well, wrong. Joan Crawford had nothing on me. Worse still, glancing up I saw Cal leaning against his kitchen door, arms folded, watching this humiliating 'Mummy Dearest' moment.

I immediately rang the surgery and booked in for liposuction of the neck, chin, stomach, hips, thighs and buttocks, along with eyelid surgery, lip implants and a facial peel.

A cheating husband will do that to you. I had to win him back, any bloody way I could. My self-esteem was threatening to contact Amnesty International – but, still, I dialled.

# 24. Ladies and Gentlemen, Due to Illness, Tonight the part of Lizzie Mcphee Will Be Played By Pamela Anderson . . . Now Sit Back and Enjoy the Show

Two months and one complete ideological U-turn later, I'd nipped, tucked, sucked, plucked, bobbed, boobed, peeled and pilled. There was not much of the old body left. It had been exchanged, bit by bit, for the body of a teenager. I'd had eyes lifted, neck lowered and legs lipo-ed. I'd been collagened and botoxed and lasered to Bride of Wildestein standards.

Twenty thousand blackheads had been squeezed, forty billion hair strands dyed, forty-five thousand acres of cellulite pummelled, three trillion body hairs tweezed, ten whales' worth of blubber Hoovered. I had so much tanning-bed exposure my *eyelids* had melanomas.

Did I mention I was now a dumb blonde too? A peroxy-moron, you might say. Yep, I was totally bleach-dependent. Extensions made my hair look longer and stronger. A profiterole of lavish curls crowned my newly blonded cranium. It was a beehive piled so high it was dangerous to walk under bridges bearing Maximum Height signs. This was a hairdo that could survive a direct nuclear hit with no adverse effect on its buoyancy.

By systematically starving myself I was soon able to show off my new solarium-tanned limbs in dresses the size of a postage stamp. A very gaudy postage stamp. Believe me, I made Elton John look underdressed. It was not possible to walk, stand or sit without revealing primary and secondary sex organs.

My dresses were cut low to show off a pair of exuberant breasts. My new boobs were so huge it would be more appropriate really to say that my *chest* had had a *Lizzie McPhee* implant.

By joining the jut-set I had stepped through the mirror, into another world. I was now the Empress of a new-found land called Beauty. I was straw Rumpelstiltskinned into gold. I suddenly found myself surrounded by silent, staring men – from security guards to taxi drivers, they just stood there, ogling my boobs and blonde hair. They winked, they wolf-whistled, they offered to sacrifice their firstborn to cop a feel. When shaking my hand, they tickled my inner palm with a suggestive forefinger as though inducting me into a secret society.

Every sentence I uttered was greeted by men as the wittiest *bon mot* since Dorothy Parker presided over the Round Table. And it was so damn easy. Victoria was right. Any girl can be alluringly intelligent. All you have to do is stand still and look brain-dead.

Now I was ready to see Hugo. One bright April morning, all pink blossoms and perfumed air, I sailed majestically into his office at the Longevity Clinic. (I had not seen him since

Antigua. Marrakech, who had temporarily moved in, had been kindly ferrying our bewildered offspring back and forth to the clinic to see their father so that I wouldn't have to face him.) Agog, my husband took in the New Me. Hugo beamed so maniacally, he looked like a man who'd forgotten to take his medication.

'These are not my real breasts,' I assured him. 'I'm just breaking them in for a friend.'

'Wow! Wow! Wow!' Hugo was more excited than he'd been by the births of our babies. I thought he might take out an ad – 'I would like to announce the birth of a new chest. Mother and boobies doing well.'

Some medical practices tell you the bad news to your face. Others send the bill by mail.

I'd come, ostensibly, to persuade my husband to settle my accounts. When I mentioned the £4300 cost of the implants – 'What the hell are they made of? *Caviar*?' – Hugo flourished his chequebook. He also moved home immediately, much to the children's delight, showering us with gifts paid for by the money pouring into his Longevity Clinic. Jamie stopped being savaged by nightmares that his Batman and Robin sheets were trying to attack him. And Julia no longer left her toy horse's decapitated head in my bed. Nor were Hugo and I in the non-smoking restaurant section of marriage any more either. We were now in the Hot Curry, Cigars Welcome, Extra Butter With Everything, Deep Fry It All, High Cholesterol, All You Can Eat, Heart-attack Diner.

And a heart-attack is what I thought Hugo might have upon discovering that he was not the only man to find me attractive. When other men flirted with me, my husband sported a range of facial expressions more commonly seen on a bull, mid-castration. When I flirted back it became Hugo's turn to lie lachrymosely awake, worrying over what – or who – I was doing.

I even got my old job back.

At the theatre one night I bumped into Raphael, my X-generational ex-boss who proceeded to choke on his own superlatives.

'Lizzie! Darling, hi. Well, wow, sweetie, you look, well, wow! A-bloody-mazing. In-fucking-credible!' He was like an estate agent on amphetamines. 'Whatcha been up to?' he said excitedly to one breast. 'Been keeping busy?' he said to the other.

'Oh, unattaching various facial protuberances from my skull and having them re-upholstered helped to pass a month or two. What about you?'

'You know what?' He addressed both breasts. 'I see an opening for you back at the Beeb.' (He pronounced 'Beeb' as if it were the plural of 'boob'.) At least I now understood why men are so bad at making eye contact. Tits don't have eyes.

\*

'Hi. I just dropped by for a career,' were my first words when I walked through the BBC news room a week later. Weirdly, nobody commented on my complete transformation. They just told me that it was good to see me looking so 'well'. It made me suspect that plastic surgery is an annual event for female newsreaders of my age; a televisual rite of passage, a hardy annual, like photocopying your bum at the office Christmas party.

So now I had everything I'd wanted so badly: doting husband, fabulous job. I should have been ecstatically happy. Euphoric. On top of the world, which was, of course, my oyster. Then . . . why the hell wasn't I? My self-esteem should have deepened like a tan as I basked in the heat of my husband's lust. But, as it turns out, 'the top of the world' is nothing more than a dismal little place at the North Pole. Instead of glowing, I felt shrivelled and cold inside.

I raged at myself to get a grip. This was what I'd always wanted – to be beautiful, blonde and busty like my sister. But here I was, having fulfilled my quest for beauty beyond genetic inheritance, *hating every God-awful moment of it*.

As were Julia and Jamie. My kids wanted their old mother back – the one who had time for them, the one who wasn't spending every waking hour on body maintenance. As I was now, not even hatching chicks would have taken me seriously as mother material. Trying to stay young, I discovered, is a full-time occupation. It's a goddamn career. I had a Ph.D. in face creams – and the intellectual vibrancy of a hand model. Once you've morphed into a glamour-puss all that's left is grooming. A woman could spend quite a lot of serious time, possibly sell-your-house-and-move-the-family-to-a-trailer-park amount of time, at exorbitantly priced beauty salons. How was I going to keep it up? I was at my wits' end – *and it hadn't taken me long to get there, either.*

Now that I was a perkly breasted blonde, a strange change came over me. I took to twirling my hair and walking differently – a half sashay, half-mince. I found myself asking incredibly stupid questions all the time. My voice even started going up at the end of sentences. All of a sudden, I was no longer capable of joined-up writing. I'd become so dull, even my *houseplants* had filed for divorce. Which was a shame, because now that Cal no longer popped over for cups of tea they were all I had for company.

It wasn't until Easter that I actually bumped into him on my way to work one morning. He looked as wan and forlorn as I felt.

'How's life?' he asked.

'Life' as in *real life*, or the panty-freshener from Boots?'

Calim looked me up and down. 'You're so thin, shug. Remind me never to fly with you near the Andes. I mean, if we crashed there'd be nothin' to eat.'

'I can't believe I'm getting criticism on my appearance from a man wearing Ugh boots,' I irritatedly tapped a spiked stiletto on the pavement. 'Now, if you'd excuse me? Some of us have work to do,' I said primly, slipping behind the wheel of the Mercedes convertible Hugo had bought me for our wedding anniversary.

'Yeah, I've been watchin' you on the box.' He distractedly tucked a torn white T-shirt into faded black fly-button jeans. 'You've become the sort of woman you hated, do you know that? '

'And who is that exactly?'

'The sort who wants world peace, an end to sectarian violence, oh, and to drop a dress size.'

'Do you know what I think about that? Well, let me put it this way,' I said, then banged the car door in his face.

Calim pulled open the door and grabbed hold of my wrist. 'Don't you have any feelin's for me at all any more?' he asked, desolately.

'Not the ones you want.'

'Actually I was wrong. I'm not in love with you. Not the woman you are now. The old Lizzie. She's the one I loved. The funny, feisty one. Not this carbon copy of your mother. *"Don't disturb Mummy, kids, she's busy counting calories."'*

I gunned the motor to try to drown him out.

'THE REASON YOU WERE SO BLOODY GOOD AT YOUR JOB, LIZZIE,' he yelled, 'IS BECAUSE YOU REPORTED THE NEWS WITH AUTHORITY AND INTELLECT. *NOT* BECAUSE YOU BUY A LOT OF UNNECESSARY HERBAL SHAMPOOS!'

All afternoon his words ate away at me. I *was* presenting Newsak. The reports I introduced seemed to have been dumbed down to go with my looks – hard-hitting exposés on lesbian tendencies among lap-dancers and shower safety for women prisoners. It was also true that I'd turned into one of those mothers whose biggest parenting decision was which nanny to take to Nevis. My own mother had children in the way we had the eaves painted on the house – to keep up appearances. It struck me that Calim had been right about that too. I had spent so much time and money distancing myself from my mother's *physical* DNA only to discover that I'd turned into her mentally and emotionally. And why? To please my husband. A dark thought had begun to nag away at me, like a dull persistent headache. *Why would I want a man who only wanted me for my looks?*

To assuage my doubts, I made love with Hugo constantly. But I felt curiously detached from it all. It was as though a party was being thrown on my body to which I hadn't been invited. One night, bored and waiting for the ordeal to be over, I went limp, oohed and ahed and writhed for a bit, then made a low moan and lay still.

'You're going to have another seven of those!' Hugo boasted and, impressed by his own sexual virtuosity, set to work again immediately.

Between thrusts and pokes, I reminded myself that this was what I'd worked so hard for – my husband was totally in lust with me . . . *Then why the hell wasn't I feeling anything?* I told myself to at least *try* for an orgasm – but gave up the idea eventually as a waste of vaginal muscle.

Just as tentatively as I'd removed my bandages after plastic surgery, I started to peel slowly, carefully, away at my marriage – and finally unravelled this fundamental truth. I no longer loved my husband. I'd surgically altered the wrong thing. It wasn't my appearance that had gone all flabby, it was my marriage. Our relationship had lost its vigour and vitality. It had become baggy, saggy, withered, weathered, juiceless. What was needed was radical matrimonial surgery – a nuptual Nip 'n' Tuck.

Guilt-tripped by Calim's lecture, I began to leave work earlier to take the kids to the heath. Watching them eating their ice creams, huge vanilla whirligigs of slime, I found myself entertaining the thought of leaving their father.

What I'd realized was that winning back my husband for the wrong reasons – well, it was like getting a solar-powered vibrator while on secondment to Antarctica.

I frog-marched these thoughts out of my head. It was just post-surgery stress, I told myself. Maybe the bleach had leaked through to my brain? I'd issue a statement to Hugo: 'We apologize for this temporary loss of service. Normal devoted-wife activity will resume at the end of this unimportant midlife crisis.'

But when Hugo started to complain about Sven's ineptitude in not getting enough malpractice insurance, laughter tickled my nose as if I were about to sneeze. When his moan segued on to the lack of expertise of the clinic's cowboy cosmetic surgeons, 'Lizzie, most of those doctors couldn't put a dressing on a salad!' – it dawned on me that if I had to listen to his voice for much longer my earlobes would fall off.

As the weeks went by, complaints intensified. One woman sued because her trilucent implant, given to her as a 'wedding treat' by her fiancé, reacted with her own tissue and swelled, agonizingly, by more than 25 per cent. 'Quite frankly, these implants have ruined my life,' she said on *Channel 4 News* to millions of viewers. 'And there's also an increased chance that I might get cancer. Dr Frazer told me there was no real risk!'

'You lied to her about the risks?' I asked my husband, incredulously, switching off the television. 'Anything else in your box, Pandora?'

'It wasn't a lie.' Hugo took another slug at his whisky. 'At worst it was a terminological inexactitude.' When he touched my arm I flinched. Whiny self-absorption is just *so* attractive in a man.

Another woman went to *The Times* when one side of her face-lift collapsed. In photos she looked like a constipated rodent.

'God!' Hugo threw down the paper and for the first time imagined the true cost of his Mephistophelean pact. 'Any more bad publicity like this,' he melodrama-ed, obviously running late for his Self-pity Group, 'and I'm going to kill myself.'

'Well, that's easily done. Just run into the roach-motel under the fridge. Commit insecticide,' I suggested abruptly, and left the room.

Then a class-action suit: a group of women sued because Hugo had given them breast implants filled with soya bean oil. Their gynaecologists had now advised instant removal because of medical concerns about the effects on embryos.

'Yours aren't soya – I checked with your surgeon – they're saline. You're okay,' Hugo assured me meekly.

'Oh, I feel *much* better now,' I replied sarcastically.

'The soya was approved! By the government! Besides, extraction isn't such a major operation.'

'Really? What if you'd had a penile implant, Hugo, and then it was *recalled*? How would *you* feel then, Doctor, hmm?'

A complaint a day kept the doctor at bay. I was beginning to understand why doctors wear those little green masks – so if anything goes wrong they won't be recognized. There was pectoral slippage (one patient woke to find his pec implant on his elbow). There was eyelid paralysis from botox injections. A pair of realigned nipples were leaking yellow toxic yoghurt. A handful of breasts were stealthily seeping fermenting carcinogenic fluid. There was permanent oozing and crusting from chemical face peels. Gore-Tex fibres used to build up an assortment of lips poked out like bedsprings from an old mattress.

There was speculation in the press about the massive sums the court might award in compensation. Then other people, smelling money, got in on the act. Like the man who had been slammed in the head by the enlarged breasts of an enthusiastic lap-dancer. He likened the experience to being hit with cement blocks and demanded fifteen thousand pounds compensation from the Spread Eagle Nightclub, which sued the Longevity Clinic for the hardening of the implants in the first place.

'At least I now know why doctors call what they do a *practice*,' I told my husband, icily. And what would happen, I asked, when customers who'd paid exorbitantly for models' egg donations had babies that grew up ugly? 'I hope you haven't counted your eggs before they hatch. Have you included a baby-back guarantee? I mean, how did you become a bloody doctor? *By correspondence course?*'

The media continued to fix the clinic in its mesmeric eye. A man who looked a lot like undercover reporter Roger Cook applied for a job as our au pair. And there was a van constantly parked in our driveway, which I didn't remember buying . . .

When Hugo muttered to me about the time Sven pushed him into recommending unnecessary laser work (Sven was a shareholder in 'Knuckles' Milano's company, whose laser machines the clinic had purchased), I didn't even look up from my nail-file.

'You seem to have mixed me up with someone who gives a shit,' I replied, intent on my thumb buff. 'Anyway, I know you don't perform unnecessary surgery . . . you only operate if you need the money.'

To top off the horrors, a week after her breast augmentation Heroin Chic's weight had risen by a quarter. She died from toxic shock due to an infection contracted through surgery.

'The operation was not a serious surgical procedure and the infection she developed was not a typical infection,' Hugo told the inquest. As her family wept, Hugo fobbed them off with flourishes of medical sophistry. I found myself wondering how

I could let him know discreetly that his services as partner for life were no longer required? Perhaps throwing my hair dryer into his bath would do the trick.

And then Sven became the subject of an exposé when he was secretly taped by an investigative journalist who was posing as a fashion photographer. The transcript of Sven admitting to arranging breast augmentations for underage models was widely reported. Ironically, it was the kind of story for which at one stage in my career I would have given my now perfectly capped eyeteeth.

Sven told us that the press pack could kiss his ass. To which I replied, 'That sounds more like a job for my husband.'

'I need your guidance, Elisabeth. I'm disgraced publicly. And I don't know how to handle it.' Hugo was slumped before the 10 o'clock television news. His suit drooped funereally on his broad shoulders. 'You've always given me such wise counsel in the past.'

'Sorry.' I shrugged. 'I'm a blonde. I don't do "counsel" or "wise guidance" any more. That was the old me. The one you discarded. The one you didn't want. Remember?'

'What's up?' he asked, in a peeved voice.

'The warranty on our marriage,' I replied sadly.

Fourteen hours later, slick with sprays and glistening with lip-gloss, I sat frozen at my half-moon-shaped newsreader's desk, flanked by cameras. Cables, thick as eels, writhed across the scuffed floor. Makeup artists and hair-stylists puttered about my face like moths. I tried to ignore the pain in my breasts. The silicone implants were less Exocet shaped now. In the half-light, they could almost pass for real. But the pain had never really passed. It felt like having jogger's nipple on top of mastitis. Then there was the constant terror that someone might hug me too hard and they'd burst like over-inflated space-hoppers.

One of the TV monitors was switched to a commercial channel. Ads sang the praises of 'mature' women – played by teenage models. You'd have to work out 365 hours a day, I reflected, to look like that. In fact, any model who looked roughly thirty-nine was warbling about the benefits of bowel regulators or orthopaedic footpads.

I started to feel slightly dizzy. Waves of panic began to rise in my chest. Despite the extra-strong styling mousse, the hair on my head was standing up. What was I doing sitting at this desk, in a body that wasn't mine? This body belonged to K-Tel. This body was Barbie's. I'd tried to disguise my identity – the identity imprinted on the strands of my DNA just as a celestial map is carved upon an ancient Abyssinian necklace. And without the map, I had lost my way, everyday navigation suddenly impossible.

The red cone atop the tracking camera ignited and the floor manager cued me to start oozing charisma for the three minute news update. I just stared at the plasma screen. My eyes tightened and ached as I tried to read the autocue about Jeffrey Archer's escape from prison. And then it just hit me. Reality aftershave. A slap of it, right in my refurbished face.

'May I have your attention for an important news bulletin.'

The cameramen, floor managers and makeup artists turned their receptive countenances in my direction.

'Some of you might have been wondering about my return

to the news desk. You might assume it's because I'm good at my job and because the producers have respect for mature women viewers. Well, actually, I'm only back in front of the camera because of *this*.'

I ripped open my shirt and flung it floorwards. This produced a flurry on the studio floor. Crusoe and Dweezil, looking stunned, spoke rapidly into headsets while above, in the control room, Raphael gesticulated wildly. Then he flicked a switch and bellowed emphatically into a mike. Too late. I had torn out my earpiece. With no alternative but to stay on me for the allotted three minutes, all three cameras pivoted and bowed in my direction, lights ablaze.

'I mean, are these plastic tits really going to make me a better news-reader? What do *you* think?' I unhooked my bra and sent it, slingshot-style, straight at Camera One. 'Would you look at these ri*dic*ulous boobs?' I prodded at my chest. 'They're not breasts. They're an awning. I could put patio furniture under there. I mean, *look* at them. They've given me the relaxed spontaneity of a . . . I dunno, a store mannequin. And actually that's *exactly* what I've become. Women who have implants are always bleating on about how they did it for themselves. Well, it's bullshit! We do it for men.' Hot juicy tears plopped off the end of my nose. 'I did it for my husband because – because he was cheating on me.'

Rage welled up inside me. I snapped off my acrylic nails. People were streaming into the studio now . . . but a tidal wave of temper swept me up and hurtled me forward. I kicked off one vertiginous shoe in the direction of Camera Three. I wriggled off my leather mini-skirt and over-armed it at Camera

Two. I tugged at my hair extensions, weeding them from my skull and scattered them, Ophelia-like, on the studio floor. Panting with exertion, I harrumphed back on the chair in nothing but my hot-pink knickers.

'Here are my demands. I want Britney Spears' and Pamela Anderson's original boobs mounted in a museum somewhere. With Cher's missing rib. Yes! And all the gallons of fat that's been sucked out of Roseanne – along with her humour, for Chrissake. It'll be a museum dedicated to female stupidity. And it will be funded by all those shitty magazine articles and TV adverts that have "Beautiful People" practically *forni*cating with their *face* creams.'

The side door of the studio suctioned open and three bald security guards scurried in. Through the jangle of urgent, whispered conversation, I could hear one of them asking if I was armed. Possibly because I was obviously on the brink of a nervous bloody breakdown, I found this extremely funny.

'Do – do you – do you know what's going to happen?' I sputtered, between huge, snorty laughs, 'In this age of boring, airbrushed women, imperfections will become hugely refreshing. A Barbra Streisand nose, a Hillary Clinton thigh.' I was laughing so hard that my naked boobs were pogoing up and down on the news desk. With Herculean effort I regained control. 'But what if we just stopped? Hey? What if we just stopped being age-ophobic? Imagine the relief if we all just *let go*. Just accept that women come in different shapes and sizes. As *we* damn well accept the bloody blokes in our lives, with their beer bellies and bald bits . . .'

The vinyl seat had stuck to the backs of my hot and sweaty

bare legs. Every time I squirmed, half my thighs stayed behind – finally following me with a reluctant, sucking, smacking sound.

'Men can get older – who cares? Women get old and we're fired off the femininity stakes. *I* was fired. Did you know that? Oh, yes. For the crime of being *thirty-nine* and flat-chested. And I only got rehired when I opted for this superannuated porn-star look.' I gestured at my bimbo cast-offs scattered haphazardly around the studio. 'Why the hell can't women come of age in the public arena with wrinkles and self-esteem intact? Like bloody blokes do. Why do Jack Nicholson and Michael Douglas still "get the girl"? What is it? A charity engagement for "Help the Aged"? Puh-lease! If time flies, then *they* have frequent airmiles. Why is it that for men, every cloud has a silver-haired lining?'

I sprang up, toppling the news desk over. 'Why do older women have to become invisible, damn it?' Stiletto in hand, I then executed a wounded elephant charge across the studio floor, and smashed the vanity lights around the makeup mirror, which exploded like popcorn in a pan. The glass shards splintered televisually through the studio lights, like snow.

Now *that* had TVQ.

\*

After being released without charge from police custody some five hours later, I went home to leave my husband.

'What about the children?' Hugo asked, dumbfounded. 'How can you sabotage their mental well-being?'

'I've decided it's pointless even trying to be a perfect mother. Because you know what happens? Your kids grow up and start whingeing, "Why didn't you screw me up more, when I was young? I've got nobody to blame now!"'

'Lizzie. Calm down. You're not in your right mind—'

'You're right . . . And I diagnose disenchantment with husband. Although you probably know it by its more technical name – DIVORCE.'

'You can't divorce me. We've been through thick and thin—'

'More like 'thin and thin' of late, pal. I would have loved you for ever, Hugo,' I said, suddenly overwhelmed by sadness, 'till jowls, golfing cardigans, bingo tournaments and bald shins where the hairs had been rubbed away by the nylon of your sad old socks do us part. But you threw us away.'

'You really don't love me any more?'

'Let's just say that the hallucinatory drugs finally wore off.'

'But I can't live without you, Lizzie. You can't divorce me! On what grounds?'

'Irreconcilable differences. We seem to have different ideas about dental hygiene. I mean, you seem to think its okay to put my sister's genitalia into your mouth.' I handed him his suitcase. 'On behalf of the Academy, we would like to offer you this award for the best fake marriage.'

Then there was only one thing left to do.

# 25. 'I'm a Natural Blonde, So Please Speak Slowly'

·····················································································

How do you make five pounds of fat look good? You stick a nipple on it.

When I turned up at the Longevity Clinic the next day, there were breast augmentations booked all morning. A mastoplexy was scheduled for twelve p.m. Suction lipectomies for one. Eyelid, neck and brow lifts at two-fifteen. Four p.m., a nose job. Three-ish – a 'lip flip' (for that bee-stung look). Three-thirty, a designer vagina. Body-fat transfers from thighs to cheeks at four o'clock. Three litres of fat liposuctioned from buttocks and a brow suspension at five. And then me: a Bimbo Reversal. To counteract bad publicity, Britney Amore was at the clinic doing an interview for *Hello!* magazine. She reared her head suspiciously like a cornered cobra. 'What do *you* want, *Blondie*?'

'I want to go back to being my old self.'

Taking me aside, Britney delivered the cruellest cut of all – that the explantation would cost more than the augmentation.

'Um . . . I'm a natural blonde, so please speak slowly. *What* did you say again?'

'It costs more to take 'em out than to put 'em in.' She laughed scornfully and put out her palm. 'That'll be five and a half thousand quid.'

Lying in the operating theatre, I informed the nurse that I was already anaesthetized. I had, after all, been married for twelve years. She jabbed me anyway. At first I thought the drugs weren't working. But then I considered the purple poodles prancing on my forehead. And why were they reading Balzac? Oh, and what was my name again? One thing remained clear; soon, I would be my old brunette, nine stone, small-breasted slobby self again, wearing whatever I liked, no matter how unflattering; clothes which looked as though I'd just thrown them on – and missed. 'Give me back Lizzie McPhee,' I said deliriously to the surgeon. (I'd requested the only other surgeon Hugo had told me wasn't a quack.) 'Oh, and while you're in there, take out a couple of organs I can sell to pay for this operation, okay?'

But, on reflection, it had all been worth it in a way. I'd mastered one of Life's most important lessons. (Apart from the truism that any woman wearing real pearls is having fake orgasms – and *vice versa*.) The very best thing about us is grey: the substance between our ears. That is the only unique part of our bodies.

And then I plummeted under.

# 26. The Boobed Job

After my live-to-air meltdown, during which I bared to the nation my silicone implants – and the fact that my husband was a liar and an adulterer – I felt like a road accident. Friends slowed down to look at the gory details, then sped on, horrified, without stopping.

During my recovery period, the doorbell became a signal to hide upstairs. My doormat read 'Welcome. Now Go Away'. Not that I was depressed – the opposite, in fact, because even during the worst of the post-op pain, I was elated. With the hideous plastic expunged, I felt lightweight and floaty; relief flooded my empty chest like a cool, oxygenated blast of air.

As the summer ripened, the botox and the collagen wore off, and I could see my old face again. I was no longer travelling under an assumed mane either; the peroxide grew out and my crown of unruly curls sprang back. Oh, the relief of no longer pretending to be a tooth-flossing abcruncher. I embraced my previous, pore-clogged self with joy. I delighted in shaving my legs only to skirt length. At night I wore a flannelette pyjama top that didn't match the bottom and fell asleep in full makeup. I was free to suck the soft centres out of chocolates then put them back in the box; to sniff the armpits of T-shirts in the laundry basket to see if they could be worn just one more time – they were the kind of T-shirts that said things like 'My Other Body Is In the Shop'. Once in them, I shook my upper arms like fleshy maracas, without giving a damn. It took a lot of self-control and determination, but I even managed to give up dieting!

Ironically, with my new notoriety came a deluge of job offers – a case of 'thanks for the mammaries'. Every satellite station in Europe and, of course, Channel 5 was bidding for me, but I wasn't venturing out in public yet – well, only to pick up the kids from school. At the gate I could feel the furtive glances of the other mums behind my departing back. But Julia and Jamie welcomed the return of their old mother with the kind of fervour that could have resulted in hairline fractures.

So, I had lost a husband (Hugo had moved permanently into a flat above the Longevity Clinic) and a half-sister, but I had recovered my self-respect. When friends asked where Victoria was, I said I hadn't seen her since Antigua. 'She may be dead or she may be modelling,' I'd shrug.

One evening after I had got the kids to bed – a parental exercise that makes you understand why some members of the animal kingdom eat their young – there was a tentative stutter of knuckles on wood.

I opened the door with some trepidation to find Victoria huddled in the portal. In the dim illumination, I could see she had been beaten up quite badly. She was weeping from a face twisted with pain. Was this the same woman who kept her emotional thermostat at a constant sixty-two degrees? Who showed no feelings as to do so would only lead to lines?

'Jesus, Vick!' I forgot my anger and a deep wave of pity

washed through me. I led her gingerly inside. Holding on to me for support, she lurched down the hall. Without her elegant hairdo and elaborate makeup, my sister resembled a coat-stand, her clothes swallowing her gaunt frame. Her face seemed to have stopped trying. For the first time, I noticed the lines etched on to her complexion; the shadows beneath her haunted eyes, the fragile erosion of her upper lip, the grey roots in her flattened hair. Crying had matted her lashes together like the legs of a crushed centipede.

After guiding her into a chair in the sitting room, I returned with antiseptic swabs and knelt before her. 'Vicky,' I tried to keep my voice calm as I pressed a cold flannel to her tattered cheek, 'who did this to you?' Her lip was split and scratches raked across her forehead.

With great effort she managed to speak. 'Sven.'

'What?' I reeled, rocking back on my heels. 'But *why*?'

'Marrakech and Sven did a deal. He paid the US lawyer to bring a case for that Death Row convict. And agreed to give her a breast reduction. In exchange she would do some modelling for him.' In a dead-pan monotone, her words blurted out like a printer. 'But instead of reducing her, he – he made her bigger. He told me that advertisers are requesting fewer super thin models and more buxom girls. And that Marrakech could be the most busty of them all. Thirty-four E. He just altered her, Lizzie. Like an unsatisfactory dress.'

It was not news to me that Sven was a chauvinist pig, but this double-cross was a feat unparalleled in porcine history.

'And I— I signed the consent form.' Victoria made a pained, flinching expression, as though her face was being sucked out the back of her skull. 'I thought it was a permission form for her to model.'

'Didn't you read it?'

'I trusted him.'

'How could you trust a rat like him?'

'Because we have a love-hate relationship. I love him and he . . . he hates me.' She buckled forward, her voice broken and juddering. 'What kind of mother am I? Why didn't I protect my little girl?'

I poured us tumblers of whisky and pressed one into her trembling hand. 'We'll bring charges,' I said, staunchly.

'I always thought I'd feel wise at forty. I mean, you should know a lot of stuff, right? At my age?' My sister's voice see-sawed. 'But what do *I* know? That getting your four back teeth removed gives instant cheekbones. That's it. You were right. I changed my exterior, but not my interior. Underneath, I'm still that vile, selfish brat I was at sixteen.'

I sighed. It had only taken her two thousand diets and twenty-eight surgical procedures to realize she'd be more beautiful if she read a book now and then.

'And now even *you* hate me.' Her mouth curled downwards. 'And I hate it when you hate me.' Her face caved in on itself and tears spilt down her lacerated cheeks. 'Can you ever forget what happened?'

'I'm told a lobotomy would erase the memory permanently.'

'It meant nothing. I was eaten up with jealousy that you, my mousy little sister, should have this perfect family. This perfect husband. Getting Hugo into bed was just a way of

217

proving to myself that he wasn't so damn perfect. I didn't do it to hurt you. But you caught us. God! I had no idea that ego-maniac had a thing about watching his own performance on video. And you were hurt and I am so so sorry.' Victoria's battered body was shuddering with sobs. Unexpected feelings overwhelmed me and, without thinking, I wrapped my arms around my sister.

'Listen, Victoria,' I urged her, 'let's skip the maudlin, self-indulgent accusations and go straight to the bit where we blame our parents. Agreed?'

'Agreed.'

'Typical,' I teased gently. 'Didn't your therapist say that you never take responsibility for anything?'

'Yes. And I blame our mother for that. She never met my growing intellectual, emotional and *haute-couture*-clothing needs.' She managed a smile, despite her cracked lip. 'Do you know what Sven calls his cock? The Incredible Hulk. I had to call it that too.' When I laughed acidly, she overcame her fragility and hugged me fiercely. 'How did *you* see through him?'

'The "Hitler is Fab" tattoo kind of gave it away.' I stroked her forehead, dank with sweat. 'What are you going to do about Sven?'

'Well, on the way here I walked into a petrol station to buy a can of gas. The attendant asked me which brand my boy-friend wanted me to get. I said my boyfriend didn't know yet that I was going to set fire to him. I ran away while he was dialling the police.'

'Immolation's too good for that bastard. Sven – can't live with him, can't cut him up with a chainsaw and dispose of his body in black bin-bag liners 'cause the neighbours might notice.' Then I asked the question I'd been dreading. 'Who . . . who performed Marrakech's operation?' I braced myself.

My sister winced. 'Hugo.'

*Hugo?* A volt of ice went through my body.

'If only we could do unto *them* what they've done unto *us*.' Victoria took another gulp of Glenfiddich.

'Yes!' I fantasized. 'We should give *them* plastic surgery and see how they bloody well like it.' I snatched up the whisky and took a giant slug.

'But who would we get to operate?'

'Some surgeon could talk us through it over the phone.'

'Yeah! The way they land planes in the movies when the pilot's died,' Victoria said animatedly.

'How would we get them into the surgery?'

'Kidnap them.'

I tossed back another shot. I would need to down the whole bottle to think *this* could ever work. 'Trouble is, kidnapping requires a cool head, a hard heart, good timing and, if the police get wind of it, *Olympic sprinting*.' I sighed. Freeing an arm from around her shoulders, I reached for the phone.

'What are you doing?'

Suspecting that we were lacking many of the talents necessary for success as Criminal Masterminds, I began to dial 999.

Victoria's face went ashen. She slammed her hand down to cut the connection. 'No! For Christ's sake! If we report him to the police Sven will have me killed.' Her voice was eerily shrill. She wrenched the receiver from my hand.

I realized she was serious. 'You mean he'd hire a hitman? I hate the man too, but is he really capable of that?'

With tentative fingers my sister probed her face. Her famously beautiful features now resembled a relief map of some war-torn wasteland. 'I went to his house to confront him about Marrakech. I threatened to report him to the police for mutilating her and *this* was my warning . . .'

With the perfect timing that eludes most of life, there came from somewhere at the back of the house the unmistakable sound of glass shattering, then the spine-chilling crunch of heavy shoes moving across splintered shards. The whisky tumbler fell from my sister's hands. My toes curled up like dead leaves in my shoes. The door thwacked open to reveal a hulking beast of a man, as hirsute as he was bulky, a rattlesnake tattoo coiled around his biceps.

Cystitis, childbirth, divorce – these are jewels in life's crown compared to the sheer terror of confronting a psychotic hitman in your own living room. How did I know this man was dangerous? Well, call me Sherlock Holmes, but not even London is cold enough to be wearing a balaclava in June. There was also something potentially explosive, something barely contained about him. He approached, his movements jerky and violent. Body odour with a tang of onion (and was that car oil?) began to fill the room. A mossy tongue lolled in a lopsided mouth, the top molars all missing, save for one furry green fang.

As the creature I assumed was Sven's hired hitman began a lunge towards me, I shrank back, petrified – until I realized it was extending its hand to shake mine. 'Bruce the Tooth,' he said jocularly, in a thick, redneck accent. 'Ex-con number 14567 Gainsville Maximum Security Prison. So pleased to make the acquaintance of you fine ladies. Gee, I'm sorry. How rude.' He ripped off his balaclava, to reveal a low simian forehead wormed with scars and a lank ponytail. He scrutinized my sister. 'You ain't Marrakech, are ya? You sure do look like her photo, but . . . You must be her sister.' (Victoria's battered spirits seemed to rise remarkably at this mistake.) 'That gal sent the cash to hire me some good lawyers. They won the appeal – not only got me off of Death Row but proved me innocent. Marrakech done give me this here address. Apologies for the grand entrance. Force of habit,' he rasped, in a ten-packs-a-day voice a couple of cartons shy of lung cancer. 'I've come to thank her for savin' me from Big Sparky.' He ground his prognathous jaw and welled up a little. 'If there's anythin' I can ever do for her, she's only gotta ask.'

Victoria attempted to straighten her appearance. 'I know it's hard to believe, but actually I'm her mother.'

The man broke into a one-tooth smile. 'Well, then, ma'am, that there goes for you too.'

My sister and I looked at each other, our eyes widening. This guy could be the best thing since slim regulars. It was like finding the toy surprise in the cereal box.

'Well, actually,' Victoria said, 'now you mention it, there is a little something . . .'

## 27. I'm So Miserable Without You, It's Almost Like You're Here

Men are perfectly agreeable and totally wonderful as long as you never let them within a ten-mile radius. After twelve years of marriage my only other insight is that, when meeting a soon-to-be-ex-husband, it's best not to resolve your differences with firearms.

To this purpose I asked Hugo to meet me on neutral turf, a seedy hotel (patrons were kindly asked to check in their chainsaws at the door) in King's Cross, an area of London culturally enriched by a diverse selection of prostitutes, escaped felons and British librarians. There was a greenish-grey tinge to the evening air as if it were about to rain. I waited for Hugo in reception, next to the spindly racks containing cheap postcards of London attractions.

When my husband pushed through the revolving doors, I looked at the handsome forty-five-year-old man I'd once loved so deeply – and was shocked to feel a profound pang of grief. When, I wondered, had it gone from '*Fuck* me!' to 'Fuck *you*!'? It was just one of life's *haikus*, like 'from womb to tomb'. As Hugo approached, I looked down at our marriage as though it were a dead corpse on a mortuary trolley. We stared at each other blankly, like two people passing on up and down escalators.

'Thank you for last night,' I said, steering him into the dingy bar.

'I wasn't with you last night.'

'That's why I'm grateful.'

'Is that the kind of sarcastic tone you're going to adopt for the duration of this meeting?' He called for coffee, then slid across the stained velvet banquette of the nearest booth and took in his sordid surroundings. The only other patrons were a couple of cockroaches the size of Arnold Schwarzenegger, sitting around cracking their knuckles, and a few million intestinal parasites.

'Where the hell have you brought me?' Hugo produced a monogrammed handkerchief and wiped the pock-marked laminex tabletop before gingerly resting his designer-jacketed elbows upon it. 'Your solicitor called me today.' His gaze lingered on me and he sighed. 'Oh, Lizzie, dearest, where did our love go?'

'To the Oxfam charity shop, with the rest of your stuff,' I said, stiffly.

I slipped off my cardigan and Hugo's eyes fell to my newly flattened chest. 'They told me at the clinic you'd had an explantation. Why, for God's sake?'

'Well, curiously enough, the thrill of carrying around two pounds of cancer-inducing silicone in your chest cavity palls quite quickly.'

'Do you know what those boobs cost me, Elisabeth? They're etched on to my Visa bill for ever!'

'You should have just left the price tags on them, then.'

'It's not just that I paid for your operation! I made a huge emotional investment in you and in our marriage. And now

223

I've lost everything. Twelve years of wedlock and what do I have to show for it? An overdraft, a failing professional reputation and a broken heart. I've a good mind to sue you for the cost of those implants!'

'Litigation. Ah, yes, well, I'm glad you brought that up, Hugo, because there's the little matter of my niece. Tell me, did you think Marrakech was going to be happy when she woke up with her big breast surprise?'

'Your sister signed the consent form.'

'Sven tricked her into it.'

'What? I didn't know anything about that!' Hugo's famously luxuriant hair began to clump in damp spikes on his increasingly pale forehead.

'How is it going to look in court when Marrakech tells the jury how she was lying there, unconscious, when against her wishes, her trusted uncle gave her a breast augmentation? She's only fifteen. My lawyer says you need to have her informed consent . . . not a form signed by an uninformed mother.'

'Sven, her mother's lover and agent, remember, came in during the operation and said, 'Make 'em big and perky. She insists on becoming a top model.' So, that's what I did. I believed she wanted them.'

'You *know* how much she hated having big breasts!'

'For God's sake, Lizzie, if *I* hadn't operated on her—' he broke off while the barman deposited our two cups of coffee – brewed, I suspect, at the outset of the Second World War – before whispering '– one of Sven's butchers *would* have.'

'Couldn't you *see* that he might be lying?' But I already knew the answer. My once honourable husband had turned into the kind of doctor who went blind once the cheque cleared. 'Can you imagine the scandal? Dr Hugo Frazer, who cannot be named for legal reasons—'

'Elisabeth,' he interrupted, in clipped tones, 'if you really want to torture me, ask me to renew our wedding vows.'

'You know, maybe it would be good if you did some time in jail, Hugo. It'd be an effective weight-loss plan for you.'

Hugo sucked in his stomach. 'You've got the house, the children and custody of the Merc convertible. What else can you possibly want?'

'Actually I have a little surgical request.'

He slurped morosely at his stewed brew and grimaced as though drinking warm sputum. 'What else do you want taken out?'

'Not for me,' I added hastily.

'Well, for whom, exactly?'

'Sven.' I took a sip of my coffee, as scalding as the look my husband was now giving me. 'Yes. Lipo, botox, a butt lift, oh, and breast implants.'

My husband spluttered into laughter, spurting coffee down his shirtfront.

I met his gaze defiantly. 'I'm pleased to see that Sven's predicament is affording you such hilarity,' I said, in Hugo-speak. 'We kidnapped him over six hours ago. He's prepped and ready for surgery.'

My husband levelled me with a peculiar stare. 'You're not serious?'

'Yup.'

'To say that you're psychotic, Elisabeth, is to indulge in the drollest of understatements. First your hostile TV hysteria, in which you denounce me to the entire world, and now *this*. How could you ever think I would countenance doing such a diabolical thing?'

'You do it to women every day. Including your own relatives.'

'Breast implants on a man?' he said, stupefied. 'I can't do it. It's – it's mutilation.'

'*Exactly*.' I lifted my T-shirt and pointed to the two-inch scars etched forever beneath my breasts. 'You *will* give Sven surgery.'

Hugo hunched belligerently over his coffee. 'You can't make me.'

'No,' I admitted, 'but *he* can.'

I nodded towards the darkest corner of the deserted bar, where Bruce the Tooth sat slouched over his Budweiser. He tipped his baseball cap. You could dimly make out the slogan on his born-again T-shirt: 'Though He Slay Me, Yet Will I Trust in Him' – Job 13:15.

''Less you co-operate, Doc, things could get very Last Judgement,' Bruce the Tooth called out, by way of greeting.

'Is he threatening to *kill* me?' Hugo scoffed, trilling his fingers impatiently.

'Well, sir, I find "killin'" too broad a term. Let's just say that there's gonna be an arbitrary deprivation of life.' Sauntering over to our table, Bruce the Tooth smashed a bloated fly with his fist, its innards splattering on to Hugo's sleeve. He picked up the insect and dropped it into Hugo's coffee cup. 'I call it "goin' postal".'

'Jesus Christ. He *is* going to kill me!' Hugo recoiled, eyes swivelling around the bar for witnesses, or preferably a SWAT anti-terrorist squad.

' "Police Find Plastic Surgeon's Head. Body Still Missing",'
I said, rattling a spoon around my cup. 'Now that's what I call
a headline.'

'A headline. I geddit.' Bruce snorted.

'Listen, my good man, whatever my wife has offered you,
I can treble it.' Hugo steepled his hands, fingers entwined
in that doctorly way, as though about to make a diagnosis.
'I have always found Americans to be so reasonable, so good
with people . . . I'm sure we can do a deal.'

Although my ex-husband extended his hand, Bruce the
Tooth pointedly refused to shake it. His muscular tattooed
arms remained firmly knotted across his heavily furred ribs.
'Hey, do I look like a fuckin' people person? Pardon my
French, ma'am.'

'Yes, it's probably best for a man like you to keep your arms
folded. Otherwise your knuckles would drag on the ground as
you walk.' Hugo slid abruptly across the booth.

'Fine, don't help us, Hugo,' I said nonchalantly. 'As long
as you're prepared for the testicular trauma and compound
fractures that will no doubt follow.'

'Don't you worry,' Bruce the Tooth drawled. 'I ain't never
castrated a man I didn't like.'

'Don't try to intimidate me. The answer is *no*,' said Hugo,
recoiling from Bruce the Tooth's natural marinade of oil and
onions. 'Now, if you'll excuse me, I have a vat of penicillin I
need to go and soak in . . .'

We watched him stride through the squalid foyer into the
dusk. Then we followed him past bag-ladies holding animated
conversations with invisible aliens and participants in what
appeared to be a public urination festival against the eastern

wall of the British Library. The air was gauzy with heat and car fumes. Beyond the towers of St Pancras, welts of grey cloud bruised the sky. A summer storm was simmering on the horizon.

Hugo was walking faster and faster, glancing furtively over his shoulder. Bruce the Tooth panthered behind him, weaving in and out of shadowy doorways. I reached my car and skidded out into the traffic. By the time I caught up with them, Hugo was virtually sprinting. Scrabbling to open his car door, my husband only had time to turn and scowl like that famous bust of Stalin before he was star-fished on the pavement. As I drew up, Bruce the Tooth flicked my husband effortlessly over one shoulder and threw him, as if he were a bag of golf clubs, into the back of my people-mover.

Rent a psycho: believe me, every girl should have one. Bruce the Tooth had attitude – and he knew how to use it. But then again, so did my half-sister. I'd left Victoria alone with Sven who was tethered helplessly to an operating table. I floored the accelerator. I'd known for a long time that life didn't imitate art. But I had a curious feeling that mine was about to imitate *The Jerry Springer Show*.

# 28. Relying on the Kindness of Passing Serial Killers

....................................................................................................

As a general rule, 'Do you know who I am?' is almost always the wrong thing to say when you're being held hostage by a six-foot-five felon with a switchblade.

These pompous words ensured that Hugo got another punch to the guts before being dragged through the basement stairwell of the Longevity Clinic, thrown into the lift and hauled into the fourth-floor surgery. It was a Sunday evening, and Harley Street was empty – no one would hear the muffled moans that were emanating from the operating theatre. I muscled open the swing doors to find Sven spreadeagled, stark naked, on the slab, arms and legs strapped down. Despite the gaffer-tape gagging his mouth, there was a scream of dismay in his terrified eyes. White curlicues of depilation cream had been squeezed across his eyebrows.

Victoria, skirt rucked up, spatula in hand, was sitting astride his bare tethered thighs, hot-waxing the model agent's bikini line. Little runways of pale flesh had been mown through his pubic growth and upper thigh forestry. They looked red and raw and prickled with blood.

'Do you think I should go for the full Brazilian? He likes shaved pussies. A 'beetle bonnet', he calls it, don't you, sweetie?' she reminded her ex-lover. Sven began to writhe on the table, struggling against his restraints. All this time I'd thought he was a top-order predator, the male equivalent of the Great White Shark, but Sven looked more like a Great White Prawn. Victoria pointed at his shrunken appendage, which seemed to wither even more. 'Now *that*'s why you're supposed to judge people on their personalities. Scrub up, Doc,' my deranged sister ordered Hugo, her tangled hair falling over her flushed face. 'Its time for Sven here to get in touch with his Inner Model.'

Victoria's dishevelment was at odds with the deep sense of purpose and determination radiating from within. 'Good thing you finally made it, Hugo,' my sister continued, conversationally, 'because I was about to start the lipo without you. It seems quite easy. Just make a cut, shove a tube in, wobble it around until you hit a pocket of pale yellow globules, then suck 'em up through a straw, like a McDonald's shake. Sluuuurrrrp. Right?'

Hugo's head suddenly tilted backwards as though he feared his eyeballs might fall out. 'Lipo?'

'Yes. There's a vacuum cleaner in the hall. But I didn't want my patient to die from shock. Then I wondered if I should get started on the botox,' she said, conducting an invisible symphony orchestra with a syringe.

'Botox,' Hugo repeated, dumbly.

'Yes. I was all ready to inject him, but what if I gave him too much? Wouldn't his larynx become paralysed by the bacteria? And then he'd stop breathing, right?'

Beside me, Hugo gasped.

'And we don't want to kill him – well, not quite yet,' my sister decreed, and leaned forward to remove the depilatory

230

cream with two deft sweeps of her pretty little hand. As Sven's eyebrows came off on a tissue, he made a noise like a deflating tyre. 'We'll start with the breast implants, I think, as a pay-back for what you did to my daughter.'

Sven was shaking so much he looked to be in the advanced stages of Parkinsons.

'Perhaps we could shave a little off his tailbone, Hugo? To give him the sort of slender waist he demands of his models.'

Bruce the Tooth snorted gleefully. 'An eye for an eye . . .'

'Yes! And a face lift for a face lift. Why not? The face is just peeled off the bone. They pull the skin right up over your head like a Spandex polo-neck,' Victoria informed her victim casually.

'The smartassed sonofabitch is a platinum-plated dick-fondler, right?' said the Tooth, getting carried away. 'Well, why not jest give him a world-class dong? The biggest damn dong in the world.'

'Oh, you evil genius!' my sister thrilled. 'The phallic equiv-alent of Pinocchio's nose. When he gets out of bed in the morning he'll have to be careful not to tread on his own willy. He'll need a truss-fund!' she cackled.

Sven made a squeak like a lost puppy. Rancid sweat was oozing from every terrified pore.

'It's "preventative medicine",' Victoria explained to the rest of us, who were gazing on, aghast. 'It'll prevent him from ever again having sex with a woman and breaking her heart – or her body,' she added bitterly.

Out of the corner of my eye, I became aware of Hugo crabbing his way towards the door.

'I don't advise you to do that, Hugo,' my sister called out.

231

She picked up Sven's limp dick, brandished a scalpel and ran it along the shaft, menacingly. 'Otherwise it'll be the Plastic Surgery *That Needs No Surgeon.*' Sven began to snivel with terror. 'After all, you don't actually need a penis to run a modelling agency. In fact, there's no medical proof that you need any organ at all. Obviously a *brain*, complete with moral conscience, is not remotely necessary.'

Sven made some ugly grunting noises, which I imagine involved a quick conversion to religion.

An involuntary shiver shimmied up my spine. Revenge, I was realizing, is like unsugared coffee: it smells better than it tastes. In my living room, fuelled by whisky, the nimble rationalization had been easy – let us do unto the body fascist what he'd done unto his women. But we were only supposed to scare him. Seeing him chained to an operating table, eyebrow-less, strips of hot wax hardening on his groin, my stomach began to churn sourly. Torturing was not high on my Fun Things To Do Today list. 'Okay, Vick, I think we've made our point now,' I interceded.

A clump of Sven's pubic hair hung from Victoria's waxing spatula like weed from an anchor.

An anaemic murmur emanated from beneath Sven's gag. My husband gave me an imploring glance.

'Victoria, look at his face,' I pleaded. Tears were streaming from the man's eyes.

'They're just crocodile tears, sweetie – droplets that squeeze out of the giant reptile's eyes from the pressure of chomping their victims.'

'We've scared the hell out of them. It's enough,' I entreated.

Ignoring me, Victoria hurled a surgical gown at my ex-husband. 'Don't mess with me. I'm all out of oestrogen and I have a scalpel . . .'

We all looked at Victoria, and mentally debated the wisdom of a response.

'Hurry up, Hugo. My next psychotic mood swing should be in about, oh,' Victoria checked her watch, scowling, 'five to six seconds. One, two, three . . .'

'Look. You're wasting your breath—'

So was Hugo because Bruce the Tooth walloped him once more, this time in the mouth.

'Blood! Oh, my God.' I squirmed. 'Blood should definitely be on the inside. Okay Victoria. This has gone far enough.'

But judging by the reckless look on my sibling's face, she wanted to go much, much further. Hell, she was in the kind of mood where she'd accept a car ride from a Kennedy.

Hugo drew himself up. 'How dare you?'

Before he could say any more, Bruce the Tooth whacked him again, right in the solar plexus. 'Now, fuckin' scrub up, like the lady fuckin' tells you,' he growled, in his native brute vocabulary, ''cause you're really startin' to frost my shorts.'

'You can't do this to me! I'll press charges!' Hugo said, querulously, mopping at blood trickling from his split lip.

'What? Under the Prevention of Cruelty to Animals Act?' my sister snarled.

'You're a man!' Hugo implored. But the Tooth just stood impassively, arms now folded. 'How can you allow this mutilation to happen?'

'Listen, pal, I spent ten years on Death Row. I was twenty-four hours from gettin' fried by Old Sparky, all for a crime I never done. Though, okay, I done a few like it.' His accent was so thick it sounded as though he were constantly chewing. 'An' that little gal! She was the one who raised the dough to pay for real lawyers – not them lousy public defenders who screwed up at my trial. Marrakech got me freed. And that fucker,' he pointed at Sven, 'hurt her bad.'

'I won't do it,' Hugo stood firm. 'You can manhandle me all you want.'

'Tell me, Hugo, did your plans for this evening involve living till morning?' My sister turned the scalpel towards my ex-husband.

I clapped a hand to my mouth. I felt like the sidecar attached to an out-of-control motorbike. 'Victoria, come on, let's all calm down.' My hand extended to take the weapon from her as my sister and I gyred around the operating table.

With implacable calm, Bruce the Tooth bent my arm up behind my back. 'You ain't goin' over to the Dark Side, is ya, sis?'

'Lizzie, you have the right to remain silent so, for God's sake, SHUT UP,' Victoria ordered.

Bruce shackled my wrists with his belt and, as I struggled, gaffer-taped my lips together. 'Thank you, Bruce sweetie,' Victoria said, serenely, the operating light directly behind her bonfiring her hair.

'My pleasure, ma'am,'

Victoria, a bubble of berserk laughter hiccuping from her lips, slid open a drawer in which fake breasts puckered, like row upon row of sun blisters. 'So, which cup size?' She began rooting through them, frisbeeing implants floorward until she found a size 34E, which, I remembered, was exactly what Sven had forced upon Marrakech.

'I *can't* operate.' Hugo insisted. 'It's not sterile.'

Bruce the Tooth, who had bound me to the radiator with surgical cord, rolled up his sleeves and said, 'Lemme do it, then. I washed me hands, after lunch.'

'Why not? It should be easy enough,' my sister enthused. 'After all, the patient is spineless, gutless and totally heartless.'

'If you do it you'll kill him,' Hugo said sternly.

The Tooth grunted severely through his missing molars. 'Yeah, and then I'd have to kill a hostile witness, wouldn't I?' He took the scalpel from Victoria and pointed it at Hugo. 'Death can seriously damage your health you know, Doc. So, would you like to meet your Maker before or after?'

The drawback of dying, of course, is that your life will never be the same again. The morality of choosing one deformed life rather than two deaths finally got through to Hugo: slowly he nodded his head before it slumped into his hands. 'God, I'm going to regret this in the morning,' he murmured.

'So?' shrugged my demented sister. 'Sleep in.'

\*

After the anaesthetic had kicked in (a syringe drip cocktail of short-acting barbiturates), Hugo began to operate, his face pinched into a mask of concentration. I grimaced as he sliced open the skin beneath the pectoral muscle then tried to insert a balloon of saline through the slit beneath Sven's nipple. It was like an airline passenger attempting to shove an inappropriate object into an overhead baggage compartment. Watching Hugo wrenching the flesh with grim determination made me cringe with revulsion. The next time I dared peep towards the operating table, I saw the bruising that had erupted across

Sven's mangled torso. He was half man, half aubergine. Hugo then began the extension to Sven's penis. This was achieved with a long silicon rod. An hour later the model-agent's dick was so inflated it could have appeared in the Macy's Parade. Now Sven really would be a *hardened* criminal. Hugo was just finishing up when we heard the bell on the lift door, chime loudly.

Bruce the Tooth hit the lights. In the gloom the poisonous green rays of the monitors blipped and blinked eerily in a Morse code that signalled danger. All I could see was the inevitable prison sentence stretching endlessly before me. My internal organs felt as though they were in a blender. I thought I might be going into labour – except I wasn't pregnant. Believe me, being caught giving breast implants to a man has to be the ultimate laxative.

We all stood rigid, holding our breath as the surgery door squeezed open momentarily, then began to suck shut. That's precisely when Sven, who was only half sedated, gurgled and gave one long moan.

The hinges made a hiss before the door sprang open once more. Light immediately flooded the theatre, the pitiless scrutiny of fluorescent tubes freezing us in the frame. One fluorescent was faltering, spasmodically, like a dying fly. 'What thuh fuck's goin' on?'

Britney Amore had a voice that sounds very nice to people who've been deaf since birth. Her piercing tones could cause nerve damage at a hundred paces, which is why I heard her before I saw her.

When my blinking eyes adjusted to the light, I was looking down the stubby barrel of a 34-calibre Smith and Wesson.

# 29. *Premature Cremation*

Our small gathering looked more surprised than the congregation at Michael Jackson's wedding. As my eyes adjusted to the searing light, I was blinded a second time by the perfect row of white picket-fence teeth that were gnashing before me.

'What thuh fuck's goin' on?' Britney demanded again, all pretence at actressy glamour obliterated.

There really is no good way to say to a woman that her fiancé has been abducted and deformed by homicidal maniacs.

My sister rallied first, probably because the gun was now aimed at her head. 'Your husband-to-be's getting in touch with his Inner Model,' she said, evenly.

Britney's eyes then registered the freshly augmented patient lying comatose on the operating table. Sven's magnificent, though bruised, breasts, which had recently increased from zero to a bouncing, bountiful 34E in defiance of all gravity and gender specifics, rose spectacularly ceilingward. His new and improved appendage protruded with surreal menace. Her mouth dropped open. 'You – you evil fucks! You're all goin' to the Chair!'

Bruce the Tooth snickered. 'This ain't Texas, ma'am.'

'An' zaccley who thuh fuck are *you*?' Britney trained her gun in Bruce the Tooth's direction. With her other hand, she wrenched the gaffer-tape off my mouth, taking half of my top lip with it. 'Elisabeth? Who is he?' She untied me from the radiator.

My brain was busily trying to jump-start my heart. 'Marrakech's prison pen pal,' I said finally, discreetly checking I hadn't peed my pants. 'The one she rescued off Death Row.'

'Couldn't she just have adopted a *zoo animal*?' She eye-balled Bruce, disdainfully. 'Although, then again . . . I guess she *did*.'

I watched with apprehension as the cords on the sides of Bruce the Tooth's neck swelled to the thickness of cables.

'Call the cops,' Britney brayed, rummaging one-handed through her bag for her cell-phone. 'Then get an ambulance.' She tossed her mobile at me. I froze. 'Didn't ya hear me? If ya don't move I'll shoot the crap out of ya'll.'

'You *can* call the police, Elisabeth,' my grim-faced sister spat, scarlet-rimmed eyes burning with hate. 'I want to tell them how Sven had my beautiful daughter butchered against her will to make her breasts twice as big.'

'Only because she ain't got the brains to make that decision herself,' Britney snarled. 'Y'all obviously both come from a long line of first cousins.'

I dug my fingernails into the pads of my palms. Bruce the Tooth's neck veins were starting to throb.

Britney, oblivious, blundered on: 'If only Marrakech's old man, whoever *he* was, had just settled for a blow-job, eh?'

The eruption, when it came, was Vesuvial. Howling like a chainsaw, and with no terror of death, Bruce the Tooth lunged at the actress's larynx.

He was still mid-air when Britney's finger squeezed back on

the trigger and the bullet thudded into his chest. It was like watching the dynamited demolition of a tower block. The big man collapsed, taking the medical tray with him. Surgical shrapnel scattered in every direction. Victoria made a sound not dissimilar to an above-ground nuclear test before flying to his side.

Hugo used the general mayhem to chop his hand down hard against Britney's wrist. The gun scuttled across the polished floor. Britney's retaliatory knee was in his groin before he could say, 'Castrati.' Hugo concertinaed to the floor. Unarmed and outnumbered, Britney decided to dash for it. Down the Corinthian-column-lined corridor she ran, high heels gritting on the ornamental gravel.

I bent down to pick up my fallen idol. 'Hugo, for God's sake, we're all in this together! You see to Bruce. Victoria, you get Sven out of here. I'll try to catch Britney.' Keen not to go to prison for something I hadn't done, i.e. run fast enough, I found that despite my previous contempt for muscle-toning ventures, I could sprint down the stairs two at a time. The back door leading on to the cobbled mews yawned open. Hurtling through the lane I crashed on to Harley Street, breathing hard.

While we'd been in the clinic, the storm had broken. Frantically I looked up and down the wind-whipped streets. Gusts howled along deserted pavements, banking rubbish against the buildings. My eyes raked left to right as the leaves circled and scuttled underfoot like giant cornflakes. And then I saw her. She was at her Porsche, car keys rattling against her ridiculously long stiletto nails. Hearing my pounding footsteps she fumbled desperately, dropping her keys down a grating. In her urgent bid to escape me, she abandoned her precious Blahnik heels and streaked towards Marylebone Road. But at this hour the carriageway was deserted. My quarry skidded across bitumen, slick with rain.

The deluge beating hard against my face blurred my vision. I dashed across the cement apron and, on instinct, sprinted towards Regent's Park – just in time to catch sight of her squeezing through a gap in the iron railings to disappear into the conspiring shadows. Where the hell was she heading? I wondered. Then, with a sickening thud in my guts, I realized: the police station at Chester Gate. And what a cock-and-bull story she had to tell them – *literally*. If I didn't catch her and force her to see sense, we'd all be stamping due dates in a prison library pronto.

Leaving the lozenges of street lamplight behind me, I plunged into the pitch black of the park. The storm had grown melodramatic, trees keening and shuddering beneath the onslaught. The sky was boiling. Clouds writhed like black sacks full of eels. A crack of lightning razored through the dark canopy of leaves – as if God was signing autographs. And there she was, darting between sculptures and flowerbeds, her legs flashing like scissor-blades as she cut through a clearing. As I stampeded after her, a stitch sliced into my side. Thick skeins of water seemed to be draped across the trees. I would need an outboard motor to catch her.

The path gave way to a sweep of luxurious lawn where the rain fell in sheets. My eyes skittered across the field. No Britney. Just menacing dark. Another great jagged prong of light split the sky, affording me a strobing glimpse of her as she darted for shelter beneath a tangle of trees necklaced in silver lightning. It had turned into an Old Testament of a night. Rainwater was sluicing in rivulets down the back of my neck. And I needed windscreen wipers on my eyes. I crashed to the ground. Winded and soaked, my body was begging to pack it in. I was just not equipped to be a criminal. Hell, I didn't even know my nylon stocking head size. But I was so fuelled with anger for that giggling, pouting, mincing, quivering, venomous, silicone-pumped-up, ice-covered volcano of devil's spawn that I was propelled up on to my jellied legs again, and tearing after her.

I was gaining ground. My advantage was simply this: when scrambling up an embankment a pair of jeans is more practical attire than a little leopardskin Prada dress, which was snugger on *her* than it had been on the leopard.

At Queen Mary's Rose Garden, I leapt forward, snaring her hair extensions with my fingers. I just hung on, no longer running but skiing after her on the soles of my sneakers. She reeled around – kicking, biting, scratching. Nails like flick-knives shrieked down the side of my face. I could taste the blood running into the corners of my mouth. We rolled and wrestled in the muddy ground. That was when the lightning hit.

The closest I've ever come to an out-of-body experience was when Hugo Frazer MD first kissed me. Being on the receiving end of a lightning rod is not dissimilar – except for the third-degree burns. The jolt lifted me up off the ground where I seemed to hover ablaze, as terror licked like flames all over me.

The last thing I remembered before being pulverized into darkness was the smell of singed flesh. It was Mother Nature's electrolysis machine – a premature cremation.

# 30. *That Was Then, This Is Noir*

.....................................................................................................................................................

I think therefore I am, but I can't hoist open my eyelids. I seem to be listening to an arrangement of 'Stairway to Heaven' for accordion, pan-pipes and kazoo. I try to move but my body is like a bucket of cement. My mouth is sour; my throat feels raw; a metallic taste is bubbling on to my tongue. I become blearily aware of someone mopping my brow. One leaden eye squints open.

'Where am I?' I rasp, in a voice that sounds as though it's been sandpapered.

'Hospital, Lizzie darling,' says my sister.

There's a searing pain in my chest, neck and shoulders. I realize that my torso is swaddled in bandages. 'Good God! I've had more plastic surgery, haven't I?' I say groggily, trying to focus through befogged synapses. But it's a regular NHS hospital. Not the clinic in Harley Street, I realize, with relief.

'You were hit by lightning, Lizzie.'

'I was *what*? . . . Oh, God, I remember. Are the kids all right?' I panic. The room is a gizmo-intensive enclave. Monitors murmur and blip neurotically.

'Oh, yes. They're both on the London Eye. With their dad. Hugo's spent more time with them in the last five days than he has for the last five months.'

'But the police?' I panic. 'Has Britney laid charges?' My heart is dancing a fast fandango. 'Where's Sven?'

'With *his* figure, he's probably being signed up by his own modelling agency,' Marrakech scoffs, moving closer to sit on the edge of the cot and stroke my hand.

'And Britney Amore? Well,' my sister takes a ragged breath, 'she's gone to the big Green Room in the sky, darling.'

'What?' My head clears instantly, as though I've dived into an icy pool.

'You were both struck by a massive bolt of lightning, beneath the trees. And I'm afraid it was curtains for the actress. The doctor said Britney had burn marks on her chest, near the left cup of her underwired bra. The metal wires acted to conduct the charge to her heart. Unbelievable, huh?'

'That a bra could kill you? I *know*,' Marrakech marvels.

'No. That the bitch had a *heart*. The coroner recorded a verdict of death by misadventure,' Victoria reports neutrally. As she speaks Bruce the Tooth, who is also bandaged around his chest, spoon-feeds her from a tub of ice cream. 'He said it was an act of God.'

Struck down by lightning! Holy hell, it is kind of biblical. All that's missing is the burning bush.

'Youse was both enveloped by this massive amount of electrical energy.' Bruce the Tooth is now feeding Victoria chocolate mints. 'I spent ten years on Death Row readin' all about electric sparks. Me lawyers, see, they reckoned the electric chair was unconstit-chew-ional. The pathology of lightnin', or keraunopathy, that's what they done call it. Well, the contact voltage of a typical industrial electrical shock is, like, twenty to sixty-three kilovolts. Lightnin' strike delivers about, oh, three hundred kilovolts. This lightnin' was so damn strong it melted your clothes and fragmented. But 'cause you weren't wearin' no, um . . . foundation garment . . .' The big man blushes and fidgets then looks towards my sister.

'Because you weren't wearing a bra,' my sister decodes.

I struggle laboriously to a sitting position. 'Are you trying to tell me that my small tits saved me?' I'm really coming round now, my singed synapses snapping back like knicker elastic.

'Well, yeah. I reckon that's so, ma'am.'

'We were right about Britney's boobs too, sis. They *were* always getting bigger. She had implants with a valve just under the skin to pump them up with more silicone, whenever she wanted,' Victoria clarifies. 'The bra that killed her was a thirty-four double F.'

'Any bigger and her bust would have been mistaken for a breakaway republic,' Marrakech puts in.

'At least she died happy,' Victoria assures us. 'The blinding flash of light . . . I'm sure she just thought it was a swarm of *paparazzi* taking her photo.'

I start to laugh hysterically; great haw-haw guffaws. 'Yes! She finally was the – the – toast of the town.' It's such a shame that, being dead, Britney can't savour the poignancy of fate's twist. I laugh so hard they have to call a nurse to sedate me. But not before I take in the fact that my sister has eaten from Bruce's hands ice cream, mints, a crème brûlé, two packets of crisps and a chocolate éclair. And all without regurgitating. My sister bounces towards me like a basketball. She is buoyant, winged.

'Victoria,' I croak, 'you're eating?'

'Brucey likes me to eat more. He says he likes something to hold on to.' I notice then that she's wearing no makeup. When she raises her arms to hug the Tooth, I also glimpse armpit reforestation.

'She's got an appetite for life back, too, haven't you, Mum?' Marrakech puts her arms around her mother, who laughs heartily – without once worrying about lines.

'An' she's gonna say bye-bye to her thirties for the tenth and last time.' A newly dentured Bruce the Tooth pats my sister's bottom. 'J'hear me?'

Victoria plonks herself down on the bed and takes my hand in hers. 'All my life I've been looking for a man who can meet my needs.'

'What? A heterosexual *haute-couture* designer with a ten-inch tongue?' I reply, perplexed.

'Even though I've always thought my Mr Right would be an old guy who is really rich and quite ill – meeting Brucey, well, my oestrogen just whipped me into a hormonal frenzy. We have this amazing attraction, Elisabeth. I've finally found the perfect man.'

I glance over at the maximum-security ex-con who is nonchalantly picking his teeth with a switchblade. 'Really? I fully intend having my revenge and sleeping with *your* man one day, Vick,' I whisper, 'but I doubt it's going to be *him*.'

'Darling, he studied hair-dressing in prison. I get a blow-job first thing every morning.' She leans towards my ear. 'I'm even tempted to grow out my hair dye, just to see what colour my roots are.'

'Mum, you can't even remember your natural colour, can you?' Marrakech teases, snuggling up to her mother. It's the first time I have ever seen them so affectionate. Victoria's eyes have glazed over in motherly rapture.

'Marrakech! Are you all right?' I rasp, suddenly remembering her surgical trauma.

'Apart from these giNORMous boobs.' She laughs.

'That's not a chest,' I tell her, 'that's an inflated life-raft. Why didn't you have the implants taken out?'

'The clinic's closed. Remember Sven's brainwave to invest in cryogenics?'

'Oh, yeah, fifty thousand for neuro-suspension. And a hundred and twenty for the whole body!'

'Well, the company went into liquidation. *Literally.* The electricity bill didn't get paid and all the heads defrosted. That's why he's gone to ground – to dodge all his creditors. Anyway, now I've got the tits,' she gazes down at her thrusting mammaries as though regarding a pair of rather exotic pets, 'I think I might just go into modelling for a while. To make loads of cash. You know. For my Causes.'

'Over my dead body . . .' my sister warns darkly.

'Isn't this *great*?' Marrakech thrills. 'Now we even have normal mother-and-daughter fights!'

'How long have I been out cold?' I ask the Irish nurse who's come to sedate me.

'Five days, now, you've been lyin' here, my dear. Watched over by your guardian angel.'

'Hugo?' My hope level rises meteorically. Maybe he's repented. Maybe he's stopped taking those Bastard Pills.

'Your man from Belfast. And what a lovely fella he is.'

I look to my sister to explain.

'Cal's been by your side constantly. We insisted on relieving

him this morning. Why he's so obsessed with your return to
life, we don't know.'

'But it does seem more than good-neighbourliness.'
Marrakech giggles. 'Uncle Hugo visited you once too'

'He did?' I ask eagerly, taking heart once more. Has the
leopard changed his stripes?

'Yes. He extracted the keys for the sports car from your
hospital property. The Merc is in his name, he said, and he's
going to sell it.'

'Oh.' I sink down into the pillows. It's Calim who's been
watching over me. My lovely Cal. All laugh lines and loud
jokes and languid legs . . .

The nurse boils around my bed removing dressings. I see
the lightning's point of entry on my chest and touch the point
of exit near my right shoulder blade.

'The jogger who found you, now *she* was wearin' a proper
sports bra,' the nurse gently reprimands. 'For the love of
Jaysus, if only that American friend of yours, that TV star –
what a waste! If only *she*'d been in a proper sports bra she
wouldn't have got fried. You can never have enough support
in my view.'

Wasn't that the truth? A Best Friend's job is to act as a
human Wonder-bra: – to be always uplifting and supportive. I
realize, as the drugs kick in, that I've been about as supportive
to Calim as a trainer bra on Dolly Parton.

# 31. Ugliness Is In the Eye Of The Beholder: Get It Out With Optrex

When I wake again, I'm lying on the narrow bed, as pale and flat as paper. My wrists are manacled in nametags and clear plastic tubes and my hands are being held. Cal is perched beside me. In his baggy Levi's and tattered T-shirt, he looks like a scarecrow – coat-hanger shoulders, his arms set at wiry angles. I am shocked to see how much weight he's lost in the last few months.

'You need to get out more – preferably to a *restaurant*,' I say with jokey affection, wriggling to a sitting position. My hospital lunch is sitting untouched on a plastic tray.

'Yeah. I know. Homeless people could move in under me clothes. Whole housin' estates.'

I bayonet a piece of chicken on a fork prong and thrust it towards his mouth but he pushes my hand away. 'Wouldja look at the state of the two of us?' he says. 'Can you imagine our wedding vows? "In sickness and in sickness, I now pronounce you . . ."'

I drop his hands. 'Our *what*?' I become engrossed with the swirly pattern on the thin bedspread, tracing the faded embroidery with a finger. The lemony light of a summer sunset filters through the smeary windows. We sit in an uncomfortable silence for a moment. I feel like a parachutist about to take my first jump. I hover at the conversational hatch, take a deep breath and leap into the unknown. 'Cal, I'm so sorry. I've been dreadful to you lately. I guess I've just been freaked out about turning forty.'

'That's okay.' His mouth quirks upwards with amusement. 'Old people are like that . . . Happy birthday.'

'Oh, God. What's the date?' I flop back against the pillows. 'Is it my birthday?' I switch on the bedside light to read the date on my watch.

'June the sixteenth.' He toasts me with lukewarm Lucozade. 'Happy fortieth,' he says, with a weary, wistful smile. 'I'm sorry I wasn't here when you woke up the first time. You've been a bit under the weather lately, what with all that defyin' death and everythin'.'

I watch his smiling lips curl around his glass. I suddenly imagine that if I kissed him the taste would be warm and tangy in his mouth. The thought shocks me and I look away. I feel unexpectedly dislocated. We sit for a moment in awkward, squirmy silence with nothing but the softly piped Muzak to distract us.

'"Born to Be Wild" was definitely *not* written for the xylophone,' I say finally. I feel like a teenager all of a sudden, *not* a good look on a woman who is contemplating her first incontinence pad.

'So, you were freaked out about turnin' the big four-oh?' he interrogates, watching me closely.

'Not any more. Nothing like a near-death experience to recalibrate your feelings about the passing of time and put a fear of wrinkles into perspective.'

'I know. Growin' older isn't so scary when you think about

the alternative, eh? It doesn't matter how your body looks – as long as it's healthy. Hey, we can share baseball caps, now,' he says, plonking his cap on my singed cranium. 'It's so dumb that it takes a brush with mortality to teach us that life is made precious by the tiny daily miracles – a poem, a piece of music, a cold pint, that certain smile from a woman you love . . .' He looks at me intently.

'Actually, smiling and laughing are the best ways to get healthy again,' I prattle, flustered by how nervous I feel. 'Laughter brings about a drop in the levels of the stress hormone adrenaline. It boosts the immune system too,' I jabber on, animatedly. 'Hugo told me that once. And, believe me, in that baseball cap you've got a *lot* to laugh about buddy, I'm telling you.' I toss the cap back at him. It lands in his lap. It's a Disney freebie, emblazoned with 'It's A Small World After All'– totally at odds with what I accidentally glimpse packaged in his fly-button Levi's beneath.

'I'm facin' me fears, okay? When you get out of hospital I'm goin' to wear that purple tie you gave me last Christmas.'

I hit him, playfully.

'I've been plannin' a new novel. With a little trainin' and a lot of heart, I just might be able to turn myself into a medi-ocre writer.' He gives a cheeky grin. 'If only I had your wit, Liz. Beauty is a diminishin' asset, whereas wit can only get better.'

'I read an article in *Ugly* – the magazine for people who don't deep cleanse their pores – that women in their middle years feel younger than their actual age. Besides, I've worked out how to stay young.'

'How's that, then?'

'Well. First off, if you've got a crêpy neck, *wear a polo*. Number two, if you've got cellulite, *wear trousers*.'

Cal smiles, joining in. 'Number three, only hang out with friends at least twenty years older.'

'Number four, get a wider mirror.'

'Five, only be seen out with much, much uglier women.'

'Oh! And get a dimmer switch, greatest sex aid known to womankind.'

'Civilization's crownin' achievement! You should also fix your bathroom scales so that they can never go past eight stone.'

'Yes!' Our words trip over each other in the effort to get everything said. 'Because as old as we look now,' I offer, 'well, this is the youngest we will ever look again, right?'

'Hey, some day we'll wish we looked *this* young.' He smirks mischievously. 'It's great to be forty 'cause, well, you're not fifty yet!'

'That's right,' I agree staunchly. 'Serenity and courage – these are my new catchphrases . . . Oh, and control-top tights.'

'I've been thinking that the only logical solution to this age crap is to shoot all models.'

'Yes!' It strikes me that Cal and I have been singing a duet for years, but I've never heard the harmony before. 'Personally I favour the death penalty for all directors of cosmetic companies. I mean, face creams promise that you, too, can look like Isabella Rossellini at fifty – but only if you looked like her at fifteen.'

'Anyway, a good fuck is better than a face cream any day.'

I gulp, my nerves are thrumming like a twanged string. 'Really?'

'Once a woman's over forty, she develops a languorous sexuality. With so much more experience under her suspender belt, she can enjoy it all so much more, yer know?'

There's a strange springy feeling in the pit of my belly.

'It's only when you stop worryin' about your body that you can concentrate on your pleasure. At forty if you ain't doin' what gives you pleasure then you'd bloody well better start.'

I'm smiling so widely I think my face might rip. 'And anyway, we plain people have a role to play. Without *us* the Beautiful People wouldn't look quite so beautiful.'

When Calim looks at me there's a light in his eyes, like sunshine filtered through a blue pool. 'But you are beautiful, Lizzie.' Then he glances away, embarrassed by this mawkish display. 'Has anyone ever told you how beautiful you look vomitin' up your dinner after you've been hit by lightnin'?' he adds, hurriedly.

'And *you*'re handsome, too, Cal.' Startled, I half turn to see who has made this banal declaration – unable to believe it escaped from my own caustic lips.

Cal smiles at me radiantly. And, by God, he *is* handsome. Why had I never noticed this before? Embarrassed, I, too, retreat into glibness. 'One of the most handsome men I've ever seen – besides k.d. Lang, that is.'

He mock-punches me, but doesn't withdraw his fingers. They're wrapped around my forearm. This turns into a gentle stroking up and down my needle-pricked arm. 'Good drugs?' he asks.

'Great. They say that morphine leads on to harder drugs. But, hey! There *is* no harder drug! Right?'

He smiled. 'Only love.'

'Well, that's *definitely* some kind of drug talking now.'

'I love everythin' about you, Lizzie. I love what you wear. I love what you don't wear. I even love your *toes*.' He takes my foot out of its scuzzy slipper and kisses my toes, one by one.

'God, you've got so pathetically mushy lately. Stop, Cal. Right now. Before you ovulate!' But I'm overawed, hugging his words close to my injured chest. 'You – you honestly think you love me?'

'Enough to make you forget that you were ever married to a cheatin', lyin' bastard.'

'Really? Without a prescription?'

He leans forward, and kisses me with his slow, soft mouth.

'So you do like me a little bit, shug,' he says gently, when we finally break, breathless, blurry with longing.

'Definitely not,' I reply.

'Lizzie, a woman can fake an orgasm, but not a heartfelt kiss like that.'

'It must be the after-effects of the strike. The doctor said that lightning survivors often experience residual effects, neuropsychiatrically. Obviously I'm off my head.'

His fingers softly trace the pinpricks on my arm. And if I joined the dots, what would they say? 'Ha bloody ha, love from the Fate Fairy. The love of your life was right under your nose the whole bloody time, you idiot.'

I grip his arms now with an urgency that seems at odds with my frail state. 'I'm feeling loads better, Cal, you know.'

'Oh. That's grand!' But, with no excuse for soothing me now, he stops caressing my arms. He folds his hands back into his lap and sits there, self-consciously, on the edge of my bed.

'But, hey, I think I've got a patch of dry skin around the

place,' I say zealously, lifting up my PJ top. 'And there's a raised mole somewhere too . . .' I place his hand on my warm belly.

'Well, then, I think you'd better get naked immediately while I look for it.'

And then our mouths touch, our heads graze. His skin smells of nutmeg. Outside the University College Hospital, Bloomsbury creaks as it cools after the heat of the day, expanding, slumping, sighing – much as *we* are. And then I'm lost in the slippery softness of our lips as we melt into each other.

When we pull away I can see my nipples pouting through the soft cotton of my pyjama top. And it's the opposite of cold in here. Cal slowly lifts my shirt and looks at my breasts. My first instinct is to shield myself. But then I realize that there's no need to cover up – Calim Keane went deep below my surface, long ago. And so I sit there, exposed to him, my plain, true, post-breast-feeding, reverse-surgeried, unadorned, naked self.

'Oh. You have the loveliest breasts, Liz. Pinky and Perky,' he christens them.

I feel sore, brave and weak, but a great surge of emotion buoys me up. I hug myself for joy. Only I don't need to as he's enfolded me in his arms already. He cups my breasts in both hands and rolls my nipples between his firm fingers.

'The Perkins,' he formally addresses my boobs, grinning coyly, as seismographic needles all over the world's oceans scribble and twitch.

When I lie against him, breathing hard, the pang of happiness in my heart almost feels like grief. For a split second I think I'm going to weep. It's so romantic it should be in black and white, really.

'But no irritatingly insipid pet names for each other in public, okay?' I say, breathlessly, biting back tears. 'No nause-ating baby-talk ever, okay?'

'Okay, my iddy-biddy pussy-wussy.' Sliding down my body, his tongue flicks and licks from one breast to the other. My nipples are so erect I could pick up the World Service.

'Don't you know it's rude to talk with your mouth full, you big Irish bastard?' I pant, effused with a fledgling, shimmering joy.

When he looks back at me, his eyes are tinged with an impish light. 'So, what do you want to do now?'

'Well, I thought I might turn forty.' I flick the door closed with my foot – but feel another door opening. 'Now . . . where's that dimmer switch?' I reach for the bedside lamp.

Cal stays my hand. He then utters the five nicest words in the English language: 'Leave the lights on, Lizzie.'

# ACKNOWLEDGEMENTS

Thanks to all the first-draft endurers: Peter Straus, Nikki Christer, Mari Evans and Suzanne Baboneau, and especially to Alison Summers for her warm encouragement and editorial perspicacity, and to Geoffrey Robertson, as ever.

Thanks also to:
- Ed Victor, the Ed-ocet missile of agents.
- Beauty guru Jo Fairley who taught me that father time, while he may be a great healer, sure ain't no beauty therapist.
- Simone Hugo, for slaving over a hot keyboard.
- My doctor buddies, Robert Lyneham and Iain Hutchison, who taught me the best way to give breast augmentations to a man while he's under partial anaesthetic. They even taught me how to spell anaesthetic.
- Kathryn Grieg for checking my trouser-hound's dialogue on her Texan-ometre.
- And thanks to all my girlfriends, Aggie, Victoria, Penny, Jan, Susie, Jean, Jenny, Cara, Liz, Ange, Mimi, Michelle, Kate, Catho and co., who agree with me that if Barbie's so popular, then why do we have to buy her friends?

P.S. Iain Hutchison, a maxillofacial surgeon, runs a charity called 'The Facial Surgery Research Foundation Saving Faces' which funds research to improve treatment for patients with cancer, disfigurement and injuries affecting the face. So if you've got a few bucks, feel free to hurl them his way at: Saving Faces, PO Box 25383, London NW5 2FL. To find out more visit *savingfaces.co.uk* or email *savingfaces@mail.com*.